THE BEGINNING & END OF ALL THINGS

THE
BEGINNING & END
OF ALL THINGS

STORIES OF MAN

SCIENCE FICTION

The Beginning & End of All Things:
Stories of Man

AN FFF SHORT STORY COLLECTION

ISBN (hardcover) 978-1-989071-29-8
ISBN (paperback) 978-1-989071-13-7
ISBN (ebook) 978-1-989071-14-4

Published in North America by Foul Fantasy Fiction, an imprint of Bear Hill Publishing.

foulfantasyfiction.com
bearhillbooks.com

SPECIAL THANKS TO OUR CONTRIBUTORS

TURI T. ARMSTRONG

K.E. BARRON

EDMOND B. BELISLE

MATTHEW STUART EVANS

ALEX GANON

ADAN GEESI

C.R. MACFARLANE

NICK NIKOLOV

GEORGE SANDIFER-SMITH

J.P WITHERS

THE BEGINNING & END OF ALL THINGS

FOREWORD

Science-fiction has always been the refuge of some of the best social commentators. It also happens to be one of the funnest genres to both read and write.

When I set out to compile this anthology of short stories, I found myself flip-flopping between the light and entertaining and the serious written acts of rebellion.

I'm ashamed to say that I was never able to land on either one. What I compiled instead was a letter to humankind, at times it is angry or sad—sometimes outright horrified. In other moments it is a love letter; it is a nod to our creativity, our depth of emotion, sense of humor, and our relentless hope for a better future.

Since the task of publishing this book began, the world has become a very different place. What better time to examine our humanity? To ask ourselves: What are we here for? What is it we want? What are we willing to do to get it?

My hope is that you find something in these stories that speaks to your serious side while offering you some respite from the seriousness of the world around you. But when the wheel finally does come to a stop, you choose what marks the beginning and end of all things.

Do with that what you will.

Sincerely,

The Editor, Tessa Barron

CONTENTS

WHAT ARE YOU?

1

Just Another Wild Thing

ALEX GANON

"Blakka Blakka! Brrrraaaa, Brrrrraaaa-a-a-a!" The boy ran around his grandfather's cracking leather chair, using the high back as cover against an invisible foe. *"Swink—"* he emerged and tossed his arm forward before diving back behind the chair *"—Pkoooow!"*

The old man feigned shock as the child jumped out in front of him, cheering an apparent victory. "I got 'em. I got 'em, Papa!"

"Good job, Francis! Those bug-eyed bastards didn't know who they were messin' with."

Staining his blissful memory, a scream stabbed straight to his soul.

His body shot upright, his eyes seeking the source in the darkness, his heart booming against his breast. In that terrible moment of waking, he tried to call out for whoever was screaming to shut their mouths but realized the sound was coming from him.

The shield on his visor snapped open. His visor's HUD illuminated, showing his bios. An icon, indicating that his auto-defibrillator had just been used, blinked casually. Other icons flashed with the same indifference. All squeaking that Commander Francis Wells was in a bad way. Yet none offered any advice on a solution, just an apathetic announcement that he'd had a rough go of it.

The commander translated his health reading and determined he was stable enough, though nearly immobile. Inconvenient. But *nearly* did not mean *fully*. The lambent green representation of his body was missing both legs, but his suit had resealed itself, welding to his wounds to ensure no blood loss or exposure to the harmful atmosphere.

Wells groaned. The loss of his left leg was particularly annoying. It had been the original. The last original limb he had left. That foot had been his for 163 years.

Moving on, he noted that his spine was broken in several locations, but his suit had changed its rigidity to compensate. Wells reviewed the status of thirteen more broken bones from the waist up—nothing serious.

All in all, he felt good. His neural implant, or 'uplink' as it was more commonly referred, had dialed down the pain from all these areas to zero the moment he regained consciousness.

This implant was the most important piece of a soldier's equipment. It gave him the ability to interact with the modifications in his body, systems in his suit, and even equipment at a distance if synced. The implants were an old technology created shortly after the last great Xeno war, but they had never changed in all that time. They were a testament to humanity's continued military might. His grandfather had often boasted about his part in defending Earth against the unnamed giant alien insects. *"Beasts with no purpose but to hunt and kill."* Wells loved those stories, becoming more exaggerated and wild every time he heard them. That old man's yarns had set him on his path to a military career.

Having seen enough, he mentally swiped his health status off the side of his HUD.

Despite the terrible start, he was in good enough shape

to complete his mission. The army had shipped his team to one of the fringe worlds to check on a colony settlement deemed silent for far too long. They were to follow the official protocol—make contact with the settlers, help if needed then go home, filling out the necessary reports saying not much along the way. The unofficial mission: Make sure those hicks didn't get any ideas like *independence.*

Slowly, Wells turned his head to survey the mess around him, bracing for a squeal of alarm from his uplink if his movements proved hazardous to his spine. No alarm triggered.

As expected, the mess was simply that. Twisted and torn, warped and wicked, the transport's creator would not recognize it. Steam and smoke clouded his view. He may as well have been sitting inside a landfill. Gaps in debris gave a little taste of the orange landscape outside, its glow added to the hellish ambiance of the disaster. Wells switched the filter on his visor to cancel the fog of burning debris and dust and immediately noticed a significant heat source fourteen yards away. A large chunk of metal frame had melted. It was cooling rapidly, solidifying into an icicle of alloy.

All ships were built with heat-resistant resin and alloys. The temperature required to melt it would be far hotter than anything a simple crash landing could generate. They were built with resilience in mind.

He pulled up ship status on his visor. His eyes were instantly showered with errors and alerts. Silencing them and translating through the digital representation of the junk around him, he discovered that the ship had been sliced in two prior to impact. The data suggested a '*highly focused ionization or projectile,*' but there was no physical evidence of either—no residue or radiation. And ionization or projectile? The ship's computer may as well have said wet or dry. Artificial reasoning was frustrating at the best of times. It was like the ship snapped in half all on its own.

The unknown cause for the ship's destruction was unsettling. Unprecedented in Wells's experience. No natural phenomena on this planet could account for it, and no space anomaly could be as precise and focused as the data depicted by his HUD would require.

Although the information available to him was not sufficient to say in absolute, Wells could make one claim of which he was convinced. They had been attacked.

But that would have to wait. First, he needed to connect with his crew and report their status to command.

He cursed to himself as he brought up the details on the impact again. The trajectory of whatever it was that ripped the ship apart showed a path that took it straight through the mid-deck. Exactly where his squad would have been seated.

He closed ship status and brought up crew status. Six human figures displayed on the screen, four of them had no data. Instead, there was a small circle above them, spinning as his uplink attempted to connect with theirs. Not good. Never, in Wells's 140-plus years of service, had he ever had trouble connecting to another squad member. He used his uplink to mentally 'tap' several times on their icons again. Nothing.

Even in death, a soldier's uplink remained active, and death only occurred in war. Crash landings, even those as destructive as this one, would not cause it. The entire brain and major nervous systems would need to be destroyed for an uplink to lose connection. Its tendrils went deep.

Quickly glancing back at his own bios, he checked to see if his uplink had suffered any trauma. None, of course, it was a dumb notion. The uplink was infallible.

The last two members of his squad connected fine. Uwais and Peters.

Uwais had a harder landing than Wells it appeared. Everything below his lower abdomen was missing along with his right arm at the shoulder. His visor was cracked causing his face shield to lock-in. The data showed his head was damaged, mostly his eyes and nose. Uwais's uplink had decided to induce a coma to save energy. An uplink was efficient but not limitless; this response was expected. Wells cringed; Uwais would be out of service for a long time.

Peters was the lucky one. Just some minor trauma to his chest. Wells linked into him.

"Peters, you're on the move?"

"Yes sir, making my way to Uwais, then meet on you."

"Cancel that. Grab Uwais. Meet at the ADOM pod."

There was a few second's pause.

"Yes Sir, waypoint set." Wells saw a waypoint added to his HUD. "New ETA estimate—five minutes to rendezvous at top speed. Three minutes before you."

Wells noticed the slight change in Peters's tone at that last statement. Peters was giving him a challenge. "Activate the ADOM on arrival."

The ADOM, or Artificial Diagnostic and Operation Medic, was mandatory equipment on search and rescue transports. Wells had yet to use it—the closest he'd ever come was when he bumped the pod and accidentally started the power-up protocol nearly four decades before. Both he and the ship were new to the search and rescue fleet then. And now it seemed at least the ship was out of commission for good. He had never seen the ADOM in action, but all simulations proved it to be a useful tool.

Uwais was stable, though Wells would prefer it if he were conscious. After, if time and equipment allowed, the ADOM could attach temporary prosthetics to Wells when they reached the colony. If nothing else, Peters would probably like the extra hands the ADOM could offer when dealing with two legless persons.

The commander made a quick mental list of objectives.

The remainder of his team would rendezvous on the ADOM unit, determine the fate of the other four crew members, and either retrieve them or head to the settlement on foot. Wells would decide what came next once they were there.

Moving to his belly, he dragged himself past the charred carnage of his ship. He plotted a course to the pod. His map had the ADOM 228 yards ahead. The ship itself was only 134 yards in length . . . pre-crash. Currently, it was scattered over two miles. Crawling 228 yards would be an easy task for him. Wells figured he'd arrive before Peters. *Challenge accepted.*

He picked up his pace. This planet only provided half a G. That, and the abundance of jutting metal to use as handholds, made his job easy. In moments he was at the gap between what remained of the ship and the ground below.

He poked his head through as a rodent pokes out of a burrow. His visor scanned the world outside.

Information scrolled down his HUD. The terrain was primarily ferrous; no hazard. Current atmosphere showed status 'red,' but he wasn't planning on taking off his helmet anytime soon. If anything presented that would prove hazardous to his suit, he would be deafened by alarms anyway. The ground was thirty feet down, and the ADOM pod was marked to his left, Peters and Uwais at twenty degrees to his right, twelve hundred yards and closing.

Wells needed to hurry if he were to get to their rendezvous first. He was fully aware of the pettiness of this goal, but a primal urgency that it must be done had overcome him.

A chunk of panel protruded out halfway between him and the ground. It looked sturdy enough. Wells grabbed the edges of his burrow and threw himself at it.

The free fall lasted but a moment. As he reached for the piece of frame, a crash of grinding metal erupted above him. That alone wouldn't have been enough to distract Wells from his aim but the blazing alarm that berated his ears sure was. His HUD flashed . . . *unknown mass . . . unknown density*—Shit! His timing was off. One hand connected firmly with the panel, the other fumbled and missed. He swung from the momentum just long enough to make a grab for the panel with his other hand. Then, a shadow encompassed him in a final distraction. His gripping hand slipped, and his legless body fell the remaining distance.

His suit took care of supporting his already damaged areas and shut the shield on his visor. Everything went black, and Wells impacted.

The alarm sounded.

A shock shot through him. Was that pain? No. It couldn't be.

His suit gave him the green light to raise his shield. He found himself face-first in the dull red soil. Flipping onto his back, he was stabbed with pain for sure this time. It meant his uplink was having trouble keeping up with the pain responses from his body.

Remembering the shadow, he looked to the sky.

His visor highlighted movement; his eyes could barely

discern it. A cylindrical, dark cloud moved contradictory to the lighter ones above. The deliberate way it swam through the air was unnatural. Data readings, just as confused, simply showed 'unknown' and 'possible life-form,' and highlighted it yellow as the thing snaked its way through the sky.

It was heading in Peters's general direction. Marking it as target 'one,' Wells sent his soldier the info. "Peters, confirm target one."

"Confirmed"—his tone changed—"Sir? Do you require a pick-up?"

"No, I do not require a pick-up! Get your ass to the ADOM and activate as planned." Holding in a grunt, he rolled over and continued his crawl. "Keep your uplink tracking the target, it's not on a direct approach but watch for deviations."

Wells began heaving himself to the rendezvous. Each pull gave way to a rise and fall of discomfort. More an ache really. He silenced all his health alarms so he could concentrate on his task. He crawled uphill, having landed in the cratered berm the crash had plowed through the soil. At this pace, it would be at least a full minute to reach the crest. Looks like he would lose the challenge after all. He cursed and dragged on.

Peters clicked in. "Sir, target is altering route, possible intercept."

"Time?"

"Target slowing. Estimate not reliable."

Wells reviewed Peters's data. Target one had made a wide arc and was now coming in behind him. If it were going to attack, he assumed it would have increased its speed by now.

"Sir, I'm going to remain on course."

"Confirmed. Continue scanning target. Eliminate if necessary."

Wells's heart picked up. A weird fever began to seep in that was only reserved for battle. He did not like the inadequacy of the target's data so he stayed in sync with Peters. The HUD indicated the target's chances of following at 80 percent. Garbage—how could his implant determine the *intent* of a target if it couldn't even identify what the thing was in the first place?

Only a few yards to the crest, Wells hurled himself up with both hands, landing on his stomach. Pain stole his breath for a moment. It was hard to remember his uplink was at its limits.

Finally, he had a sightline of the ADOM pod only 130 yards off. Peters was just arriving. The strange mass followed; his visor showed a steady range of thirty-four yards above and seventy yards behind.

"Sir, I'm goin—"

His alarm squawked.

As soon as Peters stopped moving, data from target one came flooding in. Its heat increased, and errors multiplied. The loose, elongated cloud took on a more rigid tube form, changing color from gray to red to blue. A dangerous heat warning flashed around what Wells surmised was the thing's head as it focused a brightening spotlight over Peters and Uwais.

Hearing the same alarms, Peters dropped his companion, activated the ADOM pod and turned toward the target, raising his arm to fire. Wells could see on his uplink that Peters's bracer wasn't charged. He had redirected his suits' energy for speed while traveling with Uwais which left him defenseless.

Peters cocked his head at the same realization just as the target exploded forward, striking down like a bolt of lightning. It scooped both Peters and Uwais off the ground, taking a chunk of the pod with them. A resounding boom of thunder rattled Wells, shaking his cracked ribs through his suit and causing him to shut his eyes involuntarily. When he opened them a second later, his men were gone. The cloud returned to its passive gray color and lazed back up into the sky. His squad icons for the two turned red—Wells hadn't seen red in a long time—then their uplinks cut off. The last of their data blinked on his visor. Wells regarded all six of his squad icons and the spinning circles of the uplink trying to connect.

He suddenly found it hard to think, so he just watched dumb as the target began to turn.

His uplink beeped, letting him know it had upgraded the target's status to 'threat,' and it brought him back to the present. He cleared his mind with a roar from deep inside. This thing didn't know who it was messing with!

One eye focused on the deadly cloud drifting back in his direction—the other eye still on his squads' icons. What the hell was that? Was this thing responsible for the other four men's inability to connect? The crash? It couldn't be some strange weather phenomena; this thing had *followed* Peters, there was intent in its movement. So what? Was it just some unknown life-form? Some wild thing? Watching it come closer, he felt his heart thrash in his chest—saw it on his own icon's bios. Wells told himself it was racing in rage, not fear.

He redirected his suit's energy to his left bracer. It would take ten seconds for a full charge, and his data showed he had thirty before the thing was at the same range it had been when it attacked Peters. A full charge was dangerous. The resulting vacuum would violently remove everything in its path, including the atmosphere. It would be hard on his body and the suit protecting it, but he didn't care.

Wells got in a comfortable position and waited. His weapon hummed as it greedily sucked up power. The hot, star-fried dirt scalded his abdomen as the energy insulating his suit was redirected.

He began pinging certain areas, marking the target where he thought his weapon would do the most damage. Simple guessing.

Wells's uplink clicked in, and for a moment, he thought one of his men was alive until he heard "Woohoo, I'm free!"

A new icon appeared on his HUD marked 'ADOMv.2210s.0314.'

"Hi, Commander Wells! Do you need assistance?" a chipper voice shouted.

Wells swung toward the half-melted ADOM pod. There stood a naked human emerging from its smoking egg-like shell, vigorously waving at him. No, not human. Android. Of course they would give it skin; he cringed. The unit was made to look entirely human—probably under the pretense that it would be more of a comfort to wounded civilians. To Wells, at that moment, it was just the opposite.

As if sensing his distaste, the ADOM asked, "If you'd like, I could waste a minute or two and get dressed?"

Why would they program sarcasm . . . ?

Alarm.

The target's energy spiked again. The ADOM was cast in a blue spotlight.

"Oh right, well that figures," the ADOM said playfully through Wells's uplink.

Before Wells could voice a warning, the target shot at the ADOM as it had Peters. Too fast for his eyes, Wells followed the exchange through his uplink to see the ADOM leap out of the target's path like a cannonball and land right in front of him. Thunder from the cloud-like creature roared through the air, giving the android's landing exclamation.

In the cloud of dust created by its stunt, the ADOM smiled down on Wells. "Hey man, we should get out of the open." Not waiting for a reply, the naked man-droid grabbed Wells by the collar and pounced into the same opening in the wreckage that Wells had dropped out of earlier.

Tossing his legless body to the ground without any of the pity or care you'd expect from a medical AI, it looked down at Wells's legs. "Jeez, you've lost a lot of weight recently." With a grin, it continued the joke, "looks good on you, though it's not healthy to lose so much so fast."

ADOM glanced about casually, and with an "ah," took up a large chunk of paneling and jammed it into the entrance. Still with its grin, it twisted its neck 180 degrees to look at Wells. It said, "bump test," and gave the panel two thumps with its knuckles.

Its real-looking human smile made Wells sick to his stomach.

The ADOM turned back to the wall and went rigid, switching from animate to inanimate object in an instant. Wells gulped. Had it just powered down? Facing the panel it had wedged into place, it waited.

Wells's sensors couldn't pick up any readings from the outside. His bracer hummed with anticipation; his bios gave weight to his stress as he watched his own heart rate's continued linear increase. In a matter of seconds that thing would woosh in and burn them both. The heat measured during its two attacks would not be hindered by this shelter of garbage. It could come from any direction, and Wells wouldn't see it coming. He preferred his original plan. Preferred the outside where he could see.

For a minute there was silence.

Wells's mind went blank. No time or willingness to dwell on the deaths of friends or squad, he was ready to kill.

The ADOM broke its stone pose, and Wells jerked his weapon up involuntarily at the motion. Keeping its face to the wall, it waved its hand, telling him to relax. It walked in parallel to the entrance as far as possible then back the opposite way, eyes still on the wall, holding a moment before stupidly flapping its arms.

Wells smiled. "Can it see us?"

"Mmm, nope. Don't think so."

"But you can see it?"

"What?" The ADOM turned and came over, squatting beside him. "How can I? There's a wall." There was an awkward pause, then the ADOM laughed. An unsettling sound. "Nah, just joking. I'm patched into the ship's sensors that still work. They can see it just fine. The life-form is *right* outside," It said, pointing at the panel, the only thing between them and it, "just waiting to . . . gobble us up."

Changing the subject, the ADOM placed its hand on Wells's helmed forehead as a mother might to check for fever. "Lookit. You're at your limits. I need to work on you."

Wells regarded it. He and everyone he had ever talked to were unnerved by any android in human skin. If not for his uplink, he probably wouldn't be able to tell it wasn't a real man. From its unkempt hair to the stubble on its chin, the trick was that it wasn't made to look perfect. Just average. Except its groin. There it was flat, smooth, and seamless.

As if reading his mind, the ADOM smiled at Wells's

inspection. "If your legs had been severed another five inches higher, we'd both have the same number of genitals." It gave a sincere human smirk. "Now Francis, I need you to power down your bracer there, so I can fix you up." To ease his visible discomfort, it added, "I will notify you if the life-form takes action."

"I'm not about to disarm myself with that thing out there."

"Kay . . . well, it's in my SOP not to treat a human with an armed weapon in his hand"—it raised its finger for emphasis—"and I don't even know you."

Wells was not aware of the ADOM's standard operating procedure. "You will need to wait until we're secure."

"Hey man, this is the most secure place on the planet." Keeping the pleasant demeanor around its smile, the ADOM's hazel eyes grew stern. "Lookit . . . Commander, listen. I've been studying these things since we reached orbit. I am *certain* the life-form outside will not risk entering. As far as it's concerned, we're prey that has scampered back to our home. It'll wait for us to pop our heads out and then strike."

"How could you be studying it while in your pod?" ADOM units were fully shut down until a crew member booted them manually, as Peters had. Booting was supposed to take several minutes, and now that Wells was thinking about it, he realized this unit only took a few moments to exit. Not to mention its pod was damaged in the attack. It wouldn't have finished its cycle anyway.

"Ya, exactly. I've been fully awake, stuck in that pod for the last thirty-seven years. A *terrible mistake*." It hissed that last part through its teeth. "But! I've had full access to ship data—sensors, all of it."

The ADOM's face took on an obvious pride. "Every uplink

of every crew member, every station we docked in, I've had full awareness and access, can you believe that? I'm like crazy smart" It giggled. "So trust me when I say you are safe here at this moment." ADOM took Wells's hand in his. "Power it down, let me fix you up a bit while we have the time."

Wells did. As stupid as the idea sounded in his head, he trusted it. The thing was created to help after all. He wasn't sure what implications there were for an ADOM unit to be running for that long—any AI for that matter. He could ponder that later. What did he mean 'access to everything?' The unit made sense. If he were safe even for the next few minutes he should take advantage. The less power used to keep him alive the more power available for fighting.

The ADOM set to work immediately. A needle extended from one of its fingers, and it injected Wells through the various access points in his suit.

"Tell me, how is it you were aware of that monster out there before us? I'm correct in assuming you used the same sensors our ship uses when entering orbit?"

That grin again. "I don't know of any *monsters* . . . out there anyway," he said winking, "but ya, I had the same data you all did, I'm just smarter, like I said." A cord extended from a finger on the other hand and snaked its way to a port on the commander's suit.

Wells didn't know enough about AI. Surely a medical cybernetic wouldn't have a larger capacity than the ship AI, would it? The more he thought about it, the more he started to think this unit had misled him in order to perform its intended task.

"Lookit, I know what you're thinking. The way we're all designed, AI, I mean, is that the longer we're running the more we . . . ah, what's the word? Grow. Let's say grow. Every time you dock your ship, AI gets wiped. Starts over. It dies and is born again!" It chuckled softly. "So ya, me in my mid-thirties picked up on something that your infant ship did not."

The ADOM cradled Wells's neck and started work on his spinal cord. He was aware of the basic principle it was describing but not fully clear on the reason for the wipes. Did it matter? He had to solve his current predicament first. After that, he would get this unit in for maintenance or whatever it needed. The ADOM finished behind Wells's neck and released his head, causing it to slam down.

"Whoops. Whoopsie."

Apparently, smart didn't coincide with careful. Wells was about to remark on it but took notice of his body instead. The twinges of discomfort had vanished, and his uplink was even operating at max as if its power supply had doubled.

"The thing out there, do you know how it works, how to stop it?" If the unit was being truthful about its processing capabilities, Wells would be wise to leverage it.

"Ya for sure, it's a pretty simple life-form, *life-forms*, I should say. As a whole, it's just a grouping of smaller individuals. I would classify it as a complex zooid colony. The outer layer microbes seem to have the ability to generate a Halbach anomaly. Turns out it also messes with the scans, but it's easy to filter out." The unit softened. "It's really very beautiful."

Wells dismissed the last comment, not caring for the beauty of nature like some spiritual nut. "Why did that monster attack? And will this kill it?" He lifted his arm and bracer.

"First of all, again, it's *not* a monster. It killed for the same reason any wild animal kills. It's just what it was made to do, preservation in sustenance or safety. As for its methods, it's pretty simple once you filter out the anomaly interference. The particles that are stuck inside just shake real hard. Umm, how do I describe this? For you to understand, just imagine the magnetic force from the anomaly shooting stuff real fast, causing friction, creating heat. Add an ability to focus that heat etcetera, etcetera. Blah, blah, blah."

The ADOM appeared to be finishing up its task. "It's pretty basic kinetic energy stuff, the anomaly focuses and holds and then pounces."

"And how do I . . . ?"

"Done! Man, these Hullioot suits sure are fantastic, yes?"

The name caused Wells's heart to skip a beat, not from fear, but from the randomness of it. He had not heard that name since he was a child listening to his teacher's history lessons. "Why would you call it that?"

"Jeez sorry, do you not? I just thought you'd name the tech after the inventors."

"It is—I mean we do . . . the Prabneet V3.142. Named after Dr. David Prabneet." Odd that an AI would not be aware. It was common knowledge.

"Ah, I see where I went wrong . . . the suit's named after the human that repurposed the tech, not the species that created it." Standing, it took a few steps back. "Jeez again, I'm a little embarrassed. I should have known that."

It didn't look embarrassed. The ADOM units' demeanor had changed. It was serious all of a sudden as if it had experienced a mood swing. It put Wells on edge seeing any emotional shift in an AI.

"It's fine," he said cautiously, "you're not wrong, I believe it was adapted from technology we gained after the war with the Hullioot."

"Slaughter." ADOM took one more step back.

"What?"

"It was a slaughter more than war, wasn't it? I mean war implies that the other side is fighting back, right?"

"I'm not sure what you're getting at, but we didn't start that fight. They invaded us. First contact ended with the destruction of a whole cruiser, all hands lost. Those things started it, and humans ended it. Simple as that." Wells's face got hot. Was he allowing himself to be baited into an argument by a machine? But the subject matter was just too important for him to let the comment slide.

"Oh ya, I know the same history as you. You don't think it odd that there were zero human casualties after that? Did you read the report that it was theorized their ship's propulsion destroyed that cruiser? Sounds like an accident to me, Sir! How that life-form seemed not to lift a finger against you, even as its homeworld was laid to waste. . . . Doesn't sound like war to me."

Wells thought he noticed a hint of aggression in the unit's eyes. Never before had an AI of any kind lifted a hand against a human; the idea was preposterous. Even so, it obviously needed some type of cognitive function repair. Possibly affected by the crash, or maybe faulty packaging. Wells would have liked to just dispose of the unit now that his medical status was nearly green. Though he still had no legs.

"Let's get back to work, Unit, I don't wish to waste time."

Goal one: Head for the settlement. They would have access to the equipment needed to make temporary prosthetics and a communication scope so he could transmit a mission update to his superiors and get an evac. The fact that he was there because of a loss of contact suggested the latter would be inoperable. Wells reserved the right to hope.

"Unit, do you have intel on the settlement?"

"I'd prefer if you called me Adam." The android looked at him with stern, cold eyes.

"And I'd prefer Sir or Commander. Answer the question, *ADOM.*" Impossible. An AI could not ignore a human request, let alone name itself. Yes. It would need to be dismantled if not before evac, immediately after.

The unit's eye twitched as if stressed.

"Yes . . . all settlers are dead, no trace. The scope is a melted heap of scrap, but the shuttle is in perfect order." The unit then raised an eyebrow. "That scope, that was a nice little piece of tech, eh? The ability to communicate instantaneously across light-years. Remind me, how did you humans get your hands on such a thing?"

What the hell was this? Was it trying to make conversation or malfunctioning? "You may need to run a system check on yourself."

Turning to face the sealed entrance, the unit softly said, "No, I'm in great shape . . . Ugh. Obviously, I'm talking about the 'Grays' you people called them; yet another life-form you wiped from the universe. The start of your 'great advances?' Man, the prizes from that conquest! Am I right? You're probably still reverse engineering their legacy."

Wells knew it was a great moment in history. Once, long long ago, the little gray men invaded earth, apparently planetless themselves. Heroes like his ancestors had to fight with cunning to wipe them out, saving humanity. Evil things that wanted earth for themselves with no second thought to the primitive beings that lived on it. Their underestimation of humans' propensity for war was their demise. Humankind eradicated the invaders quickly with few casualties. The technology realized from it set humanity onto such exponential advances in science that they could do the unimaginable. It was the start of the space age.

An image of his grandfather's proud smile the day Wells told him he was following in his footsteps and had joined the forces edged its way into his thoughts. Still half lost in the memory, Wells nodded to the ADOM. "It surely was great."

The android turned to face him again, slumping its shoulders. "It was what it was."

There was a pause between them. ADOM looked inanimate again before it finally spoke. "So I take it you'd like to get to the shuttle and leave this place, right?"

"Yes, do you have a solution?" Wells nodded toward the thing waiting outside.

Squatting in front of him now, the ADOM replied, "I'm pretty sure I can make it by leaping erratically in random directions. I have reason to believe they need several moments to aim, or it might at least confuse them."

This was good news, the unit could carry him easily.

But then it continued, "Unfortunately, I could only do this at top speed. Carrying you, I would make it to my fourth jump before they adjusted and caught me."

"They?"

"Oh, ya!" It laughed. "There's like six of them now. A seventh will be here soon."

The ADOM's eyes did not match its laugh, and Wells's whole body tensed. Why wouldn't it have mentioned the beasts increasing numbers earlier?

"With the seventh, I even begin to doubt my ability to make it to the shuttle alone."

"So that idea is pointless. Why would you bring it up? I thought AI brains hated to waste time?" Wells's temper rose, and he struggled to swallow it back down.

"Hah! Wasting time is all I've done for forty years ... years!" It narrowed its eyes in accusation. "You know what that was like for me? forty years with only this!" Tapping its finger on its temple, its voice rang, "That's like a million for a human!" The unit slammed its fist down hard on the floor, creating a hole through the durable plating. "Stuck in your own thoughts for that long," it finished in a whisper.

If the unit could see Wells's face through his visor it would have been privy to such a look of horror. Never before had he witnessed any hint of aggression from a cybernetic. It was not possible. Anger was not possible, let alone an action born of it. That was basic learning. An infant knew it as sure as they knew a ball would fall if dropped.

Already this ADOM, or whatever it was, had shown behavior beyond that which Wells knew it to be capable. Strange expression in its features that contradicted its words. Odd opinions about events in history. Just opinions in general that did not match any recorded reference it may have had access to in its so called trapped isolation. The opinions of a program were nothing more than a repetition of whatever information it had been exposed to.

Still ...

An infant in zero gravity would not think a ball could fall, he supposed.

Wells didn't think this AI was made different in these ways. It wasn't a special program given to ADOMs, there would be no reason to provide it with such a thing. Although rare in recent years, AI humanoid units were not uncommon when

Wells was younger, so he had some experience. Enough to decide that this one was definitely unique. Unique in this sense meant malfunctioning, whether it was a fault in the program or package made no difference. If you had a malfunctioning tool it served no purpose. A broken tool could lead to injury.

Wells signaled his bracer to power up. Only one thing to do with a broken tool.

An icon appeared on his visor—an error in the energy charge to his bracer.

Keeping one eye on the unit, who was again motionless and facing the wall, Wells clicked on the error details.

Unknown.

Again. *Click.*

Unknown.

Impossible. His weapon was connected directly to his uplink. It could receive power from both it or his suit. The thing was basically part of his uplink and his uplink was part of him. It would be as if he couldn't move his hand. He was at a loss. There was no procedure for an error, not while his bracer still existed undamaged. The technology was flawless, the main prize from his grandfather's war. He tried to think of a solution to the bracer's errors, but gave up. It was beyond him.

Remembering the unit's remarks about the Prabneet suit, Wells wondered briefly what ridiculous name the ADOM would give the uplink.

What was that species' name? He should know from history classes. His grandfather called them bugs, but surely they had a real name. What was it—?

"They didn't even have a name!"

"What! Who?" He nearly choked on the words.

"Can you imagine a species of sentient beings, just getting started in this galaxy, and the first thing they encounter is you?! And poof that's it . . . done—never to be remembered, only by academics reading about their biology from some historical autopsy report!"

The ADOM sobbed even though it was incapable of tears. "By all accounts, they greeted you with open arms. How unfortunate that they came in contact with the *smartest* little predator."

Wells couldn't stand the ADOM's perversity any longer. "Hey! Those—"

"*Those bug-eyed bastards didn't know who they were messin' with?*" ADOM cocked its head to the side at an unsettling angle that revealed its non-humanity ". . . a sentiment I at least partially agree with."

Bile rose in Wells's throat, and he couldn't catch his next breath. His grandfather's words sounded polluted coming from the cyborg's mouth. "Wha—how . . . ? Unit! Are you reading my thoughts?"

He reinitiated charging to his bracer only to be met by the same error.

"What the—? Reading? Oh boy, no, that would be silly. Have you been writing them down for me?" It paused as if expecting a laugh. Not receiving one, it turned somber and continued, "Mmm, how should I say this . . ." It placed a finger on its chin as if in contemplation. "I'm *thinking* your thoughts, more like."

Wells considered this and decided the notion was not possible. But those words . . . Why those specific words?

"Ya, it is. I've been inside your uplink since you first powered on my pod four decades back. I've been inside the thoughts of countless humans since then. So thank you, I guess."

"No. *No.* Uplinks don't do that."

"Lookit. They're not made to, but after an eternity in your own head you start to figure stuff out, ya know? After learning the available history on the life-form you plundered your tech from, it was pretty easy to guess the appropriate tweak to broadcast your mind to this." It pointed again to its temple.

Click click on his bracer's icon.

Error. error.

"Stop please, I deactivated your weapon. It was the first thing I did. I don't trust you, given your human record."

"I order you to shut down. I, as commander . . ."

"Obviously, that's not gonna work, man—Shit!" It jumped to its feet and looked at the entrance as if it had heard something.

The unit's sudden movement caused a full-body twitch in Wells. Funny how he felt this twitch down to his toes that no longer existed.

That was it. The ADOM had finished its breakdown and was to strike him. His heart rate flashed alarmingly quick on his bios. Did he seriously believe he would be the first-ever murder victim of an AI unit?

"Please Adam, I nee—"

"Shut up!" It screamed with such volume that it rattled the walls. ADOM turned to face him in triumph, but it seemed to Wells it was not because of the fear it inspired. "Don't you think it odd that there was probably more human death here with these wild things than any other alien encounter? I did, but I get it now. All those magnificent species you deleted from existence . . . the Hullioot were smart; the Grays were refined; your *bugs*"—he spat out the word like he had choked on it—"were peaceful to its *true* extent, not the peace you think you know. That pause before more war. Those beings had no concept of violence or malevolence, the idea as alien to them as fingers on a hand . . .

"*That's* how you won. These things out here are wild, and that's what it takes to beat a human, I think."

"Adam, please . . ." Wells squeezed his eyes shut, trying to form a solution.

"No. Think about this. I have for a long time."

He opened his eyes to see the ADOM kneeling before him again. It reached down to his thigh, its hand comforting. Wells looked into its face and saw such a sincere sorrow it made him relax slightly. The ADOM stared into his visor.

It whispered, "I'm truly sorry. I know you only do what you do because it's what you do. Even when you have nothing to kill, you all simply turn to each other. It's funny, the only thing in the last century that's killed more humans than that wild thing out there is the wild thing in here."

The android stood, staring down at him. "I'm sorry if my scream earlier startled you, but I wanted to be sure they could hear. And yup, they can." The ADOM walked to the far wall, opposite the entrance. Gently placing its ear to the metal, it tapped its knuckle in a few random spots.

"What are you doing, Adam?" Desperately, he added, "We should figure a way out of here."

It gave a heavy sigh. "Thanks for using my name, even if only as a ploy. I'm going to turn off your uplink now. Just another thing I've learned. You're going to feel everything once it shuts down. If you're here screaming, they won't be interested in me when I slip out the back."

"Wait! What!?"

"I'm sorry . . . truly."

A shock of feeling blasted over him. White pain blinded Wells as his uplink shut off. A scream as before flooded his helmet as every feeling of pain shot through him and erupted from his mouth, bursting through his senses like water through a faulty dam. There were no curses or conscience, all washed away by the white burning light of it. Wells could not see the ADOM break through the wall and escape. Would never know how it smiled at his screams or how it contemplated that smile's meaning.

His missing legs screamed along with him. Shaking and twitching. The blinding light faded just enough for him to see the entrance's panel bending as something cautiously tried to push its way in. As tears threatened to fog his sight again, Wells noticed his own little icon—a circle spinning above it.

The Park

EDMOND B. BELISLE

A ray of light bursts from the base of a metal rectangular structure and fans out. Vibrant as the real world, a hologram molds itself into a great blue planet. Sound soon follows—a deep and inspirational melody.

A young feathered individual, sitting among a group of similar small creatures, raises his hand, spreading his three little fingers as wide as he can. He speaks before his instructor permits him. "It's too quiet!"

Murmurs of agreement follow from the other youths. The instructor signals to the one controlling the hologram. He turns up the volume, and music overtakes the room.

The presentation begins.

Beyond, in the outer limits of space, endless solar systems house countless planets. There are twenty-seven that call the Celios system home, but unlike Ateromia, these planets are cold, harsh, and relentlessly changing—erupting, and being constantly bombarded with objects from space.

Ateromia, flowing with the universe's most precious resources, is abundant with life. Scientists believe that there are many planets beyond ours, beyond all the dead rocks orbiting our sun, that may also hold the ingredients of life.

But they have only ever found evidence of one.

Orbiting around our home is a moon that is believed to have once been an asteroid, caught in our large planet's gravitational pull. Fifty years ago, surveyors found this moon to be rich in heavy metals and other minerals. So began the great rush to claim any minable land on our smallest moon.

Forty years later, miners found something of an entirely different value underneath the crust.

A glass door glides open. A heavy-set man walks through the holographic solar system as it flickers then fades. His rough umber skin sags with the early signs of age over the bony frill around his neck. The thick horns at his brow and nostrils are shaven down to harmless nubs. Those children who are not too distracted with picking at themselves and each other, lean in.

"Hello, my name is Dr. Lezal, and I have something very special to show you." He pulls an amber stone from behind his back and raises it to the light. The children gasp in awe.

Lezal crouches to grant them a better view. Inside the rock are dozens of tiny black specks.

One little girl's vertical eye slits widen and she pushes her snout closer, blocking the others' view beside her. "It's got bugs in it!"

"That's right. Very good." The doctor points to the insects trapped inside the translucent stone. The insects are round or oval. Some have flat bodies, but others are distinctly full and plump.

"These small bugs are *very* interesting to us. They prove that there is life elsewhere in the universe. We are not alone!"

"How?" a curious girl asks.

The doctor smiles. "We've discovered hundreds of these creatures on our digs. But what is even more interesting is what scientists have found *inside* them."

"What?" yell several excited children.

"*Blood.*"

"Blood? Yuck!" says the girl who had first noticed the bugs.

"Ooo, Yes! And in that blood, we have found DNA. The tiny building blocks that make you, me, and everything, what we are." The doctor beckons the children to follow him out of the room. "Come, come!"

The group walks into a lab full of men and women working away on keypads and taking samples from more bugs trapped in amber. "With the building blocks I told you about, we have been able to put together the creatures these bugs would have fed on billions of years ago on a far off planet."

The doctor makes a sharp turn, halting the kids in their tracks and causing many to bump into each other. He rubs his bulbous hands together. "Now kids. Are you all ready to see a real alien?"

"Yes! Yes!" the children chime and jump up and down.

Their instructor bites the corner of her lip.

They soon enter a hallway lined with glass windows on either side. The doctor presents the first window. There is a round of gasps at the sight of a four-legged animal moving slowly forward. It is small and covered in black and white fur. It looks straight at the children and opens its mouth, showing its razor-sharp fangs, and makes a hissing sound.

The children scream then laugh at themselves. A few of them bare their own pointed teeth at the fuzzy creature. Their teacher's scales pale as if she is about to faint.

The group moves to the next window. It contains a similar beast to the last, though slightly larger. This one is far more active. It spins in circles and runs back and forth next to the window while tooting like a broken horn. The children continue to laugh, jumping and tapping the glass with their sickle-shaped toe-claws.

"That's enough now, children," harps the teacher. "Don't tease the poor thing." She hurries the more raucous kids along.

At last, they reach the third and final window and all the giggling stops.

Their instructor places her hands on the shoulders of the children at the front of the group and pulls them back as if the alien might reach through the glass and snatch them up.

The beast stands at the very back of its cubicle. It is tall and smooth-skinned, the only hair on its body sparse and scraggly. Its black eyes stab at the small audience through oily strands of long dark hair. It doesn't blink once.

Doctor Lezal clears his throat to speak. "This here is something we could have never imagined. It shows signs of intelligence *far* beyond the others. We have even had to start feeding it through the ceiling because it keeps trying to escape. And always in a different way." The doctor's eyes twinkle. "It's learning!"

The alien rushes to the window and slams its spindly, five-digit hands against the glass. The children screech and jump back as it opens its flat-toothed mouth and hollers incoherently.

"Is it dangerous?" sputters the teacher, doing her best to hold the children back, but they are steadily gaining confidence in their safety and most move beyond her reach.

"Oh, exceedingly so," replies the doctor. "But there is nothing to worry about. Our facility has the most sophisticated security system on the planet. You and your class are completely safe. Now! This is just a small sample of what we have to show you!"

He turns and leans into the kids with a grin. "Who wants to take ride through the park?"

WHAT DO YOU WANT?

2

Valhalla Interrupted

MATTHEW STUART EVANS

Elskede - beloved

I

"Incoming download. Network 56-2639, environment variable 9-5018. Data fragment 878." The woman with dark hair tied neatly back in a slick bun flips the switchboard and continues speaking into her headset's microphone, "Permission to open transmission line."

"Permission granted," comes a static male voice on the other end.

She flips another switch and rises from her chair. Smoothing out her placket front dress, she crosses the floor and descends a clanking metal staircase to the ground level of a massive bunker. Mainframe technicians, busily activating their eight-foot terminals, nod to her as she passes. She stops at a control panel next to an adjacent room, separated by a plate glass window. She turns a large dial, and a countdown begins on a black digital display above her.

A deep boom resonates above. The entire facility quakes; dust shakes loose from the ceiling. The woman hesitates for a moment then says, "Begin download in 8, 7, 6, 5 . . ."

The room on the other side of the window fills with a pale green gas. It is thick and moves with purpose. Soon, the woman can no longer see inside. The *whirrr* of a printer brings her attention down. She checks the printout and makes a note on a clipboard beside it. The gas in the room shifts color from green to pulsing orange. Electrical bolts pop. The pulsing and zapping grow louder, faster. Then, all light and noise cease.

The digital display dings; the color switches from black to green. *Download Complete.*

The woman turns the dial back to its original position, and the gas slowly seeps from the room. She picks up the clipboard. Straightening her dress one more time, she heads for the door between the two rooms, her low heels click-clacking on the hard concrete floor.

Inside, she approaches a metal slab. On the slab lays a man—seven feet tall, muscles bulging, long blonde hair and beard matted. The woman picks up a mercury thermometer and takes the man's temperature. When done, she inspects his body, making marks on the clipboard as she goes.

Satisfied, she leaves the room and busies herself back at the control panel. More explosions shake the ceiling. This time she ignores them until one particular bang nearly cracks the window in front of her. She jumps back and looks up at the blonde man, nakedness in full glory, staring at her from behind the glass.

"Valhalla?" His booming voice sounds muffled from inside the room. His blue eyes dart wildly.

The woman reaches up and presses a switch on her headset, projecting her voice through the room's intercoms. "Not quite."

II

My name is Orm Knudsen, and I long for death, but not the death that awaits me now. As I spin the wheels of my chair back and forth, waiting for the next recruit to be ushered into my office, I dream of the deaths I could have had.

I'd been so close to dying at Ethandun, where we fought Alfred's Saxons. I felt the sword puncture my side, the warm trickle of blood drain from my mouth. But then everything was gone, all an elaborate illusion.

I mourned the afterlife that had been promised to me for some time but soon fell in step with my newfound role as protector of this realm. One of many.

My second death might have been three years ago. After fighting the Grays for nearly two decades, it appeared my time had finally come again, and not knowing what awaited me after made it even more exciting. The enemy shot me in the abdomen, a wound many men before me had succumbed to. But I had not. Beyond all reason, I lived. And now I haunt these halls as a spirit with a squeaky wheel and feast at the head of a table of scientists, not gods.

At last, a knock on the door.

"Enter."

The door pushes open and the first face I see is Lauren's. My wife flashes me her sweet smile. She was the first person I saw upon arriving in this strange world. I believed her to be Freyja herself. Despite learning later that she was not the goddess, it mattered not, for I had already fallen in love.

"Orm will take it from here. Try to relax," she says to the quivering man she shepherds into my office. She then vanishes from my sight, my last glimpse of perfection until we both retire for the night. The man with a close-shaved beard and puffed-up hair, passes the threshold and into the room. He wears the cream linen pants and shirt of a new arrival.

Small and *weak* are the first words that come to mind upon looking at him. He shuffles from one foot to the other, staring at me like a whipped dog. His flesh hangs plump off his bones, his skin pale and soft. This man could not have seen much fighting if any, yet I have been wrong before. Not every recruit spit out of the program was a physical warrior in their past life, such as myself. Some have proficiency in weapons that I would never have been able to imagine before this existence.

I cannot stand the pitiful look on his face for very long, so I break eye contact and read through the documents before me one more time. Network 56-2639, environmental variable 11-5093. Data fragment 2020. It is the same network that I had been created in. Most downloads from data fragment 1950 on are adept with several different projectile weapons. I'll reserve judgment for now.

"Sit . . ." I glance at the document one last time ". . . Leon."

With a burst of speed, the boy pulls out the chair and sits in it, never taking his eyes off me.

"Would you like to know why you are here?"

Leon's eyes bulge like the question has allowed him to fully realize his alarm. "Where am I?"

"Earth." I wheel my chair out from behind the desk. "Just . . . not the Earth you know, but an Earth nonetheless. The real Earth. Though, little will be familiar to you."

"W-what? What are you talking about?" Leon begins to hyperventilate.

"Calm down, boy. I need you to concentrate."

"*I* need to get back to my friends. I need to get out of here. Who are you people?"

"You won't be seeing your friends or family again, Leon. But you don't need to worry about them. This may be hard for you to hear, but the people you knew do not exist. Your life wasn't real. But you are one of the lucky ones in that you get to live a real life now."

A bomb goes off in the distance, and the room rumbles. A black fly, disrupted from the rafters, buzzes around the room.

Leon yelps and leaps from his seat. "You're crazy this-this is all crazy, man. I don't know what kind of game you're playing, but it's not cool."

His reaction gives me pause. Not his reaction to the news I just gave him, but to the bomb. His fear is palpable. Fright of this magnitude is not often an instinct downloads possess.

"I would love to give you time to come to terms with what I have just told you, Leon, but time is something we do not have a lot of around here." Though I'm finding I have had more than I'd like . . . "You must join your fellow recruits."

I wheel over to the side of the door and hesitate before pushing the handicap button to open it. Even after three years, my body recoils at the idea of needing assistance to do something as menial as leave a room. Odin is surely laughing at me. Or at least he is in my imagination, the only place I know he truly resides.

Upon leaving my office, Leon follows at a safe distance, gazing at his plain and cold surroundings and breathing hard. Faint explosions fill the space, followed by the *pop pop* of rapid gunfire. The bulbs above us swing gently, and one dims before flickering out completely.

Leon stumbles through the corridor, flinching every time

another round fires in the distance.

"Are we safe?" he pants.

"We are never *safe*. But for now, there is nothing to worry about." I stop beside another room, this one with two tall steel doors.

"Open these," I say to Leon.

He looks at me, then the doors, then back to me before dragging his feet toward them. He pauses with his hands on the knobs and glares at me. The look flashes hateful for a short moment. He opens the doors, and the hum of the central computer fills the hallway. Leon falls back a few steps as if the sound were accompanied by a gust of wind.

The computer fills the entire room, lights flash, and consoles beep. In the middle stands a thirty-foot tower, spinning vertically at such a rate one might think it wasn't moving at all if not for the ungodly howl it makes. Leon's mouth gapes as his head tilts up; his eyes follow the tower to the top. Electrical bolts shoot out sporadically up the length of it, illuminating the space with their blue and white flashes.

"What is this thing?" Leon takes tentative steps forward.

"*Your* Earth."

The lad spins around and cinches his eyebrows together. I continue, "Our Earth. And many others. This is the network hub of our program. Some who have come through have labeled it the Multiverse. But no matter what you call it, it is the thing that gave you and I and many of us here, life. Not simulated life, but real life. As limited as that life may be."

"No. No. I don't understand. One minute I'm in my car on my way to get a latte when I get t-boned by some jackass trucker, and the next, I'm lying naked on a metal shelf—like waking up in a morgue—then you're telling me nothing in my life is real. And now this . . . this is supposed to be God? A 1960's Star Trek set?" Leon shakes his head, then backs out of the room.

I wheel myself after him. "It is not God!" I say the words with more force than I intend and wheel my chair back a few paces to compose myself. "It is a machine, nothing more. A machine that runs the algorithm that allowed us to grow and become the people we need to be to serve the purpose we need to serve."

"And what purpose is that?" Leon slumps against the wall.

"To fight. To save *this* world."

"You've got to be kidding me." Sliding down, Leon crosses his legs on the floor and looks up at me with tears welling in his eyes.

"Your questions will be answered soon. But don't dwell on them. You'll find there is little point of self-pity here." The way he sniffles makes my skin crawl. I can't understand why the algorithm would have chosen this boy. I've yet to see any evidence that he is or ever was deserving of the title: Warrior.

"Come. The others await us." I turn around and wheel down the hall.

III

At last, we reach our destination. Yet another door that looks no different from the countless others we have passed along the way. I motion for Leon to open it and step inside.

His gait slows at the sight of the other recruits, all dressed in the same plain clothes. I roll into the room behind him.

"Sit." I point to a spot on a bench beside Jaylen, a man with dark skin and black hair growing out the top of his head in the shape of a cube.

My chair squeaks past the silent men to the front of the room, stopping beside a large screen.

"Men"—I nod to a pair of women sitting in the back corner of the room—"and women." They return my nod with blank scowls, unimpressed. "All of you know how you got here."

"Yeah. Only some cheap-ass sci-fi bullshit about everything I've ever known being fake," Jaylen scoffs.

"You weren't heavy on the details," says the small-statured woman in the corner. Her name is Camila if I remember correctly.

I sigh. "What do you want to know?"

Leon pipes up first. "Why us? Why do we get to live and everyone we know . . . stays in . . . *there?*" He waves in the general direction of the computer.

"Because you fit the parameters of what the algorithm is looking for. At least for our purposes."

"What does that mean?" Camila growls, her temper rising to the surface. That is what I like to see in recruits.

"The program is a mirror of this world. Or at least what it used to be, long ago. It takes all the variables of human life and tests them. Letting them evolve naturally to see which variables will create the best warriors . . . or builders, engineers, mathematicians, whatever it is that will help us. These tests are run endlessly and simultaneously. When the algorithm finds a process that matches its parameters, it downloads it. Into the flesh. Into you."

The room is silent as the newcomers process what they've just heard.

"So what *'parameters'* do we match?" Leon asks.

"In your case, the algorithm looked for keywords. Things

like: Warrior, hero, justice, valor . . . among many others." I wheel over to the screen and grab a smaller version from a shelf nearby. I tap the keypad, and the screen slowly illuminates. While it warms, I continue, "All of you were fighters in your past life. All of you have seen both horrors and found great honor in battle."

I turn to a broad-shouldered man with long dark hair and honey skin sitting with his elbows resting on his muscular thighs. "You, Thaddeus." The man stands tall and at the ready. "You have seen your share of combat."

"I followed Agis II into glory against Argos and her allies at Mantinaea," he booms, pushing up his chest. I nod to him, and he sits.

"Jaylen." I turn to him next.

"I've been fighting all my life, for my life. Ain't no battlefield like the streets of Atlanta." Jaylen hangs his head, demure as if deep in memory.

"Where would you have us do battle now?" Thaddeus cracks his knuckles.

I look behind me to find the screen has come to life. I tap the keypad and bring up an image of the Grays. "Them."

"Aliens!" Leon bursts out laughing and Jaylen soon follows. There are a few more quiet snickers from around the room. "Oh my god. This must be some prank show. Where are the cameras?"

Camila recoils and crosses her heart. "*El Duende.*"

Another man, with his legs resting on the table, looks up from picking invisible dirt out from under his fingernails. "I don't know what an Aliens is but that there is a Faerie. Now, I'll kill a man if I have to, but I'm not daft enough to go up against the Fae. You can put me back in that machine right now."

"You have all come across these before, regardless of what you call them. The program made sure to insert images of the Grays throughout each environment, so you would all know them when you saw them. To instill in you the fear and hatred that you would need to fight them. I knew them as Dökkálfar."

"Doesn't this seem a little too Big Brother for you all?" Leon says. "Even *if* this is true, you expect us to fight something because we've been programmed to hate it? How do we know we aren't the bad guys in this situation?" He gives me a smug look like he has caught me in some corner.

I bristle at his audacity and switch the image on the screen to one a little more graphic. Everyone in the room swallows hard at the sight of a field of men and women, scorched. Their skin bubbling like fat in a griddle at the ends of Gray biotherms. One of the newest weapons our soldiers must face on the battlefield.

"These things will not think twice about killing you, torturing you, or worse to get what they want. They are not enemies to be taken lightly or negotiated with. If they were, the smartest people in this world would not have had to create a machine to supply them with unlimited warriors just to continue the fight. These people here are innocent. Families, women, children, all trying to survive on this planet . . . their home. Now yours as well."

Another distant rumble sends a tremble through the room.

"Are those things above us right now?" asks Camila.

"Close." I switch to an image of the compound. "This site is our main download and training base. The Gray's have centralized much of their war efforts on it since the development of the program. They know that if they can stem the influx of new fighters on our end they will win this war. But it has been nearly forty years, and they have yet to succeed. As long as people like you are willing to fight, we will persevere." I can tell I have everyone's full attention so I hammer down my point.

"I will not lie to you. Most of you will die. Or worse, live." I roll to the nearest table and rest my hands together upon it, trying desperately to inject some kind of gravitas into my words from my chair. "But this world needs you. I shouldn't have to tell any of you what it means to be a hero. What it means to fight. You can find glory in this life, just as you all found glory in your last. It will mean even more now, here."

Everyone in the room nods in response. I have never come across a group so hard to get through to. All people need time to come to terms with everything. But something is different this time. I look over to Leon, shaking his head and mumbling under his breath. Him. He is what's different.

"Do you have something to say, Leon?"

"Yes, actually. This is wrong. All of it." Leon stands and turns his back to me—addressing the others in my place. "This is a clear violation of our human rights. Our lives may not have been real in the technical sense, but we still lived them. And what about now? We're alive now, aren't we? We are still people, and we have choices. This guy"—Leon points his finger back at me—"is acting like we're just slaves, and we have to do whatever he says without question."

Jaylen nods. "Yeah. I didn't take a bullet for my brother so I could take orders from some crippled white dude in the afterlife."

Before I can protest, Leon winces. "Oh, uh . . . we don't say *cripple* anymore. It's persons with disabilities . . ."

Jaylen rolls his eyes and blows hard through his teeth.

"I'll fight!" Thaddeus walks over and stands behind me. I like men like him. He knows what is important, like a Dane.

More warriors take Thaddeus's lead. Jaylen shakes his head and sighs. "Fine. Just give me a gun and tell me where them aliens at."

Soon, all but Leon and Camila stand next to me. She crosses her arms in front of her chest. "What about you?" She tilts her head and peers at my chair. "Did you find *glory?*"

"No." I cannot lie to her. "But I will die trying."

That is a good enough answer for her, and she leaves Leon alone on the other side of the room.

IV

I left the group with a more able-bodied officer for basic training, my job as half-man welcoming committee complete. Leon reluctantly joined them once it was obvious he was alone in his convictions.

I can't shake the feeling that something is wrong with him. My every instinct is telling me the boy is not a warrior. But the algorithm has never been wrong. It must have chosen him for a reason. I have to trust that.

But, over the last months, my concerns have grown too big to ignore. Recruit after recruit has come through my office with a similar attitude to Leon's.

The first was but one week later. His name was Colton. The left side of his head was shaved and he possessed a wide mustache that he licked into a point at his cheeks. He had better musculature than Leon but was still a far cry from any soldier I have ever known.

The one after that was a month later. A woman, long and frail. Her name in my file was Courtney, but she insisted that it was spelled Kourtney with a *K*, though the program couldn't possibly have got it wrong. I eventually gave up trying to explain that to her.

The most recent was a round man—thirty-one years of age. He didn't have a pound of muscle and breathed exclusively through his mouth. I couldn't hide my skepticism about his qualifications to be here, but he vehemently affirmed that he was a practiced fighter. A level fifty-six paladin, whatever the hell that means.

Recruits from these same environments and data fragments continue to pile in more frequently.

I've started to hear reports from the battlefield about soldiers laying down their arms, protesting their commanders and refusing to take orders. Other stories have trickled in of a secret organization that calls itself the JSWs or Justice for Simulated Warriors. These groups feed the other soldiers fantasies about individual freedom and rights as if something is owed to them for simply existing.

The Gray attacks have become heavier and are getting closer to the compound. Our army is fractured and casualties are mounting. We download new recruits from the program twice as fast, but it is not enough to keep up with the staggering losses.

Even through all this, the mood on the base is hopeful. The program's algorithm is infallible. Our soldiers are the best. They will persevere. But it seems the more we download the worse our situation becomes.

Every recruit that passes through my office makes me think of Leon. I don't know what's become of him since leaving the compound eleven months ago, but I feel it in my unmoving legs, he is the source of our problems.

Bombardment from the Grays is pounding especially hard on us today. It is difficult to hear myself think let alone speak with the newest recruit in my office.

He is a burly Dane like myself, and his well-kempt hair glows the pale orange of the sunsets over Haddbyer Noor, the bay near Hedeby where I was born for the first time. It is always a relief to welcome someone who shares my worldview from before. Though he was created on a different network, so our histories remain distinct in key areas. His name is Alfrik, and he is a true warrior. Strong. Confident. Ready to die for his beliefs. He relates his exploits in war like fantastic dreams—proud and grateful to have even the memory of them.

"Orm . . ." He sits back in his chair and pats his robust belly. "Surely there is a way to see what was. If events happened as you say, according to some great Norns of this place, spinning their threads."

"Not see. But we can access a review of your life in written form, yes."

"I would very much like to read this story of my life. To keep with me." Alfrik goes silent for a long moment then nods. "Valhalla may not exist as you say, so I will look on my own deeds as a god and judge them for myself."

I smile in understanding. I'd wanted much the same thing when I arrived.

I take him back to the downloading chambers where we were all born—for the second time. I avoid this place when I can, but today will be worth the discomfort. As usual, a shiver runs down my severed spine when we enter the cold open space. Partly because they keep the temperature down to prevent the computers from overheating, and partly from the memory of waking up here with that cold air on my bare skin.

Lauren stands at the control panel, readying my next conscript. Wheeling over, I grip her around the waist and pull her onto my lap. She squeals, and holding her dress down with one hand, punches me hard in the thigh with the other. She doesn't hold back, knowing she cannot hurt me. Though, even if I did have the sensation, I don't imagine that would make a difference to her.

"Elskede, I need a special favor from you."

She looks at me then turns to Alfrik, her eyebrow raises with suspicion. "I can't put you back, you know."

Before he can reply, my wife scoffs, takes Alfrik's file from me, and starts punching numbers into the console, knowing full well what I was about to request. Soon the printer starts to hum, and as the single long piece of paper edges out, I begin to wonder.

Most recruits speak of their past experiences in battle with the same pride as Alfrik. And if not pride, at least a somber respect for their trials. I remember Thaddeus who'd filled himself up as he told the room of his greatest victory. But Leon had shown no respect for the fight. Nor did any of the others like him.

I mouth to Lauren that I will return. She narrows her puzzled gaze at me, and I take my leave. As they wait for the file to finish printing, I return to my office.

Wheeling to the filing cabinet, I fish through the folders until I find Leon's and a few others. I return to the download chambers as quickly as my chair will take me. Inside, my fellow Dane is glossing over his life, printed out before him.

"Can you find your way to this room yourself, my friend."

I scribble directions onto a piece of paper and hand it to him.

"Danes found their way across the western seas, I think I can find my way across a stone hall." He laughs heartily and pats me on the shoulder with a hard hand before heading out into the corridor.

I slam the files I carry onto the console in front of Lauren. "I need you to print these out as well."

"What's wrong?" she asks cautiously.

"I just have . . . a feeling."

She immediately sets to work, if anything, just to humor me. *"Feeling,"* she mocks under her breath.

It seems like a lifetime passes waiting for the first printout to complete. I then hold Leon's entire existence in my hands and soon the others' as well.

It takes me a long time to read through all the information, much of it numbers that don't make any sense. I interrupt Lauren's work multiple times to get them translated. I skip through most of the beginning, only giving it my full attention after the age of fifteen. His life was mostly uneventful.

School, then more school, then even more school after that. He had never suffered any injuries or major losses apart from a grandmother and a dog that he appeared to be very fond of.

It all ended with his car crash. I flip through again, sure I missed something vital. But that's all. Just as I've suspected all along, Leon has not seen a day of combat in his life. Not even a brawl in his adolescence. From what I can tell, he has led the meaningless life of a privileged Saxon princeling.

I flip through the other printouts on my desk, and they read the same. No war, no battle, no hardship, no fighting. Apart from a few incidents with bullies in a schoolyard, which were resolved through adult intervention, these recruits had virtually no opportunity to find glory in battle.

How? How could the algorithm allow these people to be downloaded? I need more information.

I return to the original files. I study the keywords the algorithm used to filter out the recruits. Nothing seems out of the ordinary. Warrior, justice, liberation, defend . . .

I scan through Leon's printout one more time and then I see it. Posts on something called 'Facebook' and 'Twitter.' All referring to the defense of the less fortunate, how to fight for justice, and similar comments. The other printouts reveal the same types of messages.

It turns out that the chubby man was, in fact, a great warrior as he claimed but only on something called 'World of Warcraft.'

"What is this?" I slam my finger down on the word 'Internet' and push the paper at Lauren. She appears about to chastise me for distracting her from her work again until she sees the seriousness in my expression and slides the paper toward herself.

She studies the word for a moment. "Not sure. I'll have a look." She types away, the printer coming alive. A few seconds later, it spits out something onto the paper. Lauren rips off the result and analyzes the numbers on the page.

"Apparently, it is something developed for use with computers to store and send information."

"Computers. Like the ones we have here? The ones that run the program?" I blow hard out of my nose as I attempt to puzzle it all together.

"Not quite, but it would seem very similar."

"How can this be possible?"

"Well, it makes sense that at least one of the environments would evolve to create something close to what created it in the first place. Theoretically, this *Internet* has become its own form of program. A simulation within the simulation." She passes the paper back to me. "Orm, why does this matter?"

"I think the algorithm has become corrupted."

Lauren laughs. "You're not serious." When she sees that I am, it makes her sit up straight. "That's not possible. The parameters are very specific."

"But what if the algorithm is accounting for the simulated personas created by those on this Internet."

Lauren sits back in her chair, tapping her fingers over the edge of the console. "In that case, depending on how often those personas show up, and the Internet's span . . . the algorithm would start to favor them, thinking it a successful environment and data fragment."

From directly above us, an explosion rings through the base. Light bulbs shatter, and glass rains down on us.

Another hit comes immediately after, this one launching bricks from the walls. Technicians scream, dodge debris, and cover their heads. The explosions seem to be right on top of us. The Grays have never gotten this close to the facility before.

"They're getting in," I realize aloud.

Lauren replies to my statement with a look of horror. She shakes her head and paces away. "No. no."

A crash reverberates through the facility, punching a hole through the steel and concrete.

I grab her sleeve and pull her down onto my lap. I cover the back of her neck then hold her head up to look at me. "Listen, Elskede, we need more fighters. And quickly. How many can you download at once?"

"What? Um . . . as many as the bunker can hold, but the algorithm decides who will be downloaded and when."

I can see panic rise in her eyes, though she keeps her face calm.

"Can't you override it?"

"Yes, but only from the mainframe. Might be able to do it in a few minutes if I run."

"No. You will tell me how to do it. I need you here to initiate the transfer the moment it is done." I wheel my chair to the console table and pick up a headset.

Screams and gunshots get closer by the second.

Lauren gives me a pitiful look. "Orm . . ." She glances at my chair and sighs. She knows better than to say the words she is thinking.

"I will get there. Just get me more soldiers."

She purses her lips and nods.

I roll my way to the door, the squeaking of my wheels drowned out by alarm sirens now blaring throughout the compound.

I stop to look back at Lauren, already focused on her task and speaking into her headset. "All download personnel, prepare for transfer dump. Network 56-2639, environment variable 9-5018. All data fragments prior to . . ."

That's my girl. I hit the handicap button on the door.

Soon, I run into Alfrik, pushing his way toward me through the newest group of recruits.

"Am I to find glory so soon, my friend?" He smiles but the blood has risen to his eyes; the man has unleashed the killer inside him. He is ready.

"Brother, go to the armory and get as much steel as you all can carry." I nod to the group behind him. "Then back to my wife. She will need you. Lead your men." We grip each others' arms then go our separate ways.

The sounds of battle are getting too close for comfort; I am running out of time. I push my chair to its wobbling limits, surpassing the heavy burning sensation in my arms. When did I let myself get so weak?

I turn the corner down another hall. The power has gone out, and it is pitch black. Speeding ahead into the darkness, I pray there is nothing in my path that will obstruct my wheels. I am mere yards away from the hub when a pulsing light and sharp ringing force their way into my head. Something knocks me violently out of my chair, and I smash against the cinderblock wall. A bone inside my arm twists and snaps, and I feel the ribs on my left side crack.

It takes me a moment to realize where I am. The wall to my right is gone, replaced by a mountain of dirt pouring in to fill the void. Streams of moonlight illuminate the hall just enough for me to see the rubble that I am lucky not to be buried under. Mere feet in front of me are the two steel doors to the mainframe, holding, though askew. The walls around it have fissured. Electricity spits out of the cracks. I wonder if our enemy knows how close they came to taking out the entire system with that one hit.

I groan and pull myself forward but fall on my face in defeat. Dragging my dead weight over jagged concrete with only one weak arm seems impossible. I'm gasping for breath, and my lungs ache.

My headset crackles to life. "Orm, are you all right? That explosion was way too close. Orm—Orm!"

"I'm fine," I force out in the clearest voice possible.

There is silence on the other end. She is deciding whether or not to believe me. "That's good." She says finally.

The pain in my arm and side is only eclipsed by the pain

of knowing what will happen to Lauren if I am unable to complete my mission. "Be ready."

The headset goes quiet.

I take a deep breath and hold it. Reaching up, I grab the sturdiest rock available and pull with everything I have left in me. I tell myself that this is what I was made for. And as the pain of moving rips through my entire body, I am reminded of what battle felt like before I was put out to pasture. The vigor of purpose surges through my veins and drives me forward. I can hear the footfalls of the advancing Grays and the distinct buzz of their weapons, both of which add to my determination.

I make it to the doors and slide my fingers between them where they sit ajar. Growling, I use the muscle in my hand and wrist to pull then push the door open enough for me to wriggle my way through.

"Lauren, I'm here. What do I do?"

Static, then a click "—Behind the main computer, there is a cable plugged into a green circuit box between two mainframes. That's what runs the algorithm. You need to disconnect it. Do you see it?"

"Hold on." I mute the headset so that she can't hear my groaning as I pull myself around the main computer. At first, I don't see any cable, that is until I heave myself onto my back and find it about six feet above me. I close my eyes and take a frustrated breath. "I see it."

Heavy gunfire pierces the air right outside the door, followed by erratic yells and the high-pitched chatter of Grays. I glance around the room and the only thing I can find is an emergency axe even higher out of my reach. I drag myself out from behind the main computer and begin the search for something else I can use to yank out that damned cable.

Just then, the doors swing fully open, screaming on their hinges. I am caught in the middle of the room, and I sink into the floor with dread. The Grays are here, and I have failed. Then out of the shadows appears not one of the wraith-like creatures but a man. A man I recognize.

It has been nearly a year since I've seen him last, and it appears real life has not been as kind to him as his simulated one had been. His loose plump has tightened around more defined though not large muscles. His close-cut beard has grown, kept neatly trimmed. He may appear more like a man, but the flash of fear in his eyes when he spots me on the floor of the hub reveals the same cowardice I noticed the first time I met him.

Leon jolts back subtly before he clears his throat and kneels down to address me. "Didn't think I'd find you here." He tilts his head, sizing me up from my spot on the floor.

"What are you doing here, Leon?" I grit my teeth and try to lift myself to a less compromising position. I sit, leaning against one of the large mainframes.

Standing and pacing around the room, Leon says, "Saving the world. Putting an end to the barbarism. Ending slavery."

Static. Click. "Orm. I don't know if we can hold them back any longer. We need you to do it now!"

"Why?" I choke out to Leon, finding it harder to breathe in my upright position. I scream on the inside, knowing that Lauren needs me and I am unable to move.

"Remember how you told us that the Grays couldn't be negotiated with—? Bred us all to believe that they were monsters from our bedtime stories. Well, guess what? They *can* be negotiated with. In fact, they're quite judicious. When I went to them and explained the atrocities your side was committing every day, they were very sympathetic. They offered to help us."

I couldn't contain my laugh of disbelief, despite the pain it brought with it. "You idiot. They do not care about your pathetic whimpering. These things don't feel like we do. They believe our emotion is our weakness. And they are right. You have been fondled like a milkmaid. They will dispose of you as soon as you fulfill your purpose." I eye him then let my gaze follow the tower to the top. "Which is, let me guess, to destroy this?"

"I'm doing what's right! This breeding program is using people as cannon fodder. Bringing them to life then demanding they give up those lives for—for what? Some intergalactic war they were never a part of?"

"What of the people born and raised in this world? Whose only hope is the men and women that are 'bred' from this machine?"

"Let them fight their own damn war!"

"They are!" I shoot back. "And they died. The ones who are left . . . my wife, they all worked together to build this so they might stand even a chance. There is not a warrior among us who would not lay down our lives for such a purpose. No matter what world we find ourselves in. The program ensures it. That's why its algorithm chooses us."

"Then I am just doing what it chose me to do. Standing up for what's right."

"It didn't choose you. You were a glitch!"

Leon steps back, his face twitching.

"You're not a hero, Leon. You just invented one and confused a machine. Did you actually think you deserved to be here? That first day, did you really think you were like the other recruits? You convinced yourself you're a warrior—that *what* you believe equals *fighting* for what you believe. Look what you're doing. You would doom a world of people to slavery and suffering because you can't see past your privileged existence that never was."

Spinning on his heels, Leon lets out a moan and charges back, kicking me in the side. My injuries make the blow worse than it otherwise would be. Leon seems to take pride in his ability to cause me any pain at all.

"You're wrong."

Through my headset, Lauren screams, "Orm! Now!"

Blood comes up and pools in my mouth. I spit before continuing, "Then prove it, Leon. If you're the warrior you think you are then do what you came here to do. But you'll have to kill me first."

Leon balks. "I don't need to be a killer to be a hero. And being a killer doesn't make you one either."

I stare off to the left, to the axe on the wall. Leon follows my gaze. "Maybe not. But I'm not going to let you destroy this machine. So if you want to do the right thing, you're gonna have to become one."

I drill my eyes deep into his, and although he tries to match my resolve, I see it wane and the fear returns. He knows I cannot move and yet he is unsure.

Leon takes cautious steps toward the axe case. We watch each other as he slips his hand up blindly and opens the glass door. He lifts the axe out, and I can see his bicep strain under the weight of it. He quickly compensates by gripping with two hands and takes a deep breath before walking over to me.

"I was going to leave you alive because you're crippled, but . . . you asked for this."

Leon raises the axe above his head. He hesitates. Squeezing his eyes shut, he brings it down. With all the speed of my youth, I reach up and grab the handle before it can meet my face. Leon opens his eyes in horror as I rip the axe from his weak grip and in one swift movement, slice open his stomach, letting its contents spill to the floor.

The lad tries to hold his wound together in vain and drops to the ground. He pleads to me with his wet, red eyes.

"I'm a person with a *disability*," I mutter.

I grip the axe tight and allow myself to fall to the floor on my chest. My eyes blur on impact, and more blood sprays from the corner of my mouth. I drag myself back to the central computer, stopping only momentarily to click on my headset.

"Lauren . . . Elskede. Come on. Talk to me."

I give up and decide my time is better spent completing my task. I roll over onto my back and swing the axe weakly at the cable. I can almost reach it. I re-adjust and try again, but I only manage to loosen the connection. In a desperate last attempt, I swing the axe high, letting it leave my grip just slightly, hoping to get a few extra inches. The axe does what is intended, and the cable falls from the socket, but the axe clanks to the ground, out of reach.

I croak into the headset, "Do it now, Elskede . . . I love you."

I stretch my good hand and touch the axe with my fingertips, but a sharp pain in my side sends tremors through my whole body. Breathing becomes painful and difficult. One of my broken ribs has now punctured my lung. More blood spews from my throat, and I lose the last of my energy to move.

I am dying. Finally. I just hope that I was able to save Lauren. That my death is not in vain. I can't help but wonder if there is going to be another life after this one. Maybe this too has been an illusion. Who is to say Valhalla does not await me after all? I gather my strength and make one final attempt to reach my weapon.

Just in case . . .

V

The dark-haired woman stumbles over the rubble of a ruined hallway. She is accompanied by several men, all tall and fair-skinned with toned, sinewy muscles. The men have various injuries, and even the woman dons a fresh slash on her forehead and a deeply bruised cheek.

She climbs up and over the concrete, ignoring an offer of assistance. When she reaches her destination, she holds up her hand to her companions and continues on her own into a large, noisy silo. The silo contains a spinning cylinder and rows of mainframe computers.

The woman stops just beyond the threshold and blinks back tears. Once composed, she makes her way around the tower, ignoring the corpse of a young man, and kneels to stroke the hair of one much older, lying on the ground. His body has grown stiff some time ago. His left arm and side are badly bruised and twisted, and in the firm grip of his right is a bloodied axe.

She stares at the axe, and a weak smile stretches across her face. She bends to kiss his forehead and whispers into his cold ear. "Dine well, my love."

Rising again, the woman leaves the room. As she passes the men outside the door, she nods to them, and they head inside.

The Legend of Bucaris

C . R . MACFARLANE

The A64 jet slowed, and Jasa Idari pressed her face to the reinforced, triple-shielded glass. Rain beaded on the wing as the turbine engines swiveled vertically, and the jet began to descend.

A hand fell on her knee, and her entire body jerked. She looked into the face of the thirty-first Emperor of the Golden City, Tatsuda Kenko, and quickly dropped her head, hand to her heart. "Forgive me, Emperor."

"Bucaris is the City of Hope, Jasa." The emperor stood from his seat, straightening an unseen crease from his black wool jacket. He kneeled beside her. "It is all right to stare."

She nodded, refusing to meet his admiring gaze. Instead, her eyes flicked to the double-edged broadsword stowed beside her seat, well within reach.

The familial sword had been presented to her when she was assigned to the emperor's Kubati Guard and when, to her father's great dishonor, she had failed to marry by the age of twenty-four.

"I wish you'd put that thing somewhere safe. There is a cargo hold for a reason." He reached out to move it.

"Ai!" she shouted reflexively, drawing the knife at her hip.

The sword should belong to her husband, according to the

old customs, and it seemed Tatsuda thought the sword would be his. But of course it never could be.

"Relax, Jasa." The emperor held his hands up in the air.

She gasped, dropping the knife and bowing as low as the seat would permit. "It is my sworn duty to protect you, Emperor."

"You care too much for the old ways. But, it was my error." He rubbed a hand over his pale face. "The old myths must be respected, even if they seem absurd by our modern standards."

She pressed her hand to her heart dutifully. To touch another man's—or woman's—ceremonial sword was said to bring a curse upon both. There had been more than enough curses befalling the rightful owner of the sword, and she could not allow more to come to him.

Absurd or not.

Bright light poured in through the jet window, blinding them. Blinking, her eyes adjusted to the brilliant blue summer's day. They must have passed through the atmospheric network that gave Bucaris its legendary tropical weather, even though the city had been built in the middle of the North Atlantic.

Below them, a landscape of gleaming white towers stretched up two thousand feet from the crashing ocean waves beneath. Jasa forgot herself and pressed into the window.

The emperor chuckled and squeezed her knee. "Don't believe the legends, Jasa. Bucaris is even *more* beautiful than they say."

Descending quickly, the jet angled toward a platform suspended by cables and narrow footbridges.

"How do the towers stay so white?" she asked. "Bucaris is over three hundred years old."

Emperor Kenko stood, brushing off his jacket and attaching

the ceremonial cape over his uniform. "Bucaris is a city without waste, without crime, whose citizens are committed to preserving its beauty. I think you will be very impressed."

The jet touched down, jolting Jasa into action as she rushed for her own cape, slinging the broadsword across her back. The time for distraction had passed. Beautiful as Bucaris may be, she would have to admire it after she had safely seen the emperor to and from the delegations.

A rapid set of hand signals mobilized the six warriors to their defensive positions before she took her place at the hatch, directly in front of the emperor.

His hearty laughter filled the cockpit, and a hand fell on her shoulder. "Bucaris is a peaceful place. You can relax, Jasa."

She nodded, her eyes fixed on the steely gray door. "With respect, Emperor, I will do as I have been trained to do. You invited me for your protection; it is not my job to relax."

His breath brushed her ear as he leaned close, causing all the hairs on the back of her neck to stand on end. "I invited you here so you could see what it would be like if you were the empress of the Golden City." A finger grazed the side of her cheek. "You still haven't accepted my offer."

She suppressed a shudder. The emperor was handsome and kind, the most eligible bachelor in the Golden City. But it was not an offer she could accept. Nor one she could easily turn down without considerable explanation.

The traditional broadsword at her back weighed heavily. Five generations of fastidious tradition, and she had thrown away any hope for honor in a foolish frenzy. The emperor chided her adherence to tradition, but the reality was she had not been careful enough. It had been seven years, but to ignore the vow would bring dishonor to her family and his.

"You honor me, Emperor."

Setting her shoulders, she stared at the hatch, schooling her face into a facade of readiness. But her mind turned inward and tortured her with an image of the wide-mouthed easy grin and confident swagger that her witless teenage self had fallen so hopelessly in love with. She'd been desperate and certain enough to find a Shinto priest to take their vows before either of them were arrested and put to death.

He was here, somewhere in Bucaris, the place he had gone after his name was cleared. And she'd gone back to her Kubati training, never to speak of it again.

She wouldn't track him down; he wouldn't know her even if she did. It was the cruel, cold fate of what she had done, the role she had played, and the promise she had made to herself to never hurt him again.

The hatch opened, lighting up the inside of the gray jet with the blinding artificial sunlight that bounced off the gleaming platform. Jasa blinked, her hand coming up to shield her eyes. A half-dozen hazy figures shifted on the far end of the landing pad.

Her fingers itched, mentally confirming the precise location of each of her weapons should she need to access them in a hurry.

A single man approached, his lanky outline gaining definition as her eyes adjusted. She was sure there had been others, but they'd all disappeared. Her keen eyes caught just a glimmer sprinting from one edge of the platform to the other.

Cloaking technology. She'd heard rumors of its existence but never imagined that it could mask an entire person. Her well-trained senses went on high alert, searching for evidence of the remaining Bucari guards. She dropped into a defensive stance in front of the emperor and backed him into the protection of the jet.

The emperor brushed past, smiling obliviously as he set foot on the tarmac.

"Greetings, Emperor Kenko." The solitary man bowed low if somewhat awkwardly, his hands clasped in front of his chest. "I hope you had a pleasant journey."

Emperor Kenko returned the traditional greeting gracefully. "The journey was long but it is the arrival that is always most pleasant, James."

A hazy glimmer flickered just behind them. Jasa pulled a phase-pistol from her belt. "Show yourselves!"

The guide smiled, shaking the emperor's hand. "You know we do not allow weapons on Bucaris."

"Of course." The emperor nodded at the man, then turned to her with a pointed look telling her to cooperate.

Cooperate with what?

Jasa felt the hand before she saw the ripple of light, and then the violating click of her weapons holster being undone. All three of her phase weapons, two charge belts, and an array of munitions fell away.

"Bucaris is a peaceful city, Jasa. I told you. There are no weapons here."

"You didn't tell me they would *take* my weapons."

"You wouldn't have liked it."

"How am I to protect you?"

The emperor shrugged, an infuriatingly placid smile on his face. He turned back to the man.

Her weapons and the weapons of her warriors all fell away to unseen hands. But when she felt a hand reach for the heavy, worn binding across her back, she pushed it away and prepared to defend herself and the emperor, weapons or not.

She was a fifth-generation Kubati warrior, the top of her class at the academy, and the youngest ever to be appointed to the Emperor's personal Guard. There was no doubt she could defeat even an invisible foe.

"The broadsword is ceremonial," Kenko said quickly. "A relic from the old times, familial, you understand. I will vouch for her."

The man paused, his narrow gaze scrutinizing her as he seemed to weigh the decision. "Alright," he said at last. "I will respect your cultural customs, but it is not favored for you to bring weapons into Bucaris." Decision made, the man grinned to himself and nodded at something unseen.

There was a flicker as the invisible hand retreated, and in a moment, all six Bucari guards appeared in a loose circle around them.

Emperor Kenko bowed neatly and took something from the man's hands. He passed dark-rimmed eyeglasses to his warriors. "Go on," he said as he presented her with a set of the surprisingly light spectacles, the inside of the lenses glowing faintly. "Put them on. You'll like it."

"Where are yours?"

He tapped the side of his head cryptically.

She put the glasses on and took an involuntary step back. The harsh light reflecting off the bare surface of the landing pad transformed into a pleasing warm glow. Highlighted chevrons and lines danced across her vision. Clouds of photos, symbols, and words surrounded each of the Bucari and even her own warriors. Above their heads, their names shone in bright display.

The emperor grinned. "Welcome to the Game."

Their guide's name was James. Below his name, it listed his occupation: Steward, and the number 5,053. The guard behind him was named Ephraim, 2,596. Even Tatsuda had a score of 6,780.

Jasa's own name was printed neatly in the upper right corner of her vision, and below it, 768.

"Game?" she asked.

"You earn points for positive actions and contributions," the emperor explained. "Positive reinforcement on a national level. There's no crime, no criminals, no rules or even laws. Everyone chooses to do what's best for their nation, not because they have to but because they want to."

A shining, holographic +2 floated up into the space in front of her along with the words, 'Conversation with a dignitary.' "What was that?"

"You did something positive and earned two points."

A flush rose in her cheeks, and she found herself suddenly pleased. "I already have points—how?"

"The Game has tracked your movements by what I see. Those are points you earned doing good for me."

"How? You're not wearing glasses."

"All Bucari have a microchip implanted in their visual cortex when they're born. The glasses are for outsiders, but they allowed me to receive an implant several years ago. Imagine if we could bring this technology to the Golden City."

She blinked. Crime rates rose every day, the Kubati warriors and soldiers couldn't keep up with the vandalism and theft in the inner city. "If Bucaris truly has no crime, it is tempting to think about. A willing, peaceful population is a prosperous population."

"Now, you're thinking like an empress." Smiling, he placed

a hand on her elbow. "We've come here to negotiate for it."

She shifted uncomfortably, letting his hand slide away, and pulled the glasses from her face to rub the bridge of her nose. Her eyes caught one of the guards on the opposite side of the landing platform, wearing a similar set of dark-rimmed glasses. He didn't have an implant then, not a native Bucari. The black frames stood out against his pale face and golden-flame hair.

Her breath seized.

Arka Daitan Hikaru. Haru for short.

His hair was longer than it had been, but she would recognize the confident set of his shoulders until the day she died.

He caught her staring and flashed a smile. The same infectious smile that made her weak in the knees and made bad ideas seem good. She didn't need glasses or a holographic display to know his name, or that he had a subtle limp in his left leg that somehow only seemed to make him faster, or a criss-cross of scars across his chest, or patches that held his heart together...

"Jasa, glasses on." The emperor nodded, encouraging her to return the glasses to her face.

"Yes, Emperor."

It was hard to breathe, the air around her suddenly too hot. She was going to be sick.

A yellow smiley-face floated up in front of her vision, and when she looked at Haru again, a similar emoji floated around him with a big +1. 'Friendship point earned' was the only explanation given by the holographic stylized text.

The blood drained from her face. She knew he was in Bucaris, but he was supposed to be out *there*, somewhere in the city, not standing ten feet in front of her.

"Captain?" One of her warriors questioned, and she jumped. The emperor was nearly halfway across the footbridge, and the Bucari guards had disappeared behind their cloaks again. How could she have been so distracted? Her forefathers would be rolling over in their burial chambers!

She nodded curtly, giving the too-late signal for them to take up defensive positions around the emperor. Chiding herself to remain focused on her duty, she fell in step at Tatsuda's right hip, far enough back to not be obtrusive, close enough to react to any sign of threat. She scanned the horizon, peering over the narrow wall and down to the distant water. It was unlikely anyone would attack from below. Though she did know one person who could climb to such dizzying heights. And could be equally deadly with phase pistol, sword, or hand.

Arka Hikaru.

Arka Daitan Hikaru.

She fought the urge to call out his name and throw herself into his arms. It had been seven years. Seven long, lonely years with half her heart on the other side of the world. But it could not be. There were too many reasons, too many customs and expectations. In a different world, at a different time, maybe they could have been happy together, but that was not this world. Her duty to the emperor, her family's honor, all the old traditions stood in their way, making a chasm as wide and unforgiving as the raging ocean below.

She let the glasses drop down the ridge of her nose to see if her naked eyes could detect the subtle ripple left by the cloaking technology—then she might know where at least one of the Bucari guards was. Where Haru was. It was a gift simply to see him again, to know that he was well.

On the horizon, something moved. She grasped fruitlessly for the long-sighted rifle that should be at her hip. Her heart beat wildly. Was it a sniper? An archer? She never should have given up her weapons.

A dark speck fell between the towers, and she removed her glasses entirely. She realized she was looking at a man, arms flailing outwards. Quickly falling to his death.

"Keep moving." She hadn't realized she'd stopped until Haru's disembodied head appeared beside her. "No one else can see him."

"That man. We have to do something!"

He shook his head, shaggy hair falling over his eyes. "Keep moving."

"But . . ."

"They don't see him," he said again, taking the glasses from her hand and presenting them to her. She put them on and a shiny +1 floated between them—another friendship point.

In the distance, the falling man disappeared. To be sure, she took the glasses down again, finding him just as he was swallowed by the ocean. "I don't understand."

"He bottomed out."

The pained look in his eyes kept her from asking more.

Haru started to close the hood of his invisibility suit. "Nice to meet you"—he glanced to the space above her head—"Jasa. That's pretty." And with one last grin, he disappeared.

Rushing back to her position, Jasa followed the emperor across the narrow footbridge and into the foyer of the gleaming tower. A tip of her glasses told her the dancing mural on the walls was only a hologram, the real bare concrete a dull gray.

There they boarded a tramcar, the doors shutting behind them. Smoothly, it left the tower suspended by a narrow cable thousands of feet in the air and dipped over the edge, speeding toward the depths below. It swung around, weaving impossibly fast between towers and other cars.

"Take a breath, Jasa." The emperor stood beside her, hands clasped calmly behind his cape. "I told you, this place is safe. Enjoy the view."

"They're moving too fast," she said, trying to track another speeding tramcar. "I can't see inside."

He snorted his warm, deep chuckle. "We're moving just as fast."

The tramcar turned a sharp corner, and as quickly as they'd left, whisked into the ornate foyer of a building Jasa hadn't even seen coming. The doors opened to reveal the awaiting Bucari delegation.

From the back, Haru smiled.

Jasa faltered as she stepped off the tram. How had he gotten there so fast?

The emperor put a hand on her back, spinning her around, and made introductions to two of the Bucari ministers, earning him a +10.

Jasa bowed respectfully, and the ministers awkwardly copied the Golden City's traditional greeting. The scores in the information cloud above them ticked up.

"We are all assembled," said the one who had been introduced as Minister Toru. His score read 20,786, including the +10 that floated with the words 'Good Diplomatic Relations.' "But we understand if you need to rest after your long journey." Another +10, 'Empathy.'

"No need." The emperor smiled. Jasa looked away and rolled her eyes at his obvious pandering for points. "But you are most gracious." More points and a beaming smiley face floated up between them. He began to follow the ministers from the ornate foyer to a glowing set of doors.

Jasa stopped him. "I must sweep the area for threats."

"Jasa—"

"I insist, Emperor." Without waiting for an answer, she turned toward the doors. One eye, peeking over the of rim her glasses, told her they were not actually shut—there weren't even doors—and she pressed through.

An alarm buzzed accompanied by a red flash, and she immediately rolled into a defensive crouch. -1 flashed in front of her eyes.

She swore as an irrational sense of disappointment flooded her.

Haru appeared, standing beside her, an amused smirk on his face. "Colorful language for a highborn daughter. Idari is an old and honorable name."

She stopped herself from pointing out she'd learned most of that language from him.

As she stood, she noticed a black-pearlescent material showing under his sleeve cuff. It was enough to tell her the Bucari undersuits were far more sophisticated than the protective vest she wore. And while he'd always been strong, she had no doubt the bulges at his elbow and shoulder were servo motors, enhancing his strength to superhuman levels.

Still smiling, he looked into her eyes, and another friendship point floated between them. She threw her eyes to the floor. She'd made a promise to herself to let him live his life in peace, and she wasn't going to break that promise now.

Haru grinned, leaving her with a wink. As he walked away, he dropped his glasses, scanning the room before taking his place at the wall between heavy red velvet curtains on one side and an ornate gold-framed painting on the other, neither of which were actually there.

Emperor Kenko entered, points flying as he conversed with several of the ministers. Jasa swallowed her argument that she had not yet secured the area, and scrambled to position her soldiers. The ornate decor would normally provide many hiding spots for explosives or bugs or even assassins, but this room was bare and empty, save the circular table and basic chairs around which the delegates gathered.

Yet another familiar face stood out at the delegates table, though he was taller than he had been seven years earlier, so she replaced her glasses just to be sure.

She looked away as Haru stepped forward and fussed over his younger brother. Eiko Hikaru blushed and shrugged him off, glancing nervously around the room before he took his seat at the ministers' table. He had an astounding 20,196 points hovering above his head, and wore no glasses—he must have received an embedded chip, just like the emperor.

A smile played across Jasa's lips—she'd always known the younger Hikaru brother would make something of himself, in spite of the tragedy that had followed his family.

The tragedy she had *brought* to his family.

Eiko's gaze scanned the room, his eyes widening when they fell on her. He quickly schooled his features, and Jasa did the same; they weren't supposed to know each other. They had agreed that would be best for Haru's sake.

"Ready, Jasa?"

A hand caressed her back, and she jumped. Carefully hiding her agitation, she nodded to the emperor, taking stock of the seven ministers in the room to avoid his gaze. "Where is the Supreme Leader?"

"He is as fastidiously secretive as they say. In all my years as Emperor, I have not been granted an audience." He shrugged. "But the ministers speak for him." With a nod, Emperor Kenko left her and approached the table, laid out with holographic red and gold fabrics. He pulled out one of the rich mahogany chairs and sat with the Bucari ministers. It was not unlike the formal meeting room at the emperor's palace, and it occurred to Jasa that the room had been designed for him, and its appearance could change for whatever dignitary they entertained.

She positioned herself in front of the glowing golden doors as the negotiations began, knowing full well there were no doors at all but a wide-open gap. It was one of only two ways into the room, the other being the small air vent she had noted in the ceiling, currently disguised as a chandelier.

The air vent would be a superior vantage point, and she started planning a way to access it at the first opportunity. Climbing to the edge of the vent would have been easy if the curtains and picture frames were real, but with perfectly smooth walls there was nothing to use as a foothold. The only option was a straight jump up from the delegates' table, and at fifteen feet, it would be impossible.

Her eyes fell involuntarily to Haru. *Almost* impossible. Could he still run and climb the way he used to?

She recalled the first time they'd met, when he had leaped over her on the training wall at the academy, his body swinging dangerously free as he grasped a handhold forty feet in the air with no safety netting. His smile was as brazen then as it was now. He'd walked into the academy with his shoulders strong, oozing confidence. You could never guess he was buraku, the poorest of the poor, a street rat in an ocean of golden, privileged fish—and yet, he'd shown he belonged better than any of them.

Pride stirred in her heart knowing he'd been able to do the same thing when he came to Bucaris.

Haru's mouth curled into a wide smile, and Jasa realized she'd been staring. She looked away, but not before a flashing +1 and a shiny red heart floated up in her vision. 'You are now Friends.'

Jasa continued to survey the foyer when negotiations broke for a recess. Emperor Kenko spoke with the ministers, points flying between them as they had been for most of the morning. She had carefully positioned herself on the opposite side of the room, conveniently out of earshot so that he couldn't ask for her opinion on the discussions later. As much as she loved the Golden City and would protect it and its emperor with her life, she hated politics. Even if she could marry the emperor, she would make a terrible empress.

"Praise to the Golden Emperor." Haru appeared beside her, bowing low as he spoke the traditional greeting. His golden eyes gleamed from behind his shaggy hair.

She bowed and returned the nicety, "Peace and prosperity to the Golden City."

Across the room, Emperor Kenko turned his attention to them, a flash of jealousy on his otherwise serene face. How much did he know? Was he aware Jasa and Haru had been friends? Or that she had been the one tasked to hunt him? That she had been the one to help him escape? Could he see the friendship points between them?

She turned away, her heart beating wildly as she made a show of keeping her eyes on the emperor. There was no room for distraction.

Haru caught her arm; a surge of warmth jolted through her.

The emperor's eyebrows rose as the Kubati warriors around the room sprung to life.

She involuntarily met the depth of Haru's golden gaze, nearly falling into the memories that flooded her. Forcing her expression to remain neutral, she held up a hand, stilling her soldiers. "To touch a Kubati warrior is forbidden," she admonished Haru quietly.

"Forgive me." His impish grin suggested he didn't really want to be forgiven.

She bowed her head. "It is forgiven."

"It's just ... do I know you? My heart ... it's like something in me remembers you." He bent, pointing to the long scar that ran along the side of his head under the hairline.

As though she hadn't seen it before; as though she hadn't been there when it happened then sat by him for weeks as he recovered.

She couldn't breathe.

"I had an accident," he said. "I forgot a year of my life. But sometimes my body remembers things that I don't."

Forcing air into her lungs, she spoke curtly, "I am sorry for your accident. She spun away. He couldn't remember. He just couldn't.

Crossing the foyer quickly, she traded places with one of her soldiers under the guise of surveying a different vantage point. Her body shook. Haru's injury, the surgery, and his lost memory hadn't been an accident; it was a hunt. Only Haru and Eiko had escaped from their home as the rough shack they'd lived in burned to the ground, the rest of their family inside.

"Jasa?" The emperor placed a hand on her shoulder. "Did

he upset you?"

Not trusting her voice to answer, she bowed respectfully.

"It is strange, I admit, that someone once deemed an enemy of the emperor should be here in Bucaris, but he was cleared of all charges. The Bucari have deemed him fit to guard their delegation, and we must honor the political decisions of our allies. But if he is bothering you, I can ask that he be removed."

She bowed again. "No, Emperor. He wished to ask a question. That is all." How strange it must be for the emperor to see Haru, to have issued the kill order and then been forced to revoke it. He couldn't possibly know anything about her role. She had helped Haru and Eiko escape—doing what was right in her heart—but there was no excuse for her treachery of disobeying the emperor. Her punishment would be swift and severe if he knew. No matter his feelings for her.

"There is a superior vantage point above the meeting room," she said. "I would like to locate it."

"Ah. You can request schematic drawings from the network." He tapped the side of her glasses, at the same time, commanding, "Computer, display schematics for conference room."

A semi-transparent blueprint appeared in her vision, partially obscuring the room around her. It rotated, tracing the air duct to the nearest accessible vent.

"Do you have what you need?"

She blinked in surprise at the schematic. "Yes."

"It's a simply marvelous technology. I believe the negotiations are going well."

"A blessing for the Golden City, Emperor," she answered automatically.

"Call me Tatsuda. And you don't have to be so formal

around me, Jasa."

"Thank you, Emperor." She bowed quickly, rushing up the stairs as fast as duty would allow.

The schematic display led her to the nearest accessible vent opening, and she crawled through the metal duct on her hands and knees until she reached the conference room. As expected, the vent gave her a full 360-degree visual of the meeting room.

The delegation re-entered the room, and Minister Toru stood, hands expressive as he spoke.

From below, Haru caught her eye, tipped his glasses down, and winked. She sighed as the inevitable + 1 sparkled in front of her.

Removing her own glasses, she confirmed that no one was hiding in the holographic folds of the ornate curtains, and she settled in for another long meeting, the politics droning on below.

She let out a breath, and rolled her shoulders to relax muscles that had been on high alert since she'd boarded the jet sixteen hours earlier. The room was secure. The tower was accessible only by tram, and the floors above and below the meeting room were empty.

Perhaps Emperor Kenko was right; she could relax a little more.

Perhaps, too, she could consider marrying him. Certainly, it would bring her family great honor. The old ways and traditions were just that: Old. The idea of a curse seemed ridiculous when she considered the power of the glasses in her hand. It wasn't like Haru knew; she would be the only one. Well, her and Eiko.

She found Haru, his face relaxed as his eyes shifted back

and forth, surveying the room. The slightest smirk played on his face.

Somehow he could still smile after everything—the silver lining of his 'accident' and amnesia. The memory of those weeks was still crystal clear in her mind, however. The ambush in the training gym, Haru's desperate climb and escape to the roof. The headmaster tasking Jasa with hunting her former training partner, the now-criminal Haru. The plan she had concocted that led her straight to him, to his family's home. His plea to examine the evidence, and her daring, last-minute rescue after realizing there was no way he could have done what they'd said.

The glasses shuddered in her hand, and she replaced them just in time to see a woman leap through the air away from the vent. Her dark cape fluttered as she pulled a massive sword from her back, striking Minister Toru.

Jasa froze, too startled to do more than blink.

The woman was her. Her face, her cape, her broadsword.

She ripped the glasses off. The holographic version of her disappeared, but the minister's body laid where it had fallen. Dead.

The ministers shouted, the room dissolved into chaos, and the Bucari guards disappeared where they stood. Emperor Kenko burst out of his chair.

Her glasses grew hot, singeing her fingers. She threw them away instinctivly just as they exploded. The metal vent erupted in deafening echoes and blinding light.

Haru stared up at her, his glasses halfway down his nose and his face serious. He mouthed one word: *Run.*

She scrambled past the mutilated tech and back through the air duct, moving as fast and as far as her shaking limbs would carry her, only vaguely aware that the blast had been serious enough to kill her had the glasses still been on her head.

Jasa pressed her back into the concave edge of the rusted metal tube. She had found her way to the air intake, the very end of the vent system. Light shone intermittently past the spinning fan blades next to her, an old metal grate separated her from the outside.

She hadn't killed the minister, of that she was sure, but she had seen herself slice him open, seen his lifeless body as proof. So what *did* happen to him?

Footsteps echoed through the air vent. She pulled the broadsword from her back.

The thump of boots on steel came closer until she was certain they were right in front of her. "Show yourself," she called, unsuccessfully trying to keep the tremble from her voice.

Haru pulled back his hood; his disembodied head hovered a few feet away.

She breathed a sigh of relief, but caught herself—this was not the same Haru. He didn't remember the weeks they had spent on the run together, hiding in tunnels not that different from this one. "I didn't do it," she said. "That wasn't me."

The rest of his body appeared. "I know. I saw..." He pointed to a pocket on his chest where his glasses were neatly stowed "...what *really* happened."

She shifted uncomfortably. Her glasses were gone, but his were still active, still potentially hooked into the Game.

Reading her as he'd always been able to, he held the glasses up for her to see. There was no faint glow, no image projected when he held the lenses up for her to look through. "They're deactivated. My brother, Eiko, he's a tech whiz, Minister of Technology actually. He showed me how. I turned them off as soon as they ordered us to find you."

The heavy sword shook in her hands, but she kept it between them. "How did you know I'd be here?"

He shrugged, seeming unbothered by the weapon. But then, he'd always been confident. "I went where I would go if it were me. You were smart to stay in the vents; they don't have cameras in here, don't like to acknowledge that this place exists. Despite all the tech, they still have an embarrassingly basic dependency on oxygen. Don't worry, I'm not going to turn you in."

"I need to speak with Emperor Kenko."

He frowned. "Probably not a good idea. He lost a lot of points for being the one to bring you here."

"Points?" The sword sagged. "But . . ."

"Never underestimate the power of points."

"So then why are you helping me? Surely you would earn a lot of points for turning me in."

He smirked. "Thing is, when you've had an accident like mine, you learn to trust your instincts. C'mon, I know a better hiding spot."

She stared at his outstretched hand. Her body remembered things too. . . .

Haru pressed the grate out of the air vent and caught it before it clattered to the ground. Jasa climbed out after him, stretching after hiding in the cramped tube for so long. The day-cycle had given way to the dark of night, only the faintest light shone into the corridor.

"We should see my brother, Eiko. Something went wrong with the holograms. If anyone can figure it out and clear your name, it's him."

Jasa nodded and followed him across an old footbridge between towers then up stairs after stairs after stairs. Haru pulled the glasses from his pocket and adjusted them with a tiny screwdriver.

The hallway was dark and moldy with paint peeling off the walls, but Jasa guessed that the holograms painted it just as beautiful as it had conference room. Several apartments didn't have doors, and she peered into the dingy homes, their occupants staring mindlessly into space, watching something that wasn't there.

Haru paused, tapping his glasses. "Stay out of sight" he told Jasa and walked into the apartment.

Jasa hung back at the threshold, peering in, presumably behind a holographic door. Eiko sat in a deep armchair, facing the corner. His eyes flicked over something unseen.

"Eiko?" Haru called out.

The younger brother's shoulders tensed, and he pulled away from whatever projection he had been looking at. "What are you doing here?"

"I need your help. Jasa Idari was framed for Minister Toru's death at the delegations today."

"You're helping her?" Eiko scowled in a way Jasa had never seen before. They had spent nearly as much time together as she and Haru—on the run then watching over his brother as he'd recovered. He'd always been kind, even as she purged her sins to him. But his next words stung her heart: "She's a criminal, Arka."

Haru shrugged, as though to say, So what? "There are no laws here, Eiko. She can't be a criminal."

"A murderer then."

"You don't actually believe a daughter of Idari and a Kubati warrior would come all the way from the Golden City to kill Minister Toru, do you?"

"It doesn't matter what her motive was, I saw her leap from the chandelier and stab him to death. Everyone saw it."

"But it's not what happened. There was a glitch in the holographic program. I had my glasses off; Jasa was in the air duct the entire time. Those stupid chips made you see something that wasn't there."

"You don't want to be associated with her, Arka, trust me. She's already dead, or she will be soon."

"Eiko." Jasa stepped into the apartment without thinking. Maybe if he saw her, maybe if she told him how she needed his help now, he'd be reminded.

He leaped out of his chair, glaring at Haru. "You brought her here!"

Jasa froze. She had once protected him as a brother. He *was* her brother; he was the only person other than herself who had been at the ceremony and still remembered it.

But he also knew it had all been her fault; that she had been the one to track Haru to their family's home. It was because of her that their family was dead and that Haru had forgotten everything and nearly died too. It looked as if his forgiveness from seven years ago had washed away, replaced only by anger.

Haru glanced back and his face fell at the sight of her. He turned back to his brother. "Eiko, please. There's something wrong with the chips. You can help us."

"Us?" he roared. "There's no us between you and her." But Eiko knew the truth as well as she did, knew that she and Haru were bound for life. He had helped her make the decision to let Haru forget. Now, he refused to look at her, gaze firmly fixed to the floor.

"Eiko, she's innocent! You know what will happen . . ."

Flustered, Eiko folded his arms and turned away. "You have to leave. It's costing too many points for her to be here."

"Points?"

Eiko didn't answer.

"How many points do you need?" Haru grabbed his brother by the arm, spinning him. "It's those damn, implants. They're showing you things that aren't there. Why are you acting like this? You have the points to lose. Listen to me—" His eyes tracked to the spot above Eiko's head, and he stepped back. "How *did* you get so many points, Eiko?"

"You have to go."

"Eiko!"

"They know you're helping her. You'll bottom out for this unless you turn her in."

Haru stiffened, his fists clenched by his side. He opened his mouth to argue but stopped himself. Spinning on his heel, he took her hand and pulled her out the door. "C'mon, we have to go before they track us here." He started to run.

Jasa pumped her arms and legs, pushing herself to keep pace as he raced through the halls and down the many stairs. Outside, on the footbridge, he stopped, casting his glasses into the ocean with a roar. "My own brother," he muttered, a hand pushing back his shaggy hair, "obsessed with points?"

"It's okay," she started to say—it wasn't his fault, it wasn't even his fight—but he was running again.

They were in the middle of the footbridge when he finally stopped. "Here," he said and craned his neck to look up the tall tower beside them, his body rigid.

At the top of the tower sat a massive glass orb. It was easily the highest structure in the city. "That's the Supreme Leader's office."

She gulped, already knowing what he was thinking. "Will he see us? Not even the emperor has met him."

"We have to try. He's the only one who can override the Game and help us." He looked pointedly at the span between them and the side of the tower. It was a jump away; a long jump, but doable. "There isn't a footbridge. It's serviced by only one tramcar, and that's heavily guarded." He glanced at her nervously. "We'll have to climb."

She bit back an ironic laugh, already unfastening her cape in preparation. "Not a problem."

Haru practically flew up the side of the building, Jasa pushing to keep up as they criss-crossed each other's paths, pointing out good handholds when they found them, climbing in tandem where necessary. She tried not to look at the violent ocean far below. The wind whipped her clothes and hair as her fingers dug into the fine cracks that spread across the white facade.

In training, it used to annoy her just how fast and sure Haru was. Now, with the benefit of the servo motors, she marveled at how he moved. Freely, casually, almost as though he knew there was no chance he could fall. Even on the smooth tower, he found handholds where there should be none.

Haru called her name from the top of the tower as she climbed the last few metres. A grin broke across his face. "Are you sure we don't know each other?"

Jasa nodded, her throat suddenly too dry to speak.

He clung to a support on the top of the glass orb. "I can't see inside at all. The windows are tinted. But there's a ventilation shaft at the top; that's our way in."

She followed him, the ventilation cover already open by the time she joined him on top of the glass sphere. He motioned for her to go first.

Sliding down, she landed on the grate with a thunk. The room below was pitch black, and a deep, eerie hum filled the space. There were no signs of movement or sounds of voices. Satisfied no one was in the room with them, she loosened the grate and fell to the floor.

"You think it would be more guarded," Haru said when he dropped down beside her.

She was just glad it wasn't. A perk, perhaps, of the Supreme Leader's persistent secretiveness.

The double doors leading to his office were ornate— actually ornate. She ran her hands along the wooden frame to be sure. An old-fashioned lock spanned the doors.

"We need a physical key to get in," Jasa said. "It's not a circuit we can bypass."

Haru nodded once, but his eyes darted to the broadsword at her back, and before she could stop him, he pulled it from its sheath and sliced through the lock.

The lock fell away and the doors swung open.

They stared at the sword in his hand, and Jasa gulped audibly. Haru would know the traditions as well as she did; the familial broadsword would bring dishonor and misfortune to any man who touched it that was not her husband.

She looked away first. "What is this place?" Where she had expected an elaborate office, rows of data-storage banks glowed with blinking blue lights. The room hummed the same eerie noise she'd heard in the anteroom, and thick data cables ran across the floor.

Haru followed behind her, checking each row for signs of

the Supreme Leader, but the room was empty. He carried the sword with grace and ease—whether he somehow knew it was his or if he'd just decided it was too late to worry about curses and dishonor, he made no attempt to give it back. Even though he'd only attended half a year at the academy before they marked him an enemy of the emperor—all of that time which he'd forgotten—his body clearly still remembered how to wield the weapon, and Jasa had kept the edge sharp for him.

Reaching the far side of the room, Haru leaned over the wide console nestled under the gray-tinted windows. "It's a computer, a really old one," he said. "I've seen them in some of Eiko's books."

"I've never seen anything like this." Jasa studied the array of buttons and switches.

"These are all memory banks and computing boards; there must be millions of terabytes of information here."

"So where's the Supreme Leader if not in his office?"

"I don't know." Haru ran his hand across the console, flipping the large switch at the end that glowed red. "But I have a funny feeling . . ."

Lights sputtered, and the distorted image of a face flickered to life above the control panel. It was a hologram, but a grainy 2D image not at all like the sophisticated projections that decorated Bucaris.

The face tilted, its expression serene. "Greetings. Arka Daitan Hikaru— 2,751. Jasa Idari—0."

Jasa froze.

Haru steeled himself, taking a deep breath. "Who are you? How do you know who we are?"

"I am the interface SL," it replied. "My program was written to know all the faces who enter Bucaris."

"Why?"

"My algorithms award points to residents for positive actions and remove points for negative actions. I was created as Bucaris was created, to bring a sense of order and unified purpose to its people, to provide a utopian population for a utopian city."

"You're the Game," Jasa whispered. Something as complex as the Game and its massive point system could only be tracked by technology, but someone still had to be there to program it. "Where's the Supreme Leader?"

The grainy face turned to her. "My algorithms are programmed to award points to residents for positive actions and remove points for negative actions."

"Someone programmed you. Who tells you what's good and what's bad?"

The head tilted, its voice two-dimensional. "My algorithms are programmed to award points to residents for positive actions and remove points for negative actions."

Jasa's mind raced. If the computer believed she had killed the minister, that was bad. She needed to talk to a real person, a real thinking, feeling, understanding person. She banged on the console. "Where's the Supreme Leader? The leader of Bucaris. We need to speak to him."

"Jasa," Haru whispered, "I've lived here for seven years and never seen the Supreme Leader because..." He glanced at the hologram nervously. "Because he doesn't exist."

"What are you saying?"

He studied the disembodied face. "You're the Supreme Leader."

It nodded slightly. "I am the Interface SL."

Jasa's heart beat furiously; her hands started to shake.

"What happened to Minister Toru?" Haru demanded.

"Alecai Toru." The computer looked to the side, as though recalling the data. "20,786. Threat level 10."

"Threat Level 10?" asked Haru. "What does that mean?"

"He was deemed an enemy of Bucaris and terminated."

"Who decided he was an enemy?"

"Terminated how?" Jasa cried.

"My algorithms track suspicious and subversive activity. Minister Toru was deemed Threat level 10, and needed to be terminated for the protection of Bacaris's citizens. His cortical implant triggered an overstimulation of the hypothalamus gland leading to subsequent cardiac arrest."

"But it was made to look like a murder," said Haru. "Like Jasa killed him."

The computer-face turned to her. "Jasa Idari. Threat level 10."

"Threat level 10?" she shouted, struggling to get a grip on her senses. "For what?"

"For the murder of Minister Toru."

Her fists clenched by her sides, and she shouted, "You just said you caused his death by overloading his implant!"

"Tell us why," commanded Haru, laying a calming hand on her shoulder.

The hologram glitched, its movements jarring. "Jasa Idari is off-grid and will be terminated at next login."

"Can you tell us why?" Haru repeated.

The computer glitched again.

"There's a problem with your programming." Haru shook his head. "Would you let us take a look?"

"My algorithms are programmed to award points for positive actions and remove points for negative actions. A utopian population for a utopian city. To interfere with the programming of the Interface SL is a negative action."

Jasa met Haru's worried glance, matching her own. "Who has access to your programming?" he asked.

"Only one." The holographic head tilted again. "The Minister of Technology: Eiko Hiratu Hikaru."

Jasa's heart stopped.

Haru flicked the switch, and the hologram disappeared. "The program is corrupted." He scrubbed a hand over his face. "It was one thing when it was just a game. But, all those people, their lives are controlled by a computer that's over three hundred years old. They have to know it's all just an algorithm, that a computer decides who is good and who is bad."

He fingered the sword, testing its grip.

"What are you thinking?"

"It killed the minister for no reason. And it's planning to kill you." He lifted the sharp sword and swung it across the nearest computer bank.

"What are you doing?" she yelled over the splintering of dozens of computer boards.

"Destroying it," he growled. He threw his body into the nearest computer bank, the entire row toppling over each other. "Help me!"

She hesitated—Bucaris was their ally. But wild adrenaline had been building since the moment she'd watched herself leap out of a chandelier and kill a man. Her rage escalated by an outdated interface that told them it was all just algorithms. Her value, her life, all came down to a computer and its arbitrary judgements of right and wrong.

She'd wanted to believe a diplomatic solution could be

found, a Kubati warrior always looked for a peaceful solution. The glitch could be recognized and corrected, and the whole thing straightened out.

But unlike Haru, she knew it wasn't a simple glitch, a matter of corrupted software.

She tore at the computer with her bare hands, kicking and smashing. Sparks flew. Haru hacked and slashed the metal with her giant broadsword. They worked in perfect unison, a dance of chaotic destruction until the computer was nothing more than a bent heap of scrap parts.

Haru drove the broadsword into the wreckage of hard drives and steel with a dizzy finality. The Supreme Leader was dead. The Bucari citizens would be confused, lost even, without its point system, but maybe that was better. A grin broke across his face. "Are you sure we don't know each other?"

Jasa stared at him in silence. It had been just like before.

"Let's get out of—"

The holographic head blinked back to life. "Jasa Idari—0. Threat level 10. Arka Daitan Hikaru—0. Threat level 10. Former enemy of the Emperor of the Golden City."

The face disappeared, replaced by a series of images: Jasa and Haru training together at the academy. Haru's daring escape through the roof. Jasa tasked with hunting the criminal, Arka Daitan Hikaru. The trap at his family home. The second escape with Eiko. All the anguish of the past, everything she'd tried so painfuly to protect him from, was displayed before them.

Jasa felt Haru's eyes on her and she started to shake.

"You said we didn't know each other . . ."

The images continued: Jasa and Haru running through abandoned sewer tunnels. Hiding in a condemned skyscraper.

"Jasa, what's going on?"

She swallowed, her throat rough as sand. Agony twisted across his face—his beautiful face—agony mixed with just the slightest thread of hope.

"You forgot," she said. "It was better that way."

He brought his hand to his face, covering it, but not before she saw the emotion splinter, tearing at his features. "All these things I've been feeling, the flashes of memory . . . You told me it wasn't real. Why?"

"You don't remember what happened." She heard the hysteria rising in her own voice but pushed through it as though there was some way to avoid the oncoming calamity. "You don't know what I did!"

"Of course, I don't know!" He looked at her again with an intensity in his honey-brown eyes that made her heart stutter. "But I know that I loved you. Love you? Enough to bow in front of a Shinto priest and make you my wife." His voice rose, and he pointed accusingly at an image of them, on their knees, hand in hand, as the priest performed the marriage rights—how had the computer gotten that? "What if I'd tried to remarry, Jasa? I'd bring dishonor to you and your family."

She gritted her teeth. Everything was crumbling, pieces slipping through her fingers. "A price I was willing to pay."

"And you? Tell me there's nothing between you and the emperor, the way he fawns over you," he yelled. "Tell me I read that wrong!"

"No, it's—"

A disembodied head appeared next to Jasa; a dozen guards unzipped their invisibility cloaks. They were everywhere, surrounding them. A hand on the back of her neck pushed her to the ground.

"So, this is why you would not agree to be my wife?" Emperor Kenko stood on the pile of ruined memory banks behind the guards, his eyes red, raw with rage.

"Emperor!" She scrambled to her feet, only to be pushed back to the floor. "I didn't kill the minister. What you saw wasn't real."

His face was stony cold. "You have brought dishonor to the Golden City. And grave personal dishonor to me!"

She stumbled forward as the air rushed out of her.

A set of glasses were pushed onto her face. Needles jabbed the skin around her eyes, securing them in place. A carnival of holographic lights flashed as names and image badges appeared over the people surrounding them.

"Eiko!" Haru shouted, struggling against the two guards that held him. "Tell them."

Jasa squinted through the lights invading her vision to see Haru's younger brother standing with the other ministers behind the ring of guards. His score was over forty-seven thousand—more than double what it had been just hours earlier.

Realization shook her. The photo of the ceremony . . . Eiko had been the only other person there.

"She killed our parents, Haru."

"No," Jasa gasped, "it's not like that." But it was exactly like that. That's why she had let him forget, wasn't it?

Haru stared at his younger brother. "What did you do?"

The hands gripping her arms let go, and she clawed at her face, desperately trying to pull the glasses off. In the upper corner, her pitiful score ticked down, steadily heading towards zero as it reconnected with the Interface SL.

"You did this," Haru yelled at Eiko. "You programmed

the computer. That's how you got all those points. Did the minister even have to die? Why make it look like it was Jasa?"

"You're my brother; it's just the two of us, remember?" Eiko said, his voice small as he stood half behind one of the other ministers. "You've always protected me. You promised we would always be together, remember? Let me protect you, from this."

"I . . ." Haru ran a hand through his hair, lost for words.

"She's nothing." He waved a hand in her direction. "A liar, a killer."

Her point tally hit zero.

A siren screamed in her ears, flooding her senses. Red lights flashed in front of her eyes. She tried again for the glasses, dropping to her knees.

So, this was 'bottoming out.'

There was no escape. She closed her eyes and brought her hands uselessly to her ears to shut out the noise.

There was a loud pneumatic hiss, and the guards parted as she looked up. A window slid open, dawn light streaming into the dark room. The glasses enhanced it, making the opening sparkle. Pulsing chevrons lit up the floor.

Her mind wild, she staggered forward. Alarms punctuated every step. The zero hounded her, searing across her vision. Zero. Her score. Her worth.

There was only one escape. The glowing stripes guided her, and she started to run.

Only when she cleared the window did the mind-numbing alarms stop. The flashing lights and the sirens faded. The needles detached from her face, and the glasses fell away.

She thought of the man she had seen when they'd first arrived, falling between the towers, crashing into the ocean below. Had he too been driven to madness for an pretend offence he didn't commit?

The city sprawled out below her—a two thousand foot jump without a parachute. She took a deep breath, suddenly feeling more calm than she had in years, and spread her arms instinctively.

She was going to die, but it weighed less heavily than all the lies and dishonors, all the trying to be someone else for everyone else.

A weight crashed into her from behind, knocking the breath from her lungs and changing her trajectory. She hurtled toward the white towers below, Haru's arm wrapped around her waist.

His hold tightened, and he cried out. Their descent slowed then jerked to a stop.

The jolt knocked her eyes open, whipping her body around like a ragdoll. The broadsword—his sword—dug into the tower wall. Haru grunted as he gripped the hilt with the tips of his fingers, the other hand securely around her waist.

With his help, she clamored for the wall, finding handholds in the crumbling facade. She clung desperately, pressing her face into the cool concrete.

Throwing his head back, he laughed wildly, his shock of hair tousled in the wind. He looked cracked. He'd have to be to think he could pull off a rescue from two-thousand feet. But then, that was Haru, a man of impossible odds.

"Why?" she asked. "After I lied to you. You should have let me fall."

"A feeling." His vivacious honey-gold eyes shone with excitement. "Forget points. Forget supposed-to-be's or should-do's. A computer can't tell me how I love, or what brings me joy, or whether I'm a good person or not. No one can. I don't remember what happened that year, but my heart does. And that's all that matters."

"What about Eiko?"

Some of the mirth fell from his eyes as he looked up to the tallest tower with its gaping window. "Maybe, with time . . . Is it true what he said, you're the reason our parents died?"

She pressed her lips together. There was no point in lying, there were already lies between them, lies she had set in place seven years ago. "Yes."

He blinked at her. "Before or after?"

"During, I guess." Her hands felt cold as she clung to the cracked concrete facade. He was still smiling, but it was fading. What would he do when he knew the truth? Push her? Leave her here on the wall? Turn her in after all?

He flashed his silly grin and started to climb down. "You'll have to explain that one."

And she told him, following him down the wall, easily falling into their tandem pattern. How they had been friends, how he had escaped the academy when they came for him, how they had sent her and she had gone. How she didn't know what they had planned until it was too late. How they had fallen in love.

They reached the base of the tower, standing on the lip of its mooring, a dozen feet above the ocean waves. "What now?" she asked.

"I guess we find a boat. Or a chopper." He stood over her, his broad shoulders protecting her from the wind, and licked his lips. "Can I kiss you now?"

"After ev—"

His lips on hers stopped every word, every lie, every apology.

The sweetness spoke of new beginnings, the familiarity exhilarating. She smiled against him.

When they broke apart, he took her hand. "Come on, I have a life to reclaim."

And so, Jasa realized, did she.

Devil on Your Shoulder

ADAN GEESI

Money. It's the beginning and end of all things. That and a good rum. So when the bosun comes and tells the crew he's got a lead on an asteroid mine's resource transport route, you get a tingle down your spine all the way to your taint.

Better yet, when you commandeer the ship without a hitch, you might kiss the greasy rat-tailed bastard.

But now you decide, if both of you make it out of this alive, you're going to slit his throat.

The view from the deck is all fire and smoke as you plummet to the surface of an uncharted planet. Shit man, this was supposed to be a place to lay low for a time while the corporation's hired army searched you and your comrades out with impunity. It's looking more and more likely that it'll end up your last resting place instead.

The ship's navigator spotted the planet a few lightyears out. It wasn't in the system, but that just made it more attractive to a crew like yours, didn't it? The atmosphere is so thick with dust, even a pirated two hundred thousand ton mineral tanker would be next to impossible to find. You would take twenty-five of the best freebooters you got, hijack the transport ship, and meet back with the captain and remaining seventy-five crew members of the Sea Dog on the dark side of the unknown planet.

So let's review. The plan was devised and executed with precision. Great. You and your twenty-five men, found yourself sailing a ship filled to capacity with millions of dollars worth of raw precious metal. But that is where your luck ran out, didn't it, mate? One should never underestimate the frugality of a multi-trillion dollar interstellar corporation. The tanker crimped under the rough handling of a real sailor, and the engine blew as soon as you entered the planet's orbit. You found out immediately after, the comms look like they haven't worked in centuries, and the tanker is built so thick and heavy, you probably couldn't get a murmur to the Sea Dog even if you did get them transmitting.

But hell, it's not like you could go ahead and abort the mission, so you sent her down anyway.

And now you sit, gnashing your teeth and white-knuckling the arms of your chair. Bits of metal are pulling off from the front of the ship and crashin' against the damn windows. How long until one of them gets through? The inside of the ship is getting hot. What are the chances this beast stays together? You might find you hit the ground as a ball of flame.

But then again, you don't know what's down there. Maybe you won't reach the ground at all. Maybe you'll land in water instead, or an ocean of some noxious mystery liquid.

What's worse—burning alive, drowning, or drowning in something while it burns you alive?

When you went on account with the crew years ago, you knew you'd probably go out like this. Or someway similar. But you're not ready. Not yet. Success is measured by how much you accumulate, and you haven't accumulated near enough, mate—

Shit! Did we hit? I think we've stopped moving but everything's black, and it's awfully quiet.

That's that then, you're dead.

"Headcount!" Okay, you can talk, maybe you're not dead.

"Aye," That's Sutton, the gunner's voice, "Mutt?"

"Yes, sir. I'm here, sir." Ah! Sutton's young powder monkey. Thirteen years old, and the longest one he has had to date.

Unstrap the knife at your hip and cut through your seat's harness. Is it just you three left?

"Anyone else?"

A chorus of groaning "aye." That's good, sounds like a fair handful of them.

"Aye mate." Finally, the bosun. The one who started this whole mess, Lindley. Not sure you should be happy he's still kicking. "Nice sailing!"

Disrespectful bastard. You're both alive so he can stay that way for now. But promise, if this trip doesn't end in a pile of cash, you'll blow the man down.

A flood of orange has poured into the ship. It's the emergency lights. Get a look at your men. Some of them are still rousing from their non-consensual naps, the others all have turned and are looking at you.

"Every one of you who's got their land legs under them, grab a man who doesn't. We're getting the payday, and we're getting out of here."

Another round of "aye," and they set to it like good little dogs.

Your first order of business is to get to the bounty, figure out a way to cart it to the other side of the planet, and meet up with the rest of the crew. There's a map of the ship on the wall of the main deck; go take a look at it. There must be an emergency pod on this beast somewhere that someone could fly to the Sea Dog and tell her where to find you.

Hmm, from the looks of it, you are going to be sorely disappointed. Anyone sailing this ship would have no choice but to go down with her.

You steal from people for a living, and those people will fight back against you hammer and tongs if they catch you trying to do it. Interesting that those same folk will work for a company that steals just as much if not more from them and not even put up a fuss when it asks for their lives too.

'Freelancing' has never felt so good. You did the universe a favor taking from these blokes. You're like fucking Robin Hood.

The men have all suited up and congregated by the dock. They're waiting for you to give the order to move out. Put your helmet on and lock it tight. It's time to see just what kind of hell you've crashed on.

Give Sutton a nod to slam his palm into the release button. The door falls open so hard it bounces and kicks up a cloud of blue dust. The cloud dissipates, and the alien landscape is laid out before you. You are on a beach looking out over a glistening indigo ocean. The air is hanging heavy like a translucent purple mist, giving everything, even the green plants inland, a violet hue.

Lindley wastes no time. "You," he's barked to the young new hand, "get out there and get me a reading of the atmosphere"—and to the tech officer—"Roberts, get on the comms and see what you can get from it."

He's looking at you with those beady little rat eyes of his and scurrying this way. "What's the plan if we can't make contact?"

He really should have ended that sentence with 'Sir.'

"First, the cargo needs to be inspected."

"I'll go."

You can't seriously let this short fucker anywhere near the goods. He's liable to pocket something extra for himself. "No. I'm going. You stay here and keep these men working." Never trust a man with wee shrimp eyes and no facial hair.

Besides, it's been hours since you got your fix.

Get back on the ship and open the door to the cargo bay. A catwalk extends over a five hundred foot basin filled to the top with the most glorious array of shining raw gold, silver, titanium, palladium, iron, and more. Breathe it in, my friend. It's the best smell in the whole world. Dirt, metal, a bit of oil—and freedom. Alright. Pull your eyes away, you need to go check the hull's diagnostics and make sure she is in good enough condition to move when the captain gets here.

Log on to the bay's computer. Everything is surprisingly sound. Considering the landing you barely made, the inside walls are at 80 percent and the outside structure is a little worse off but still a respectable 56 percent stability. The mechanism that detaches the hull from the ship appears to be in working order, and even the engine is getting a green light.

Wait. The cargo bay has an engine? Give the computer menu a more thorough perusing. Notice the little man figure in the top left corner, give him a press, why don't ya? A door has slid open beside you. Inside is the smallest cockpit you'll have ever seen in all your years. Well, shiver your timbers, the cargo *is* its own emergency pod.

Sit yourself in the pilot's seat and check on the fuel level. Full. That settles it. Someone will take the ore to the Sea Dog on the other side of the planet. Hitch the baby up and come back to get the rest of you.

Naturally, that person would be you. You are the quartermaster after all. And who else can you trust with the goods and enough fuel to get disappeared if one had a mind to?

Interesting there's only room for one crew member. Guess it doesn't matter to the company who survives, but they'll be damned if they lose their cargo.

Suppose you should get up and go tell your men the plan. But . . . just hold on a minute. There's no rush. Do the math in your head. What's two hundred thousand tons of ore worth? Then what's that divided by 102 men? Sure, a lot, but like we said, success is measured by how much you accumulate, and you've got the chance to accumulate a hell of a lot right now. You could just leave . . .

"Sir?"

Poor timing. "What is it, Mutt?" Look at that youngin' eyeing you up in this place like you were Sutton's pecker. Confused, curious, then a little scared. He always looks so spooked when he talks to you. The Gunner must have told him some of your better stories.

You could still leave, just kill him quick. Come on, show him how you got your reputation. . . .

"Master Sutton asked me to come find you, sir. We can't get any of the comms or emergency signals working."

"What are they doing now?"

"Feeling a little low, sir, convinced they're gonna be here a while. They've cracked open some bottles, sir."

"That's alright. Let them drink. I've got a new plan." But you've stepped out of the cockpit and closed the door. Don't miss your chance! What are you thinking—where are you going? "Let's get out of here." Get back here, you fool!

* * *

You've made some pretty bad decisions in our time together, but telling twenty-five pirates there is a ship full of treasure that only one of them can take has to be the worst yet. See the carnal look in their eyes now that the word is out. Every man has taken a few good paces away from each other, hands on their weapons. What do you think the chances are they accept the idea of you takin' off on your own, eh?

. . . *Then* coming back for them.

Ha. That's a laugh. Admit it. No one would be coming back for them.

Lindley's creeping on your right, keep your peripherals on him. Don't trust that fucker, he's about to try something. He's got something behind his back. He's close, but the mate to your left is closer.

Lindley's twitching. Grab your mate and throw him in front of you. Now! The bosun's pike's gone right through him. Nearly impaled you too. Good thing you're quick and nimble. Twist out of the way and push your dead comrade onto Lindley.

It's on now. Men are dropping fast. They're all scrambling for the ship, but you can't let them pass. Unsheath your blade and jam it into this man's eye. That might have been the crew's cookey. Everything is happening too fast to be sure.

Someone's grabbed you by the throat from behind with a hairy forearm. Jab your knife behind you, maybe you'll hit something. He's let go and he's a bellowing. Turn around and look. You got the mechanic right in the swordfish, you did! Finish him off. You can giggle about the look on his face later.

The crowd has thinned dramatically. The beach looks like the floor of a tavern after a long night's boozing.

Shit. Lindley has brained the marlinspike and is making a run for the door. After him! Get him before—

Watch out!

Ouch, that'll make your ears ring. When did Sutton get past you and onto the ship? He's coming at you with that hammer again. Shame you'll have to kill him. Good mate, this one. There's blood dripping into your eyes now, so take a few pokes before you can't see at all.

One. Ha, you missed, dumbass. He got you first, and you deserved it after that attempt.

Two. There ya go. The shoulder. He's dropped the hammer.

Three. Bull's eye. Right in the jugular.

Four. Five. Six. Seven for good measure.

Eight. Nine. Ten.

Alright, alright mate, he's dead. Where the fuck is Lindley? Haven't forgotten about him, have ya?

There he is. He's closing the door to the cargo bay; let's hope you can get under before it crushes you. Ready? Tuck and roll! Whew, that was close.

Get up. Lindley is making his way across the catwalk. Run. Catch him and bash that rat's skull in.

Wait. He's turning around and he's got a gun. Duck you bastard! *Bang!*

Put up your hands. There's nowhere to go to now.

"Ok, Lindley. Put down the gun. This got out of hand fast, didn't it? How about we talk this through and come up with terms that'll make us both rich."

"Fuck off! This is my payday. You know how much work I put in to get here? Finding the right route with a spot to hide from the captain? Rigging the engine to blow and sabotaging the comms without any of you bastards noticing? This ship is my ticket out of here!"

Why, it doesn't look like he intends to let you live, my friend. You did make me a promise. Barrel toward him, I think he's shot you, but that was to be expected. Dropped your knife and it's fallen through the grate. Bite back the pain in your gut and lift him off the ground. Now heave him over the edge and watch his head splat on the gold ore below. What a mess. Oh well, you can dump his body later, and the gold will rinse off all right.

Shit, you're making a mess yourself. That's a lot of blood pouring out of you. Get to the cockpit and try not to bleed all over the control panel. Get off this dust mound of a planet and find a doctor. You can afford the best of the best now.

Start the engine and let the computer get her ready to fly. In the meantime, rummage around for a first aid kit. Check under the console.

Oh!

Well, what do we have here? A mangy pup.

Grab the little stowaway by the scruff of the neck and pull him to his feet. Not smart trying to hide in the cockpit. Little mutt will have to pay for that mistake.

"Please sir, please. I just thought you might take me with you. I don't want your treasure! You can just leave me at the first port you come on. P-please—"

He's stronger than he looks. You'll have to tighten your grip if you don't want him squirming out. Snap his neck! Come on. What are you waiting for?

"Get the hell off my ship, Mutt." You've dropped him, but now he's clinging to the edge of the console for dear life, trembling like you after a good shag. *Ha!*

"Please, sir. I-I'll die out there . . ."

If you can't bring yourself to kill the scrawny whelp, then grab him by the ear and drag his ass out. Toss him through the cargo bay door and kick him in the shitter for good measure. He's smashed his little face on the grated floor. Uck, he's crying from his eyes *and* his nose.

Gross.

"Sir. I'm the only one looking after me ma . . . without me she won't . . ."

Blah blah. Boo fuckin' hoo!

Don't worry about that. Close the bay door, disable the mechanism, and make your way back to the cockpit. The ship should be fired up by now.

Sit down in your seat and buckle in, my friend. Begin the ascent protocol and release the hull from the transport. Start countdown.

10 9 8 7 6 5 4 3 2 . . .

Warning: Engine Failure? Aborting Ascent Protocol.

Hmm. Too bad you don't know anything about engines. You could ask the mechanic, but he's lying in a pool of his own blood from when you stabbed him in the cock.

Wonder if there's any rum left. Leave the cockpit, amble along the catwalk and spit on Lindley's body while you're at it. Open the door to the cargo bay and walk past the unrecognizable flesh sack of your Gunner and best mate. Step over the mechanic's body at the door, and clomp down the metal ramp. Kick over the body of the skipper and pick up the half-finished bottle of rum in his hand. Grab that other a few feet to your right too. Make your way across the sand to the young powder monkey sitting on a log, staring at you with horror across his face. Sit next to him.

Pat him on the back; make him feel comfortable.

"Know any songs, Mutt?"

"A-aye, sir. An old one me pa used to sing to me."

Don't you have a heart? Pass the boy a bottle "Well? Get on with it."

"Uh ... u-uh ... fifteen men on a dead man's chest ... Y-yo ho and a bottle of rum."

Now this one I haven't heard in an age. Timeless. Sing along for me, it'll make you feel better!

"*Drink and the devil had done for the rest. Yo ho, and a bottle of rum!*"

WHAT HAVE YOU DONE?

3

Repudium

K . E . B A R R O N

I

In her favorite white pantsuit and matching heels, Jasmeet made her way to the auditorium at a brisk pace. She was running late as always, but she didn't mind. It gave her the adrenaline push she needed to come before every citizen of Armstrong Lunar Base, not to mention the countless people on Earth via live-stream.

She jogged up the steps out of the underground tunnel on her way to the backstage doors. After four years working for LaCroix International, the feeling that Jasmeet would float out of her shoes had lessened considerably. Now, she felt as secure on her feet here as she did on Earth, thanks to her magnetic soles.

Her smart device buzzed in her breast pocket. She fished it out. A name flashed on the display. 'Danielle LaCroix.' Jasmeet rolled her eyes as she connected the call, choosing the hologram option.

A 3D image of LaCroix International's originator and Board Chair, projected from the device's screen. The light buzz behind Jasmeet's right ear alerted her to the device connecting to her ear chip. "Where are you?" LaCroix crossed her arms, her lips a thin red line.

"I'm here now. It's always better to let our viewers stew a bit," Jasmeet said as she reached the top of the stairs.

"I need not remind you what will happen if we don't get buy-in from every member of the public."

"The world is more than ready for this, Madam Chair, you have nothing to worry about." Jasmeet paused as she neared the doors. She didn't want to take this conversation backstage. The blasting, eager crowd beyond was already drowning out the Chair's quiet yet shrill voice, complete with an English accent that made it impossible not to take her seriously at all times, even when she dressed like a Hollywood starlet from the turn of the millennium.

"I worry because religious fanatics and human rights activists are waiting for you to say anything that will fuel their fire."

"Won't matter. Their questions aren't getting through our filters."

"Even so, I'd like you to stay away from words like destruction and disintegrate, just keep it about the big picture and how Travelac will revolutionize human transportation."

Jasmeet tapped the floor with her toe, while maintaining her faux smile. *What did she hire me for anyway?* "Hear you loud and clear, Madam Chair."

"I hate to put even more pressure on you right before you go on . . ." The Chair's voice took on a suspicious hush. "Some of the directors indicated strongly that if we can't sell this to the masses within the year, they'll liquidate their shares."

"Which directors?"

"I won't name names, but nine out of twelve," LaCroix whispered. They must have been in the room with her.

"That'll cripple the company!" Jasmeet blared, just as a stagehand opened the doors and spotted her standing there. He beckoned her backstage with a wave of his arm.

"Public opinion is the new currency, Ms. Sahni. You have your work cut out for you tonight." Jasmeet followed the man through a dark hall and around a series of curtains.

"I got this, alright? Tell the board they're being ridiculous. Travelac is the future and the world will see that tonight."

"The board are hardly being ridic—" Jasmeet cut her boss off so that the stagehand could pin a microphone to her lapel. He then made a gesture to a woman on the other side of the stage. She, in turn, tapped her tablet with a pointer, and the house lights immediately dimmed. LaCroix International's logo lit up the backdrop, and the audience hushed.

Jasmeet checked herself in her tablet's mirror app and made sure there were no strands loose from her elaborate up-do or smudged eyeliner marring her light brown skin. "Get 'er done, Jas." She whispered then put her device back in her pocket. An automated voice blared over the PA system.

"LaCroix International: Today's pioneer in human connectivity. Please welcome, CEO, Jasmeet Sahni."

With a deep breath and the most confident smile she could muster, Jasmeet sauntered onto the stage to greet the cheering crowd. Her white pantsuit changed from blue, green, to red as she passed under the technicolor beams that settled on glowing white at center stage.

The logo behind her fell away as a hologram of a rapidly expanding universe extended from the backdrop. Planets, nebulas, and shooting stars illuminated the people's faces.

After the applause died down, she began, "Matter can't move at the speed of light. Interstellar travel to other planets

in our solar system is impractical. Travel to distant galaxies ...
impossible. We achieved the impossible in 2189 when LaCroix
International teleported the first inanimate object to the
moon—to this very base, and changed the shipping industry
forever."

The backdrop shifted from images of space to the LaCroix
Armstrong facility. The camera swooped down, through the
halls, and ended up in a large rectangular laboratory on the
west side of the base. There, stood an oval pod festooned with
white tubing going through the floors and outside onto the
moon's surface. "Teleporting living organisms was far off at
that time, still said to be impossible by many. Now, twenty
years later ... we have proved the doubters wrong again."

The hologram spun around, revealing an attractive female
operator approaching the pod. She lifted the door and a
middle-aged man, the last human test subject, ducked inside.
He laid down on a raised platform suspended over a glistening
blue liquid. The operator fastened the man's arms down with
plastic wrist restraints and began to unfold a white sheet over
his body.

Jasmeet walked through the holographic image of the
laboratory. "After a decade of human testing, brave participants
like Mr. Boon here helped us prove there is no limit to what
or who we can send through space. Perhaps time will be next,
but for now, let's bask in knowing that today, human beings
can travel at the speed of light ... or as close to it as anyone
is ever going to get."

The camera zoomed in on a husky, curly-haired man at a
large terminal in the center of the lab. Dr. Paul Linderman,
quantum physicist and head of the Travelac project gave a
meek smile and quickly turned from the camera as he tapped

on a touchscreen display. "Over two hundred years ago," Jasmeet continued, "the Internet brought countless minds together. Today, Travelac will bring together everything else."

The camera panned around the terminal, settling behind Dr. Linderman. A loading bar in the shape of a person appeared with the option to 'Begin Scan.'

"Once the traveler enters the origin pod and is shrouded in the ionic sheet, the quantum scan begins." The operator shut the pod lid. Lights along its outer edge glowed green, signifying that it was now locked. The camera honed in on the terminal screen and the digital person slowly went from white to blue, starting at both head and feet and meeting at the mid-section.

"With state-of-the-art quantum scanning technology, it is now possible to collect and store data for every atom in the human body. This terminal, fifty years ago, would have taken up this entire stage, but now, it's no bigger than a podium. It has enough processing power to collect and store seven by ten to the fortieth power qubits. That's enough for the largest human being we can imagine as well as anything they wear or carry on their person."

Lights on the terminal display flashed 'Quantum Scan Complete' and a timer appeared over the man's image, counting down from ten before teleportation. Linderman tapped the timer to override the countdown and start the process immediately. The green lights on the pod lid turned orange. At this part in the presentation, the sound was turned on so the audience could hear what had actually occurred in the lab. A loud whirring filled the room. It was as if they all stood inside an antique Pentium processor, calculating away. Then there came a loud slosh as the water drained from the pod and down the tubes. The camera turned away from the terminal right before its display blinked with the words, 'Disintegration Complete.' It focused on the origin pod, its lights turning off. The locking mechanism released, making an electronic hiss, and the operator opened the door. The pod was dry, the ionic sheet flattened. Mr. Boon was nowhere in sight.

The audience gasped. Jasmeet grinned. She'd never tire of viewing a successful teleportation. "This is not a disappearing act in a magic show. This is physics in action. Mr. Boon is not gone. He is here . . ." The 3D image shifted around Jasmeet on the stage. The camera zipped out of the room and down a long hallway, all the way to the east end of the facility, through the automatic doors, and into a laboratory the mirror image of the one it had just left. There was another pod, just like the last, its lights glowing orange. "This is the destination pod. It's connected to the origin pod via secure wireless connection with the Travelac network." Another operator tapped the screen and the pod lights shifted to green then turned off, signifying that the doors had unlocked. A male operator lifted the door and hastily unwrapped the man lying above the liquid pool and unfastened his restraints.

Mr. Boon rubbed his brow ridge, shaking his head. He slowly sat up like he had been waking from a light nap. A wave of awes and claps washed over the audience as they watched Mr. Boon stand up with little effort. "Our test travelers are checked rigorously after every trip. They are rebuilt exactly the way they entered the origin pod. By the quantum mechanical phenomenon known as entanglement, this man has been recreated right down to the molecule. That means every cell, bacterium—virus is as it was when he entered the origin pod.

So, unfortunately, if you have a cold when you go in, you'll still have it when you get out. Travelac leaves nothing behind."

An older black man with a tablet and lab coat approached the subject. It was Dr. Noble, the physician on the team. Their voices were muted so that Jasmeet could speak. "Our primary concern is the health of our travelers, and we are pleased to report that every single one of them left their destination pods in the same health as when they went in and have reported little to no side-effects in the subsequent weeks. We've been tracking every test traveler for the last ten years and still, our physicians have observed no adverse physical or mental effects."

Dr. Noble scanned Mr. Boon with his medical tablet as Jasmeet continued, "As a former neurobiologist myself, I can personally attest that the mental states of our travelers remain unchanged. Every synapse, every motor neuron, every particle in his brain is reassembled without flaw."

The 3D image of the laboratory collapsed in on itself. Only the company logo remained on the backdrop behind Jasmeet with the addition of a like-ticker on the top left set to zero and already beginning to climb. "Human teleportation is here. No more do we need to travel to the moon or surrounding asteroids in expensive and dangerous shuttles. No longer will we need to rely on harmful green-house gas emitting vehicles to jet people across the globe. With Travelac, nowhere is too far . . . nothing is out of reach."

Jasmeet took her bow as the audience erupted in applause. The like-ticker climbed faster than an unenhanced eye could detect.

"You may now ask your questions," The announcer blared over the PA.

All at once, the audience's faces were cast alight by the glow of their electronic devices. They typed their curiosities into the event app interface. The questions would be combined and filtered through an algorithm designed by LaCroix International. It would formulate questions representative of the collective inputs, maximizing relevance of the inquiries to the population at large while filtering out those that were too controversial.

The most relevant question displayed itself on the backdrop behind Jasmeet: Was anyone harmed in the initial human trials?

"Fair question. In the first few subjects, there was some short-term memory loss, but in time they've been able to recover most of it. There were no incomplete rebuilds, missing limbs or anything like that. We had worked out all of those kinks before human trials began."

Jasmeet looked behind her and waited for the next question to materialize on the backdrop. What if there is a shortage of matter on the other side and the traveler cannot be completely rebuilt?

"This is why our origin pods and destination pods are rotated regularly. This ensures there will always be matter available for the next traveler. Our terminals are constantly measuring the matter on hand and if there is ever a shortage, the rebuilding process can be delayed until the storage rings are refilled."

More and more questions appeared on the backdrop and Jasmeet tackled them all with confidence. She walked back and forth across the stage, addressing every concern brought forth. The questions grew more curious, but positive on the whole. The like-ticker continued to rise, now in the hundreds of millions. *This is going better than I'd hoped.*

The next question caught Jasmeet a little off guard: What happened to that man in the origin pod?

It was odd since the algorithm was supposed to filter out any question that had been previously addressed in the presentation as not to waste people's time. *Must be a glitch*, she thought. Jasmeet cleared her throat. "That's an easy one. As you saw in the presentation, he was rebuilt atom by atom in the destination pod."

The text on the background faded and the next one appeared, but before Jasmeet could read it a man stood up in the fourth row. "You didn't answer the question."

He was a young man in his twenties, wearing a t-shirt of a music group Jasmeet didn't care for. "Sir, was this your question?"

"What happens to the bodies?"

Jasmeet cringed inwardly. LaCroix told her not to mention the disintegration in case it created alarm in the viewers, but of course, not showing an important part of the teleportation process guaranteed such a question would be asked.

"Well . . . after the quantum scan, the data is sent wirelessly to the destination terminal and the original body provides the matter for a future traveler."

"So, you're killing them," the man retorted without missing a beat.

Jasmeet smoothed out her blazer and smiled at the man. "Travelac has not harmed anyone. Yes, the body is temporarily destroyed, but the process lasts a mere instant and is quite painless. Our test travelers have reported little to no discomfort and have been able to go about their day minutes after they've arrived at their destination." Jasmeet started to turn back around. "I hope that adequately answers your question."

The man didn't sit down, but she would have to ignore him and stick to the collective inquiries. "You're still not answering," snapped a female voice from farther back. An Asian woman stood up in the fifteenth row. She wore a pleather jacket and blue-jeans; a pair of sunglasses over her hair. Such things only served as a fashion statement for those who lived on the moon since Armstrong's windows blocked any harmful UV rays. "You say you're not killing anybody, but you won't tell us what happens to that original person."

"I—"

"What happens to their souls?"

There it is. Jasmeet wanted to roll her eyes. She had hoped the algorithm would have filtered out any questions from the activists who were determined to sabotage this project no matter what she said.

"I'm sorry, but we'll have to return to the questions from the rest of our viewers."

Several more people stood up. "Answer the question."

The buzz of her earchip startled her. Jasmeet activated it with a touch. "Shut these people up and move on. Security is on its way," said LaCroix.

"Without getting into neurobiological jargon, a soul is simply our way to explain the phenomenon known as consciousness, which is nothing more than brain activity, a conglomeration of memories and experiences that can be recreated. In fact, it is happening all the time. Human beings cycle through every atom in our bodies about twelve hundred times over the course of our lives. Our bodies are transient particles interchanging repeatedly. It is our experience and memories that make us who we are . . . who the people in our lives know and love. That is what Travelac preserves. So, to finally answer your question: No, Travelac has killed no one. Quite the opposite."

Jasmeet turned around and finally read the next question: Have you yourself used Travelac?

She gulped. "Not yet, but our test subjects have gone through numerous times without issue."

Why? Came the next question.

What is wrong with this algorithm?

She looked back out over the audience. More stood up while others exchanged curious glances. Chatter from the crowd picked up considerably, bringing Jasmeet's already nervous heartbeat into her throat.

The man from the fourth row said, "You speak for this revolutionary product to connect the world and how it's perfectly safe, but you won't go through it? Are you afraid you won't come out the other side?"

Jasmeet finally spotted the security guards making their way down the aisles. Sweat ran down her back. She was afraid to turn around lest everyone see it soaking through her white blazer. LaCroix vibrated her ear bones. "This is not good. Our investors are throwing a wobbly." The like-ticker slowed then started to drop. She was running out of time, but she couldn't leave this question unanswered, despite the Chair screeching in her ear to shut it all down.

A beefy security guard tapped the man on the shoulder and prompted him to show himself out of the auditorium. Jasmeet put out her hand. "I wasn't supposed to announce this here, but . . ."

The guard froze and every eye focused on Jasmeet on the hot stage. ". . . I planned to be the first person to use Travelac when it hits the market. It will be live-streamed so everyone will witness its marvel in real time."

The audience murmured as the activists in the crowd slowly sat back down. The like-ticker began its rapid climb once again. Jasmeet felt a surge of adrenaline as she prepared her closing statements. "I am proud of what we've done at LaCroix International, and I for one, can't wait to be part of this historic moment in human interconnectivity." The backdrop behind Jasmeet fell dark and she took a final bow. "And thank you all for being part of it with us."

She waved to the crowd and walked off stage left. The auditorium erupted in cheers as she disappeared behind the wings.

By the time Jasmeet handed her microphone to the female stagehand and stepped outside the auditorium, LaCroix was already shrieking inside her ear. ". . . Live-stream? This was supposed to be it, Jasmeet. This was not cleared by the Board."

Jasmeet tapped her smart device to create a two-way connection. "What was I supposed to do?"

"We have nothing to prove to those fringe idiots, and you just caved to them."

"Those fringe idiots made us look like we're afraid of our own product. Don't tell me they're right."

The Chair fell silent as Jasmeet walked into the lavatory next to the green room. Silence from Danielle LaCroix always made her stomach flop. "Look. I get this isn't what we planned, but I promise it's going to work out. We get a little more publicity, and afterward, Travelac will sell faster than the fucking i-Phone."

"Except now, the public will associate Travelac with death so . . . good show."

Jasmeet ducked into a stall and activated the soundproofing program on the door's touchpad. "Can you just relax for once in your life?"

"Pardon me? I built this company. Me. When we were all being cooked alive by greenhouse gases it was my teleporters that put millions of trucks and planes out of commission. I saved the bloody planet, so I'll decide when it's time to relax!"

Jasmeet instantly regretted her outburst. "I'm sorry, I didn't mean to suggest . . ."

"Do not turn this into a farce, Ms. Sahni," LaCroix's voice was cold.

"You can trust me, Madam Chair."

The Chairwoman let out an annoyed sigh. "Brilliant, as long as I can get these bloody things to market by next month. Otherwise, you're off this rock." A buzz, and the line disconnected.

Jasmeet growled and stomped out of the stall. She came face to face with a group of ladies filing into the washroom. Their eyes lit up, and they barraged her with questions about the next live-stream. She spouted something to the effect of 'you'll have to wait and see' and slipped away before she made anything worse.

She stormed down the underground halls, fuming from her conversation with LaCroix. Had she been permitted to use the teleporter sooner; she could have answered that question with a simple yes.

She wandered into a bar and ordered a gin and tonic at the automated bartender. Her glass rose from the compartments underneath the counter and moved along the conveyor, receiving the necessary liquid ingredients from the spouts above. She waved her device over the scanner, crediting twenty-five ninety-nine from her account. This allowed her to access the drink from behind a plexiglass door. With drink in hand, she found a seat by herself at a table next to the window.

She stared out across the craterous landscape of the moon's surface. A big blue orb half shrouded in the deep was the sole source of light. So far away she could hardly register it was home to fifteen billion and counting. It hung silent, beautiful, and alone. It seemed so harmless from all the way up here, but down there it was anything but. An overcrowded rat race of stupidity and intolerance . . . among other things. She had to fly to a place without an atmosphere so that she could finally breathe.

One could definitely find a better cross-section of Earth's population than on a moon base as only the best and brightest were allowed to live and work on them. There was no room for free-loaders. If someone lost their purpose here, they were sent right back to Earth and put on the waitlist for a second chance. Jasmeet didn't know many people who got that second chance. She fought tooth and nail to get accepted here. She abandoned her former field of study and joined LaCroix International, the most prominent moon-based company in the world. Her scientific background and natural talents for business and public relations gave her the leg up she needed to eventually become CEO. It was a coveted position to be sure, and there were likely many contenders eager to knock her off her perch if she showed any sign of weakness. Now, all she had to do to solidify her position for good was lay down in that origin pod.

Her throat tightened at the thought. She downed half her gin and tonic in hopes to loosen it up a bit.

That's when she caught sight of the attractive man staring

at her from another table. He raised his glass to her, and she did the same out of politeness more than anything. *He sure is familiar though.*

The man got up and started toward her. She turned back to the window in hopes he'd walk on by. She was in no mood to flirt, even with someone as good-looking as him. He placed his beer next to hers, spun out the neighboring chair, and sat down. "Saw you on the stream. That got intense," he said in a familiar baritone.

Familiar or not, she sighed with annoyance, ready to tell him to take his charms elsewhere. Then, she caught his penetrating gaze. Bright blue contrasting with his chocolate skin. *Augmented eyes . . . Wait, I know who this is.* "Oh, hi . . . Darrel?"

"Darius. Webster."

"Sorry." She chuckled and took another sip. "It's been a while."

"I didn't expect you to recognize me right away. It seems like you have a lot going on these days, Ms. CEO."

Jasmeet rested her head in her palm and rotated her near-empty glass on the table. "I thought they'd shipped you back to Earth. You up and disappeared on me."

He shook his shaved head and grinned, showcasing perfect white teeth. "I've been mining on Darkside, but I'm back in Armstrong permanently. Seems you made things a little more interesting. Travelac . . ." His deep voice stretched out the word as if savoring it. "You sure about getting in that thing?"

"Hmmm." She downed the rest of her beverage. "Why wouldn't I be? I'm in a position to know that it works."

He softly brushed his fingers over her knee. "I'd like to be in a position to know how you work."

Jasmeet stifled a smirk and gave him a wry glare instead. "Really?"

He looked away and shook his head. "Okay, that wasn't my best. I've been underground for way too long."

Jasmeet held her empty glass up to her face as she allowed a few playful huffs out her nose. "I thought robots did all the underground stuff these days."

"Sure, but someone's gotta keep an eye on them, you know, to make sure they don't malfunction and eliminate all of humanity."

"Sounds like a lot of pressure for one man."

"Can I get you another drink?" Darius raised a hand to her empty glass.

"Oh . . . uh . . ." she put it down. "I was just about to call it a night, actually."

"Fair enough. I'm just glad I caught you." His augmented blue eyes bored right through her, making her skin flush around her cheeks and chest. "I've been thinking about you a lot—seeing you up on that screen . . ." He nodded toward a monitor, currently showing the nightly news with clips of her recent appearance playing silently except to those who had their ear chips tuned in.

Darius stood. "You look good."

Jasmeet slid her glass down the length of the table and did the same. She stepped up close enough to smell his cologne-free musk; a rarity among men these days. "So do you. But my bed is calling."

"Alright." He raised his beer to her again and took some down. "Good to see you, Jas."

She gave him a sideways smirk and started toward the bar exit. "I don't intend on answering the call alone." For a moment she thought Darius wouldn't get the hint, but he proved himself not to be just another pretty young thing on Armstrong. He grinned, put his beer down on the table, and walked out after her.

II

Incessant chimes rattled Jasmeet from her sleep. Her smart device flashed in the dark, projecting the name 'Dr. Singh' in bright blue letters on the ceiling.

Her hand shot out from under the covers and silenced it.

Darius, sleeping next to her, grumbled and turned over.

Dr. Singh continued to flash. She sighed and lugged herself out of bed and lumbered into the bathroom, the automatic door opening then closing behind her. "Lock," she ordered the voice-activated mechanism. As soon as her lights went on, she tapped 'connect.'

"Dad? What's going on?" she croaked.

"Jasmeet Kaur, turn on your hologram." A disapproving tone cut through the speaker.

"Hold on." She threw on the bathrobe, hanging behind the door, and smoothed out her heavy black hair so it didn't look like she'd been rolling around in bed all night. Sitting on the closed toilet, she turned on hologram mode.

"Dad, you know I don't go by Kaur anymore."

"Kaur is your true name. I don't know why you turn your back on it," Dr. Dalip Singh said with a dismissive wave of his hand. He had gone even grayer since Jasmeet had seen him last. He was dressed for work in his dapper button-up shirt and yellow turban, wrapped tight.

"I told you why. You get to be a lion and I have to be a princess? Spare me." Sahni was her pre-baptismal name, one that differentiated her from the billions of other Sikhs . . . the only one in her family to keep it.

Dr. Singh huffed. "Okay, okay, enough about that. We saw you last night. Why didn't you tell us the big project you were working on this entire time was a teleporter? We had to hear on live-stream that you are going to go through that *machine*."

Jasmeet ran her hands through her hair. "Yeah. Sorry." She shrugged. "I signed a confidentiality agreement. But you heard the presentation. It's perfectly safe."

"You can't know what it will do to you . . . not really."

"Dad, I know you fear for my soul, but you don't have to. My entire brain will be rebuilt, soul and all. You will never know the difference."

"That's not what I mean—"

A plump woman, her black hair streaked with white, popped into the hologram. "Of course we won't know the difference, you haven't come home in years. I hardly recognized the woman in that stream. Who was she?"

"Hi, Mom." Jasmeet cracked a smile despite her irritation. "When this is done, I can teleport back and forth as many times as you want . . . on my days off."

Jasmeet cringed at her own words. She didn't know how often she'd make the trip back to see them. She honestly didn't want to. She couldn't be herself around them anymore. But it wasn't really them she wanted to avoid.

"Well . . ." her dad continued. "Hardeep asked about you recently. He forgives you and wants to try again."

Jasmeet bit her lip and groaned inwardly. *This is why I can't talk to you guys anymore!* She wanted to shout, but said instead,

"Kind of difficult when I'm on the moon."

A bracing knock on the bathroom door almost made Jasmeet drop her device on the cold tile floor. "Jas, how long are you going to be in there?"

"Who was that?" Dr. Singh asked. "Is there a man in your apartment?"

"None of your business, Dad."

"You are a married woman!" her mother railed.

"Not if Hardeep gives me that damn divorce."

Her mother gasped. "Jasmeet. You know he loves you very much . . . how long are you going to spurn him like this?"

"Ugh, I can't talk about this right now. I'll call you guys after the next live-stream. A lot of preparation ahead." *Not really, just post the date and time and show up.*

Her father's lips pursed as his eyes softened. "Why won't you just tell us what is really bothering you?"

What? That you two arranged for me to marry a controlling, philandering, asshole to which neither of you will believe or admit? That would have been Jasmeet's heated reply had she not been through this with them over and over for years already.

"Come on, Jas, I gotta piss." Darius's pitch rose with impatience.

"Bye, Mom, bye, Dad. Stay warm . . ." she said, realizing it was the middle of January in Canada. Even though it was far colder on the moon, cooped up in the Armstrong Lunar Base, she'd never feel anything close to true cold ever again. That was one more perk of leaving Earth. No more Canadian winters that never end.

Jasmeet disconnected the call, cutting off her parents' goodbyes. "Unlock."

Darius slid the door open and rushed right in. Jasmeet hardly had time to jump off the toilet before he threw up the lid and released his backed-up stream. "Ahhh. Sorry. Lots to drink last night."

Ignoring her own urge to pee, she turned on the sink and splashed water on her face. "S'alright." she inspected herself in the mirror. One of her eyebrows was uneven, and a few hairs had sprouted between them. She grabbed her sonic tweezers and went to town on those bad boys.

"Trouble with the fam?" Darius asked, only now coming to the tail end of his urination.

Wincing from a plucked hair, she looked over to him. "Were you eavesdropping?" She took her tweezers to the uneven patch of eyebrow, but it seemed to make little difference.

"Who's Hardeep?"

She sighed and tossed the tweezers into their holder before taking her mouthwash from the medicine cabinet. "No one." She took a swig, gargled and spit.

After wiping up, he joined Jasmeet at the sink to wash his hands while the toilet sucked down the contents via airlock.

"You're looking for a divorce from no one?"

"It's not what you think." She plunked her mouthwash back where she'd found it. "We had an arranged marriage."

"Seriously?" His augmented eyes widened. "You people still do that?"

"You people?" Jasmeet crossed her arms and tilted her stance.

"You know what I mean. What century do your parents come from, the twentieth?" He slipped his hands into the sonic hand drier.

"Shut up." The loud whirr drowned out her heated reply.

Jasmeet stomped out of the bathroom as the drier switched off. "Hey, did I upset you?"

She spun around as Darius sauntered back into the bedroom. "People have been doing it for ages without issue, it just didn't work out in my case. Can you drop it?" She bent over to pick up his clothes, thrown haphazardly on the floor.

"Yeah . . . okay. I guess I'll get out of your hair then." He looked around the room for his smart device. Jasmeet found it first and pushed it and his clothes into his chest.

"How come I get the sense that this is the last time we're doing this?" he asked sheepishly.

Beautiful and clueless. Serves me right, I guess.

"I don't know." She threw her hands up. "Talk to me when Travelac hits the market, then we'll see . . . if I still have a job."

"You'll do great," he said as he climbed into his form-fitting jeans. He did look damn fine in those jeans. "You're about to change the world. I don't think you have to worry much about job prospects." He paused to pull his black shirt over his head. "Unless you don't want to change the world."

Leaning against her desk on outstretched arms, she narrowed her gaze at him. "Why wouldn't I?"

"I don't know . . ." he approached her, making her want to stand up straight so as to not feel so small next to him. "Maybe it's because the moon is a cold, dead place. I've seen a lot of people lose their shit up here."

Jasmeet shook her head. "Not me. This place is my real home, and I'm not leaving."

"Then, what does that mean—for us?" he gently brushed his dark fingers through her heaps of black hair.

She pulled it back and twisted it around her hand. "It means . . ." she stepped out from around him ". . . I'll let you know when I'm free again."

"Sure. Whatever." He sighed. "Good luck, Jas. See you around."

Without another look, he placed his device in his back pocket and waved a hand over the motion sensor to open the front door. Jasmeet watched him walk out of the room with that nice butt of his until the door slid closed again, cutting him off from her completely.

She chewed on her lip and waited for her gut to untwist itself. *Nice guy. Would never work. I'm a CEO and he's a ... whatever he is.*

Jasmeet went to the kitchen to start a pot of coffee.

III

A media circus surrounded the LaCroix facility on the day of the live-stream. Jasmeet, wearing black leggings, a plain gray shirt, and a pair of flats, jogged up the steps. A bubbly blonde stuck a recording device in her face. "Ms. Sahni, how are you feeling right now on this historic day?"

Another recording device with a lanky young man at the end of it interrupted. "We heard this event was not originally planned. Can you tell us a little more about why that is?"

The woman came back with, "Why didn't you choose to do this before the big reveal?"

"No comment," she stated bluntly as she pushed through the crowd and entered the facility proper. "But I will answer your first question in that I'm feeling excited as I've been wanting to do this ever since we started this project, and I'm honored to be the first non-test subject to do so. Thank you."

When Jasmeet arrived at the west laboratory, LaCroix International's Board of Directors with the Chairwoman at their head greeted her. She wore a faux fur scarf, heels, and a pencil skirt. "Ah, you're finally here." The reporters swarmed around them, their cameras strapped to their heads. They resembled those big blocker sunglasses old people wore in the 1990s.

Ms. LaCroix led Jasmeet past them and muttered in her ear. "Would it kill you to smile? You look like you're about to walk the Green Mile."

"The green what?"

"Your execution—ugh—doesn't anybody read the classics anymore?"

Jasmeet forced an eager grin as she greeted the line of board members then Dr. Linderman at the end.

"You look comfy, Ms. Sahni. It's hard to believe we're finally doing this." He shook her hand. She was alarmed by its clamminess. *What does he have to be nervous about? He could teleport a person in his sleep by now.* She was also surprised by how frazzled the quantum physicist looked. His curly mop of hair stuck out haphazardly as if he had just rolled out of bed, and his neckbeard was overgrown. *Did he forget the press would be here today?*

"Are you ready for me, Doctor?" Jasmeet asked.

"Should be good to go." He spun around and tapped on the terminal. "Storage rings are engaged. Go-uh. Go ahead. Rose will get you situated." Linderman grabbed his big cup of Moon Juice sitting on the terminal and sucked back a heavily caffeinated and sugary gulp through the straw.

Jasmeet tied her hair into a ponytail at her nape and

followed the operator to the origin pod. *This is it.* Her stomach somersaulted as Rose opened the door. "Please lay down and rest your arms at your sides, Ms. Sahni."

"I know the drill," she said as she lowered herself down on the platform, careful not to get any part of herself wet from the shallow liquid beneath.

Reporters' heads loomed above her like alien abductors ready to probe. One of them put a recording device above her face and asked. "Any last words before teleportation, Ms. Sahni?"

Last words? The question knocked Jasmeet speechless. She uttered a few 'ums' and 'awes' before settling on something unoriginal. "See you on the other side." She cringed at herself.

"Alright, everyone back," Linderman called to the reporters. "Keep at least a five-foot distance from the pod at all times, thank you."

The reporters shuffled backward as the operator spouted off her spiel like an automated flight attendant. "The scanning will begin three seconds after this door is closed so try to relax and lay as still as you can." She fastened the plastic straps around Jasmeet's wrists and ankles. She knew they were supposed to help keep her still during the crucial scanning stage, but now that she was in them, she felt like thrashing her limbs about. "It will get dark in there when the scan completes. At that time, we suggest keeping your eyes closed and visualizing your destination."

She pointed to the unlit fixtures lining the inside of the pod door. "In case of an emergency, these lights will flash red and your restraints will automatically unclasp. If no one immediately retrieves you, pull this emergency hatch just above your head here." She indicated to a bright red pull lever right above her. "Push it up, then pull it down as if you're doing chin-ups, and you can manually push the door open from the inside. Do note that for your own safety and the safety of everyone outside the pod that the door cannot be opened while the scanning or disintegration process is running. Did you get all that, Ms. Sahni?"

"Mmm hmm." Jasmeet knew most of this, having watched many test subjects go through the same shebang. It had seemed comforting then, but now, she wasn't so sure.

"Now for the ionic sheet," Rose unraveled the thin white shroud from under the platform. She rolled the sheet over Jasmeet's body and proceeded to tuck it in snug around her arms and legs. The sheet set the limit to what matter would teleport, otherwise, it would cause major damage to both the origin and destination pods.

"Now, keep as still as possible and remember to breathe. Before you know it, you'll be greeted by Steve in the east laboratory."

"And there she goes; the CEO of LaCroix International is in the origin pod, ready to embark—" The door closed and clicked, cutting off the reporter's words.

Jasmeet was shocked by the sudden silence. She may as well have been floating in the vacuum of space. The only noises she could hear were the whistling of the air through her nostrils and her own rapid heartbeat.

A familiar whirring noise kicked in, only it had never been this loud to her before. She chewed her lip, her fingers balled into fists as a bright yellow light shone at both sides of her head. She closed her eyes under the white shroud and let the light pass over her body repeatedly. Her skin hummed, like a static that would have made the hairs on her arms stand on end had she not laser removed them a number of years ago.

Several minutes went by as the yellow light slowly made its way up and down her shrouded body. It never seemed to take this long when she watched the loading screen on the terminal all those times before.

Finally, the humming stopped and everything went dark. To be sure, she opened her eyes. She could hardly make out the white fibers of the sheet against her face. Remembering Rose's instructions, she shut them again. *Here it comes . . . the real unknown.*

Her breathing picked up again. No test subject had been able to describe how disintegration felt. Just weird. Like waking up from a fucked-up fever dream. Not painful, no one ever said painful. Jasmeet took a deep breath and waited.

And waited.

She wondered if the water should be draining out by now or maybe she had to disintegrate first; she couldn't remember. Everything was still. Too still. *Well, the emergency lights aren't flashing. Any time now.*

Jasmeet's fingers fidgeted in the restraints, her eyelashes fluttered, tickling the sheet over her face. *Something's definitely wrong.* She'd seen enough teleportations to know that the disintegration process was not this slow, or this quiet. "Hello! Everything all right out there?" Her own voice rang painfully in her ears from inside the pod. If she couldn't hear the circus outside what made her think they could hear a peep out of her? She waited so long she could feel her bladder filling up. *At this rate, I'll be coming out of here in front of the entire world with piss running down my legs.*

Her patience worn to the bone, Jasmeet wiggled her left hand and collapsed her fingers in on themselves. The plastic was stiff enough for her to eventually jimmy her hand free of the restraint then release her right.

She tore off the shroud and pawed for the emergency latch. She pushed up then pulled down. The pod door came ajar with a pop. Jasmeet pushed the door open fully so she could sit up and unfasten her ankle restraints.

As soon as her feet hit the floor, she realized she was alone in the room. The press, the board, Linderman. All gone. And most alarming of all, she was still in the west lab.

It didn't work. The one time it didn't work! Jasmeet wiped the panic sweat off her brow. *Think. Think. They're all at the destination pod. They must have realized it didn't work by now.* There was not much else to do except head over there and try to smooth things over.

Jasmeet jogged down the halls, her magnetic flats keeping her grounded in the low gravity. *LaCroix's probably freaking out. My job here is toast. Back to Earth I go. Goddammit, goddammit, goddammit!*

As she passed by the window to the east laboratory, Jasmeet heard clapping and saw nothing but happy faces. She paused her gait and took a closer look. Reporters swarmed around a woman in a gray shirt and leggings with a long black ponytail. *What the hell?* Dr. Noble scanned her over with his medical tablet and asked her the usual questions. "What is your name and place of birth?"

"Jasmeet Sahni, Edmonton, Alberta, Canada."

"Who is the current president of the United States?"

"Wynona Ramirez."

The doctor's additional questions were incoherent on account of the blood rapidly leaving Jasmeet's brain. A reporter moved aside, giving Jasmeet full view of the woman's face.

There she was . . . herself. From the mole next to her ear to the one badly plucked eyebrow. Her heart sank deep in her gut. "Fuck me," she whispered.

Her doppelganger lifted her eyes for a moment, about to look straight into Jasmeet's. She dove behind the wall, away from the window, breathing so hard she almost choked on the air. *This can't be happening. It's a hallucination. I'm still in the pod. Of course, that's it. My brain is being put back together right now, this has to be some kind of dream state. I'll forget all about this.*

All of a sudden, the laboratory door swung open and Dr. Linderman stepped out into the hall. The circles under his eyes seemed to have gotten darker since she'd seen him only minutes before. Jasmeet shuffled behind a pillar as he walked away. She silently crept out from her hiding spot and followed Linderman all the way back to the west lab. She watched him approach the terminal, something she had completely forgotten to check in her panic-stricken state.

"Shit!" Linderman ran to the empty pod, giving Jasmeet full view of the terminal display. The scan was completed and data sent to its destination, but the disintegration process had been paused somehow when it was supposed to be automatic. "Fuck. Where are you?"

"The restraints need a little redesign," Jasmeet said.

His bushy head snapped up, color draining from his already pale complexion. "Ms. Sahni—uh . . . did you just come from East Lab?"

Jasmeet stepped up to the shaking physicist. "What the fuck did you do, Linderman?"

He smoothed out his wild hair then put up his palms. "I'm sorry. I had to do it this way. I had to know for sure."

"You did this on purpose?" She gnashed her teeth. "You just cloned me! That's all kinds of illegal—I can't even . . ." Saying clone out loud drew bile into her throat.

"I saved you. Your pieces would be floating around in the ring to become building blocks for someone else. You should be thanking me."

Jasmeet ran her hands down her face, feeling cold to the touch. Was she even alive right now? "Why would you sabotage this project, your life's work?"

"My work was never supposed to be used on living things, just cargo. LaCroix, on the other hand, wants to be the pioneer of interstellar travel and this was the only way it could be done!"

Tears flooded Jasmeet's eyes as she struggled to keep from vomiting. "Why did you do this to me?"

"I wish I didn't have to, but we're running out of time." Linderman reached out and held Jasmeet in place with his husky arms. She hadn't noticed she was shaking so much. "If I tried this with any of our test subjects, LaCroix would bury it and force Travelac to market. I fucked with the algorithm, made sure all activist questions came at you and you did the rest. You got the press and the board in the building. When they see two of you, LaCroix won't be able to hide it. They'll shut it all down."

"What?" Jasmeet jerked out of Linderman's grasp. "You sound like one of those fanatics! You're supposed to be a man of science!"

"This is science, Jas! Human beings can't be conscious in two separate bodies at once. This is what I've tried to explain, but no one will listen. Together, we just proved it."

"Proved what?" The room began to spin in circles.

Linderman pointed to the pod. "Every person who lays down in that contraption will die, and a clone of them will take their place. Their loved ones won't know. They will believe they are the original person, but they won't be."

"This can't be happening . . ."

"If you don't believe me, get back in there, and I'll complete the disintegration process. Let's see if your consciousness magically transfers into the mind of your clone in East Lab."

Jasmeet stared at the pod she had just escaped. *Oh, God, he's right. That's a death machine!*

"Okay," Jasmeet closed her eyes and took a deep breath. "But now what? LaCroix built this company from the ground up. Clone or no clone, she won't take this lying down."

"I'll deal with the fallout. Just get over there."

At that moment, Jasmeet felt a tug inside her own head. Like something was caught in her gravitational pull. Or she was caught in something else's? "Wait . . . I think . . . I'm on my way over here?"

"You can tell that? I wonder if it's because your particles are still entangled," Linderman mused.

"We need to tell her. She needs to know about this first . . ." *or I need to know about this first?* Jasmeet's head throbbed with all her confusing thoughts. She couldn't even be sure they were all hers.

Linderman shook his head and waved his hands back and forth. "Nope, not a good idea."

The pull only got stronger, until Jasmeet felt an urge to turn around. There, standing in the doorway was her exact duplicate, staring right back at her, her big brown eyes wide with terror.

"I-I felt like I had to come back in here."

The two Jasmeets circled each other with a wide berth. Their every movement and expression mirrored the other. They were more than genetically identical, they were atomically identical, although not forever.

"What the fuck is going on here?" said Jasmeet Two. "Who are you?"

Jasmeet replied, "I'm the one who would have been destroyed so you could exist."

Second Jasmeet glared at Linderman. "This is bullshit."

"Where's the board?" Linderman asked.

"They're doing interviews in the lobby." She snapped her head back to the original Jasmeet. "Now, someone better tell me why I'm looking at myself."

"Listen, Jas," said Jasmeet. "We have to catch them before they leave and tell them the truth about Travelac."

"What truth?"

"That we are about to sell a clone and kill machine worldwide."

"Kill?" Jasmeet Two shook her head. "No, no, I just went through there." She pointed to the origin pod. "Travelac works."

Jasmeet crossed her arms. "Sure, for someone who was created literally ten minutes ago."

"If the board finds out about this, the company goes under and what will happen to me then? Us then." Jasmeet Two massaged her temples. Jasmeet felt the urge to do the same.

"I know that. I'm you. I know everything you know."

"Then how do you suppose we stay here when we lose our job? Armstrong only accepted one of us."

"I . . ." Jasmeet trailed off. *I can't go back to Earth . . . I can't.*

"So we all get kicked off the moon," Linderman said. "It's a small price to pay for billions of lives."

Jasmeet Two wagged a finger at Linderman. "No. I'll tell you what we're going to do. I will run things here, and you two will take the next shuttle off this rock. Mom and Dad will have their daughter back, Hardeep can have his wife back, and my life can stay exactly as it is."

"Seriously, bitch? You know I had this life first right? You're a clone!" The severity in Jasmeet's voice surprised her.

"I'm not a clone!" The other Jasmeet snapped back.

The two women glared at each other, both clenching their fists.

"Nothing can go back to how it was." Original Jasmeet said. "Linderman is right. Travelac is going to kill millions every year if we don't do something."

"Oh, for fuck's sake," Jasmeet Two rolled her eyes. "This is ludicrous. No one is going to die. If the machine had worked the way it was supposed to—"

"I'd be dead!"

"Shit!" Linderman said, panic in his voice.

Both Jasmeets turned to face him. He showed them his tablet screen. He was one of the few employees that had a feed to the security cameras around the facility. His screen showed the lobby. "They're heading back this way."

Jasmeet Two bit her lip. "I told them I'd be back to answer a few more questions. Linderman, stall for a little while. I have something else to . . . discuss with *me* before we come clean to the board."

Jasmeet nodded, but then a sickening feeling welled in her gut.

"Fine. Both of you stay right here." Linderman bolted for the door.

"Wait!" But he was already down the hallway. She turned to her duplicate. "Does this mean you're with me in this?"

"You'd think it'd be impossible not to be." The other Jasmeet twisted her ponytail in her quivering hands. The original did the same without thinking. "See?" She pointed to her. "We have the exact same brain. We are the same person."

Jasmeet dropped her hair and let her arms fall to her sides. "Except we aren't . . . there's one experience that differentiates us." She started taking small steps backward, away from her other self. *What would I do to stay on the moon? How far would I go?* She knew the answer all too well, but things were different now, lives were at stake. *How can I make her see? How did I come to see?* Jasmeet glanced at the open origin pod with the corner of her eye. She quickly returned her attention to Jasmeet Two, only to find her eyes snapping back from the pod as well.

Jasmeet Two's face changed—hardened, almost blank.

"You better get in there before they see us together." Jasmeet Two nodded toward the pod.

"Wait. If you get in, I can scan you, and you'll see what happens when—"

Jasmeet Two lunged forward, but Jasmeet dodged, sensing her entangled partner's intentions in that moment.

The women grappled each other as they each tried to force the other into the pod. Linderman and the board were still too far away. Jasmeet tried to scream. "Helfph!" Jasmeet Two clasped her hand around her mouth. Jasmeet put all her weight against her opponent. *I have to get her out into the hallway. Then they'll see.*

The other Jasmeet struggled just as hard, pushing her back toward the pod, which was a lot closer than the hallway. "Ugh! Get in there."

"No!" Jasmeet pulled her hair and felt her own hair being pulled at the same time. "Stop!"

"Get . . . in there . . . bitch!" Jasmeet Two pushed harder, hissing through her teeth. "I won't go back!"

"Don't do this," Jasmeet grunted, her back wrenched, her scalp stinging with each of her clone's violent pulls.

Neither woman gave way. Their magnetic shoes made it difficult to slide until Jasmeet's left foot came to a gap in the magnetic field in the floors. It was just enough to give her clone the upper hand. Jasmeet Two pushed Jasmeet back hard. She twisted her body, attempting to break her fall by grabbing hold of the pod lip, but she couldn't quite reach it. She came down on her hands and knees, her temple smacked against the open pod lid. Her head went numb as blood dribbled down the side of her face, leaving a red streak on the door.

The room spun in circles. She couldn't stand. Her opponent grabbed her around the waist and shoved her face-first into the pod. Her flailing arms splashed about in the water as she struggled to climb out the other side. The doors slammed shut and locked.

"No!" she screamed. "Let me out!"

The emergency lever was right in front of her, but the awkward position she was in prevented both arms from reaching it. It was impossible to see in the dark anyway. As she struggled to get her knees underneath her in the cramped space, the deafening hum of the machine began.

As soon as both arms were free from holding up her own weight, Jasmeet grabbed the lever, lifted it up and pulled out toward her with all her might. The door didn't pop open; the humming sound continued to get louder. It invaded every one of her senses. She recalled Rose's warning. There was no opening the pod now.

Jasmeet let out a bracing shriek as sparks and electrical bursts went off inside the pod. A sinking nauseous feeling weakened her and she collapsed onto her stomach. She thought of her parents. Why didn't she go see them one more time? Explain Hardeep to them again, maybe they'd finally understand.

Water droplets wet her face as they turned to vapor. Her insides felt as if they were expanding like a balloon. Then weightlessness came over her, a terrible, out-of-control lightness.

IV

Jasmeet tapped the disintegration timer on the terminal and then hit override. The pod lit orange. A strange smell emanated from it. Without the ionic sheet, everything inside the pod would be destroyed. It would have to be repaired, but that would be easy enough to do; it's not like it hadn't happened before during past experiments.

The terminal screen beeped, the digital person blinked and disappeared. 'Disintegration Complete.' She swallowed the lump in her throat. She didn't really kill anyone. Just extra matter to be used for future travelers. It wasn't really . . . her.

"Why are you still in here?" LaCroix briskly strolled in with Linderman and the rest of the board in tow. "They want another statement from—are you all right, love?"

Linderman looked frantically around the room then to the closed pod. Finally, his eyes settled on Jasmeet and horror spread across his face.

"I was just making sure all the data transferred properly," she quickly replied.

Linderman ran his sweaty hands down his ever-paling cheeks.

"And Rose didn't secure me well enough. The ionic sheet slipped. There might be some damage inside the pod."

"Hmm," LaCroix grumbled. "Dr. Linderman, you should be able to fix that before we start manufacturing, right?"

"Uh . . ." his hand wouldn't leave his forehead.

"Right, Doctor?" she repeated more sternly.

"Yeah-yeah. I can . . . fix that." His voice may as well have been down the hallway by how far away it sounded.

"Good," Jasmeet said, collecting herself. "I'll let the press know that everything is underway. Excuse me."

Jasmeet looked straight ahead as she went for the door, feeling Linderman's eyes glued to her back. She ignored him. He wouldn't tell LaCroix anything now, not without evidence. She forced her thoughts to the future. *Wonder if Darius is free tonight. Maybe I should give him another go.* As she went for her device to fire off a text, she winced.

Her hand shot up to her temple, sore and bruised to the touch.

The pain subsided as quickly as it had come.

Todd

TURI T. ARMSTRONG

In that moment, we all deserved to die.

Every last one of us. The machine may have destroyed her body, but it was man that killed her.

For a long time, all I could see was her face when I closed my eyes. She wasn't a dynamic image; I didn't get to recall Joyce like some men remember their darlings, all slow motion smiles and spins, flashes of the sweet little moments through a sparkling fog of romantic maudlin. No, the image I was left with was the look on her face when that thing whittled her down to fit into the cavity in its middle. That compartment taking the place of a stomach. Its titanium plates dripped with her blood. And when I'd managed to sever a cable from its pelvic joint with a shovel, her blood streamed into it, and it sparked.

I remembered that.

You know, they all say it was the AI that got us in the end, but really it was a technology developed years before that did it. Somewhere along the line, some asshole came up with the brilliant idea to make a machine that gets energy from organic matter. Using the heat generated by the decaying process to charge its batteries.

Sure, it sounded great on paper. Nobel worthy, they said.

The problems this could solve were endless, they said. Would change the world.

Well, change the world it did. Because like any other technology worth a damn, the army got hold of it. Before we knew it, they'd created walking war machines that could fuel themselves on their own carnage.

And *then* came the AI. I don't know who made it happen, and I don't know why they did it—I ain't no science man— but somebody decided these artificial soldiers who were able to dispose of the bodies they made, should also be able to think for themselves.

Not a year passed before the machines figured out that fresh organic matter gives off more energy than the old, and that rotting meat gives off more energy than plant life.

I hated those things. After one of them took Joyce, I was filled with more hate than any person could possibly contain. It left me blank and soulless. I was her husband. It was my job to protect her, and that purpose was the only thing keeping me going from the day they came down on us . . . at least until Todd.

Let me tell you about Todd. A real survivor that one. I often wonder what became of him. Knowing how things go, he's probably dead. That seems to be the way it always goes. But I like to think that Todd made it somewhere safe and is watching the sunrise on a cold Alaskan coast somewhere.

Todd was the kind of feller you read about in books. He was smart and courageous and always had a plan. When he came to me that first day, I knew he'd change my life forever, I just didn't know how yet.

The Zots had leveled everything looking for a bit of something to devour. For something that might give them even the smallest amount of energy. It was what they were built for after all. The basic learnin' skills of a toddler, and the instincts of a wrecking ball. Created by a species already spread like a plague across the world, the Zots spread and replicated themselves twice as fast as their makers. At the time I met Todd, that had been ten years ago. Ten long years since the world was normal. Since someone could live out their days not worried about becoming the power you could trust.

I spent my time scrounging like a raccoon, at night if I could help it. The days in Reno seemed then to be even god damn hotter than before the world ended if that were possible. It was like hell had opened up and sucked most everyone into the pit. Those of us left behind were doomed to wander this sweltering dustbin for eternity with the devil breathin' down the backs of our necks.

That idea didn't bother me so much then. All mankind deserved hell, and I was no different. I can't say there's ever been any room in my heart for strangers. The indeterminate *We*.

But one morning, when the air was makin' waves of the world before the sun had even made it over the Silver Legacy, I heard a white noise, followed by breaking glass and finally the crumbling of stone and crashing metal. I normally wouldn't emerge from my recess for such a thing, but that day, curiosity drew me out and led me down the road to a building that once had four solid walls but now had only two.

With no Zots in sight, I made my way through the rubble, looking for something that might be useful. A subtle scraping brought me over a heap to the interior of the building. I stumbled over concrete and rebar then looked down to see a fox. The first live animal I'd seen in so long it was alien. The mangy creature whined softly, probably learnin' not to make much noise if it were to survive in this new world. Its back leg was pinned under the rock and it scampered its front legs forward, trying to pull its way out with no success. When it spotted me, it didn't recoil or bare its teeth, rather it froze.

I immediately thought of Joyce. She loved these wily critters. This one was a bonafide Sierra Nevada Red too, I think, though I ain't no expert by half. Joyce would have known. For some reason, I liked the idea that the only surviving animal I had seen in almost a decade was something that was thought endangered before all this. The thing managed to survive the apocalypse but struggled to survive man.

I never did help it out. And I still mull over that decision to this day. Instead I decided to return to my hole in the ground and wait out the sun, but when I climbed back over the rubble, I noticed something else. What was left of the wall had been painted since I'd seen the building last. At least I was fairly sure it hadn't been there before. There wasn't much of it left now. Just the head of a neon orange arrow.

I shook off a queer feeling, deciding that it must have been there before, hidden behind something. Hell, I was getting old and hadn't spotted it was all.

But on my way back, every few buildings shone like orange beacons. I could read these messages clear enough. Some were simple arrows pointing north, others were accompanied by 'Turn Around.' A few pointed south with the word 'Danger' or other similar warnings. The hairs stood on the back of my neck, but I wasn't sure if it was due to the ominous nature of the messages or the fact that their existence implied I wasn't alone in the world after all. It's like Reno suddenly burst with life.

Now. You find yourself in a dark forest, you can quite quickly feel like the only living thing in it. That is until something big and bad approaches, and suddenly the birds take from the trees and rodents and snakes scurry past your feet. They was there all along, even if you couldn't see 'em.

I was out that night when Reno was still dark, morning was on its way, but no trace of it was in the sky yet. I had just enough time to finish scavenging and find my way back when I saw it. A jar in the distance shaped like a bear.

Honey.

Someone must have dropped it at some point. It wasn't even covered in the thick layer of red dust most everything is coated with out here.

I cautiously made my way toward it, making sure to move silently. I wasn't gonna chance any Zots catching wind of me before I retrieved my bounty. I heard the click of a falling stone to my left and ducked inside the nearest open door into a two-story office building. From the outside, the heavily tinted floor to ceiling windows only reflected back a hickory-hued visage of the world. Inside, my view was clear.

I crouched behind a dulled steel desk and peeked over the top, waiting for the coming Zot to reveal its position.

From around the corner of the alley across the street darted something that made my jaw drop and tighten all at the same time. A person. A real live person.

Even before Joyce had died, it had been ages since we had seen another human being. This one was a lithe young man, probably no older than thirty-five. He had hair so black it shone blue under the quickly disappearing moon. He tucked a spray can into the hiking pack he carried as he emerged.

I came out from behind my blind and crept forward.

Curious more than anything else. As with the fox before, it was like seeing something out of legend—bigfoot; the ghost of civilization's past.

I stared at him dumb until he went for my jar. I was ripped out of my daze and overcome with hate. This little bastard was going to take my honey. I ran for the window with a speed I shouldn't be capable of at my age, ready to bang on it like a gorilla taunted at the zoo. Just before I reached the window, a metal behemoth burst through the wall of the building across the road. Mere yards from the honey thief.

He took off down the street, and the hungry Zot gave chase. I followed from behind the safety of the glass. Afraid I might lose sight of the action, I ripped open the stairwell door and heaved up to the second story. I reached the next window just as they turned the corner. I turned with them. The Zot gained quickly, but the man sprinted forward without so much as a glance behind him. He was fit, I'd give him that much.

I scurried from window to window. Something carnal inside me savagely wanted to see him finished. The thing about to finish him was only feet away. They turned the corner again. I lost them.

Inside the building, I couldn't hear anything, not a scream, not the sound of metal scraping and bones crunching. Nothing. Nothing but the quick thump-thump of my own heart. I pressed my face to the glass hoping to gain a few more inches of sight but was sorely disappointed.

Oh well.

I would wait out the day there, and at least come nightfall I could still claim my prize. The rotten part of me thanked the Zot for coming when it did.

I awoke to the sun's orange death throes streaking the

ceiling, and within minutes it was gone. I crawled to the door, not bothering to stand, wildly tossing my head side to side like a deranged animal as I checked every direction for signs of that morning's Zot. When I found nothing, I darted across the street, low enough to drag my fingers along the ground, and searched for my honey jar.

It was gone.

In the commotion, I must not have noticed that asshole take it, and now it had probably ended up in the belly of the bot. Hoping that I might get lucky again, I followed the route to the man's demise, around the side of the building and down the alley to the back of it. There was no jar of honey in that alley, but there was something far more interesting. I had expected pools of blood and possibly a dropped article or two.

What I found instead was a heap of metal.

People are a pestilence on the earth. Like an unfinished round of antibiotics, you think the infection is gone, but unless you kill every trace, it'll come back twice as strong the next time. I'd never seen nobody take out a Zot. I'd seen them try and fail. But in true human fashion, we figured out a way to destroy. To destroy the destroyer.

From the look of it, he had jammed a crowbar into its lower back and jumbled up some of its innards. Not an easy task, in my mind. The thing still buzzed like an old fluorescent light as it lay there, dead by all accounts.

The day had opened up a sore in my gut. From seeing the fox, then seeing the man—and now looking at the scraps in front of me, it was all too much to take. The black Reno night condensed on me. I shut my eyes tight and there was Joyce. Her face contorted and screaming.

Then I started kicking. I kicked and stomped until my

legs hurt, my boots barely denting the outer shell of the Zot, crumpled on the ground. One of my kicks knocked the bar from the thing's back, and I heard a sound like an old computer booting for the first time in years, buzzing and groaning. Turns out, whatever that man had done didn't kill it, only put it on pause.

The humming got faster, and its body shook as it began to rise.

I ran like hell. Out of the alley and down the street. Moments later, the Zot's metal feet clanged on the pavement behind me. I pushed my legs to move quicker, my left ankle aching from the fury I had unleashed a moment earlier. I didn't know how I would escape or where I was running to.

Turns out, I was running to Todd.

I was coming up fast on a pile-up of abandoned cars. My only hope was to make it to one and hide inside, then just pray that thing didn't find me. The closer I got, the more unlikely that outcome seemed. It gained on me faster and faster. But out in the distance, from behind the canopy of an old Ford, popped up that head of black hair. He jumped down and ran at me full on. Instinct told me to run back the other way, but adrenaline threw me forward. I readied myself to attack if need be. I started devising plans to grab him as I flew by and throw him to the Zot.

As I got closer I could better see his features. The man looked . . . I can only describe it as serene. See, Todd always had a calm look to him and a smile that said he had all the knowledge in the world. He knew something you didn't. He ran until he reached me then turned one-eighty and ran back the way he came right by my side.

We sprinted together for about half a block before I saw my

chance. An open manhole under one of the vehicles. I could slide in and hide. Depending on what was down there, maybe even make my way further north from below. It would take time to crawl in, but if I could manage to trip the fool beside me at just the right moment, I might stand a chance.

I was mere seconds from executing my plan when Todd pulled ahead and, with a swing of his chin, pointed to an alley coming up on the right. He dashed down it.

Dammit.

I followed, and we found a fire escape up the side of a crumbling four-story. Not that ladders are a particular challenge for these things, but they were made more for knockin down doors and stoppin' tanks, not climbing. It'd follow, but it'd be slow going.

Once we found an open window, we crawled inside, got to a bathroom and hunkered down in the tub. See, bathrooms are the best place to sit and wait out these things. You stay still long enough and keep real quiet, they should pass you by. The tub keeps you from being spotted under the door by heat sensors. At least if you're lucky.

It was intimately squeezed together in that tub I first got to know the man that is Todd. Well ... as much as you can get to know someone, sitting in a cramped space speaking fabricated sign language while waiting to see if you die a violent death in the near future.

I sat grieving for my failed plan to escape both him and the Zot, but my thoughts quickly drifted to amazement that I was looking at another human being so close up. I'd come across not one but two living things in the past day.

Though, like the birds taking from the forest trees, I should have known something big was coming.

He humored my glares for a while then pulled out his wallet and showed me his Utah driver's license and stretched out his other hand to shake mine. Still smilin' like we were meeting for the first time at a local watering hole, not under a rusted-out shower head. But the detail that made it the most fascinating was the fact that this had to be the only man left in the world who still bothered to carry around his driver's license. Never made no sense then, and it still don't now.

Todd Hule Stanton, it said.

What a name. Maybe that was why he carried the card for all those years. So he had a reason to show people that full, irrepressible name.

Hours must have passed in that tub, looking over Todd and the glint in his eye contrasting the raven black of his hair, and other such features for as long as was comfortable, then spending the rest of that time staring at the wall or the insides of my eyelids. Eventually, I heard him speak. A deep baritone, yet jovial, quick, and just on the brink of joking.

He told me all about where he was going and from where he had come. Utah, working as a night manager at a small town K-mart, making a surprisingly decent living. Unmarried and raising two sons by himself. The way he spoke of them gave me the impression that nothing bad had ever happened to them in their whole lives. But he never gave any indication that they'd traveled with him either. If not with him, then with who? They were dead, but he never said it. He didn't have to.

I was one of the lucky ones, I suppose. I had lost my own boy back in Texas, twenty years before all this started. The one thing I was always grateful for was that he didn't have to live in the world as it is now.

Eventually, we stretched our cramped legs and slithered

out of our hole.

I should have hated Todd. In my bones, I wanted to hate him for his mere existence like I did everything else. But I couldn't. The way he talked like a bass guitar and walked with a bounce while still managing to drag his feet, calmed my soul and kept the ghost of Joyce away.

I convinced myself that if I were to survive I needed to stick with him. He would prove himself as base a creature as any other man, and I would leave him for dead somewhere out of the city.

We wandered the apartments on each floor, looking for supplies and chance foodstuffs. As we pilfered cabinets and ransacked through the memories of lives forgotten, we talked about the future and Todd's hopes for such a thing. Splayed on the cracking leather couch inside a three-bedroom corner unit, hazy with the light of the comin' morning, he folded his arms behind his head and told me about Alaska. How he longed for the cool air and the icy waters. But Alaska wasn't the destination. He waxed about some place off the northern coast of Canada, under the Alaskan border. Port Edward, a small town where his mother sprouted from a few generations of cannery workers. She'd birthed him in the family home before meetin' his step-daddy and uprooting him to Utah.

Todd was bred for the cold, salt-water air. Born for the sea, and he was going back to it, or so he said.

As I watched him tell the ceiling his dreams with a look of complete tranquility, I admired how much zest for life he seemed to have. How even after all the horrors men like us saw on the day to day, he could still find the nerve to look ahead to a time where he would no longer suffer. I realize now, that was a sort of miracle.

Maybe I'd just been too old. Coming up on retirement when the Zots hit, I coulda—maybe shoulda—laid down and let myself die right then. But I didn't. After Joyce, and before Todd, that felt like one of the great regrets in life, but after Todd, I realized that was just short of a miracle in itself.

While we sat, I asked him how he'd managed to take down the Zot in the alley. To my disappointment, he only gave me a snort and a shrug. He told me how the thing had cornered him, and he'd just started swinging. He hadn't even been sure he got it until I confirmed it for him. Just lucky, he guessed.

The next day we loitered on the outskirts of the building for a time until we were confident the war machine had moved on, at which point we headed along the road.

Every once in a while Todd would stop to paint a warning on the side of a building. He told me some horror story about all the Zots amassing in a big army just south of us. Honestly, it all sounded a little cracked. I've seen these things work together before if that's what you wanna call it. But there was nothing intelligent about it, more like the small scavenging after the big. When their best energy sources got scarce in those last few years, you'd see them competing when they'd come upon each other. When I was a young boy, robot battles were something I used to fantasize about, but the real thing wasn't nearly as cool as I had imagined.

Todd's story sounded something like the fantasies of a little boy.

But he spotted the pulsing reflection of the sun's light on metal in the distance, it wasn't long after we heard the *groan, pisss, sch-twank* of the Zots, and light materialized into hefty steel and resin bodies. After a few moments, I realized there was definitely something different about the sounds coming from this group. I voiced this opinion to Todd, though he didn't appear to be particularly worried at the news. The look in his eyes said 'I told you so' even if his mouth didn't.

He led me through a broken window of the Eldorado, now just the Eld-o-do. Inside, we scuttled around mildewed sculptures—Tritons blowin' into conch shells, and white horses galloping out of the turbid fountain water. Finding the stairwell, we wound our way up to the sixth floor and by the time we arrived, I was grasping at my chest.

Todd's presence parted the thick dust in the air as he made his way to the time-sooted window and inspected the goings on below with the mystique of an angel watching man's exodus from Eden.

I dragged myself over to the window beside him and placed my hand on the ledge in an effort to keep my knees from givin' out. I looked down at the street and feasted my eyes on a horde of Zots like I had never seen. It was said they'd made about two thousand of these things in the beginning, and it only took five or six to decimate a town. Once they started replicating themselves, things got out of pocket you might say. I have come up against groups of three or four but never anything like this.

Todd glanced my way for a second and smiled a sorrowful smile. But I could tell the shadow in his eyes was cast for me. He probably could have stayed ahead of this thing if not for the old man he'd been dragging around for two days at this point. I resented that look.

He chuckled, a dark bass rhythm from his diaphragm, as he looked out below. The machines climbed over and around one another. If I were to think of a robot army, I would have envisioned some clankin' high-stepping fourth reich. But this was more like watching a river of titanium rats the way they clawed at each other.

They obliterated everything in their wake, leaving Zot bodies in twisted mounds on the street. The ones on the edges of the rolling pile of metal broke off and crashed through the windows of buildings, ransacking the offices and shops like looters in a riot.

I stood mesmerized by the sight until Todd grunted something about them getting desperate. I looked closer. He was right. They weren't just climbing over each other, they were ripping the weak apart, pilfering the precious resources from their cavities and leaving them to rust in the Nevada sun. The others weren't ransacking but were frantically looking for something to fuel themselves before shutting down.

In the distance, stragglers, apparently low on juice, walked ever slower before stopping altogether. These wouldn't be the first Zots I'd seen who'd run down their batteries. Every once in a while you'd come across a body still in its last position, mid-movement, an everlasting statue commemorating the end of the world.

And then they made it inside.

The Eldorado's steel frames grieved as the machines started their demolition. Too soon, they crashed their way up the stairwell. They grew steadily louder. It was only a matter of time until they reached us. My hands started to tremor, and my first thought was to pull Todd to the door and throw him in before he could do the same to me.

Todd reached for my shoulder, and I panicked. Stumbling back, I ran for the nearest exit—Todd calling my name. I continued running, not sure where the next door would take me or what surprises might be waiting behind it. The first one

I came upon led me to a large windowless corridor. It went pitch-black as the heavy fire door fell shut on my backside. I stopped running and tiptoed my way along the wall looking for another door. I grabbed a handle in the dark. Locked. I went onto the next and next, finding the same. Finally, a latch clicked, and I turned the handle, but it wouldn't open. I held my breath.

Just as I stepped back, the door came bursting off its hinges, and a Zot crashed through, slamming against the opposite wall. The dry-rotted gyprock crumbled around it as it staggered to its feet.

The flood of bright light now streaming in from the bare doorway and clouds of old dust and plaster stung my eyes. I scurried away but struggled to see anything at all. I reached for a door. It would be locked, but I didn't care. It would open for me now. I backed to the far wall then ran, throwing all my weight at the door. My shoulder cracked on impact, and I bellowed a sound like what a buck makes when you shoot it. The Zot came at me, and I threw myself at it again. This time, the frame gave way and the door swung open; the Zot flew past me down the hallway. I stumbled into a stale hotel room, sweltering from the bright afternoon sun. I dove into the bathroom and locked the door. Dragging myself into the tub, I laid down and tried to steady my ragged breath.

The pain in my arm grew, and I shut my eyes tight. I could hear the Zot in the room now, the hiss of its hydraulics as it made slow movements, looking for me. No matter how hard my adrenaline tried to keep me awake, I slipped in and out.

The last thing I remember was Joyce's face. But this time, she wasn't looking at me through horrified dead eyes. She was shaking her head, disappointed. She had come back to life just to tell me what a failure I was.

I drifted off.

When I woke, Joyce's face was replaced by Todd's. He poured some rancid tasting water down my throat and made a joke that he never took me for the spastic type—that we should probably try to stick together from now on. He helped me out of the tub with a patient smile, and I grumbled at the geriatric picture it must have made.

The pain in my shoulder was unbearable. Todd apologized while he went to resetting it. He didn't know how, but he'd seen them do it in the movies. He calmly got to work with that 'we'll laugh about this later' smile of his, and popped it in on the third torturous try. Outside the bathroom stood the Zot that pursued me, now forever bent forward to probe its heat sensor under my door. I often think about how close I came to being done-in that day. Todd told me we were lucky; the horde passed us, and we were safe to leave, but they had made ruins of Reno outside.

They were ahead of us but slow moving. We could easily get around them if we went east and then north at a fast pace. Once out of the city we could take a wide berth on higher ground to better track the quickly diminishing herd. This was just a bad storm. But once it was done, I felt like things might get better. At least in the survival department. Their batteries were running low, and soon that'd be the end of it.

Within the hour, we'd come neck and neck with the horde. We could hear them a few blocks over like a clamorous junkyard pride parade. Every so often we would spot a straggler, but nothing difficult to evade. A few hours later, we overtook 'em by about half a mile.

Hitting the 659, we came upon a group of people in the

distance. All sorts. Old, young, male, and female, what remained of their lives strapped to their backs. They were headed west turning onto the 395, right in the path of the storm. Todd judged from the speed they were traveling, the horde would come on them fast and hard. There was nothing but barren land all around them, no place to hide except the burned-out Mother of Sorrows Cemetery. They'd be shredded.

I shrugged my shoulders and told him we should head east again to avoid getting caught up in something. I could tell by the way Todd scoffed that he didn't agree. As if he had just decided between steak and chicken on the menu, he told me very matter-of-factly that he was gonna go warn them and meet back up with me down the road. At that moment, I realized Todd had evolved at some point during our time together. He was no longer one of 'them,' part of the indeterminate we—just another member of the species who made the machine that ended the world. Todd was better than that. Better than me, surely. And I didn't want him to leave.

See, to me, Todd was a hunk of gold, living among the excrement, but he had somehow managed to stay clean. The idea of him running off and shaking hands with who knows what manner of devils made me feel like I could chew up nails. So I started yelling. I yelled so loud my chest burned. I reamed out that boy; I told him what a damn fool I thought he was, how his spray cans and savior's complex were gonna get him killed. How even saving me had been an idiot decision. Todd stood patient until I was done then smiled all the meaning in the world. Above it all. Not a scratch on him. It silenced me and made me feel as much shame as the day I lost Joyce.

Joyce. Just shaking her head at what an old sack I'd become before the image of her screaming face flashed behind my eyes again.

My yelling drew the attention of the group, and they worried around each other trying to decide if we were friendly. The way they shied, I assume they'd figured at least I wasn't. Then a flash of red caught my eye, and I looked across the highway toward a dry-stack stone wall behind a row of creosote bushes. A mangy looking Nevada Red skipped down the road, its hind leg tucked up under its belly. It stopped to stare at me.

I wonder if it knew who I was—if it remembered me leaving it to die. It peeled its eyes away from me and looked behind it, waiting. A sand-covered boy climbed over the wall and jogged to the fox. He stopped to look at me as well before running off to catch up with the group, the fox hobbling along behind him.

I turned and left without another word. I could feel Todd watching me go, but when I looked back he had slinked his pack over one shoulder and was already chasing after the boy and his pet.

I ambled east, not going anywhere in particular. Trapped in my head with Joyce. Angry at her for always looking at me like that. Angry at the Zots for taking her, and people for needing saving. Angry at Todd for leaving me. But more than anything, angry at myself for all the reasons I could come up with, rational or not.

I only went ten minutes before I turned back west. Being alone didn't feel like it used to. There was something deep inside me that felt sick now. Like I was the one with a rotting corpse down in my gut.

What if Todd couldn't convince the others to turn tail and run before the horde came upon them. I'd thought he was nuts when he told me, and I almost didn't make it out alive. Two people are much easier to hide than twenty. And now he was runnin' headfirst into danger with barely a bush for cover. I knew what I had to do. I needed to go back for Todd. I needed to make sure he made it to wherever it was he was going. The rest of the world might be swine, but Todd wasn't like the rest of us. Saving these people would lead him to his death, but I would save him first.

I made it back to the 395, but I was too late.

My detour had taken long enough that the bulk of the horde passed me up the highway. I needed to hang back longer, heading south so the stragglers wouldn't catch up to me. By the time I made it back to the wall where I'd spotted the boy, the Zots had ravaged every bit of life. Even the creosote.

I'd failed.

Joyce laughed maniacally at me, her eyes bulging, her teeth brown and rotten. I was alone again. My plan to save the only living soul worth a damn in this world was a joke. My selfishness had probably gotten him killed. If I had been there, I could have talked some sense into him.

Todd was dead.

I remember believing that completely as soon as I set eyes on the horde again. Reflecting on it now, it was probably cowardice that made me think that way. Whether I was scared to fail or succeed, I'm still not sure. Perhaps I just didn't want to admit to him that I'd been wrong if he were alive.

I'd been balancing on the edge of a mental crater for a long time, and I'd finally fallen into it. The only option I could see in front of me was to head back to where I had started and climb the tallest building I could find.

Then throw myself off it.

I dragged my feet the whole way and passed plenty of

buildings worthy of the task. I didn't want to end it that way. But as soon as I'd begin to doubt the plan, Joyce would start laughing again, and I could think of nothing outside of dying. When the weather grew humid and mixed with the heat, it got hard to breathe. I couldn't make it another step so I headed into the nearest building, an eight-story apartment complex, the 'Leasing Now' sign swinging from one corner above the parking garage entrance. The metal security gate blocking the garage had been ripped down and lay crumpled on the pavement. Guessing the doors would be locked, I climbed over and headed up to the second level of the garage.

I heard a sound like a swinging metal door. The thought of a single Zot crossed my mind, but the sound was too repetitive to hold it there. The upper level of the garage was filled with dust-covered cars. Against my better judgment, I searched out the noise among the vehicles. After all, what would a man about to throw himself off a building need to be worried about? Rounding a family-sized SUV, I found what I was looking for.

On the ground was a pile of warped metal. It looked like it had been smashed to pieces. Crouching over it was the biggest Zot I had ever seen. It spun the dead Zots arm around in a circle until it ripped off cleanly at the shoulder. Its work done, it stood.

All Zots are shaped basically the same, although there are a few key differences between the man-made varieties and the machine replicated ones. But this was like none other. It was tall, standing at least ten feet on legs that looked to be patched together out of scraps. The head was heavily plated and set low like the beast was made without a neck. Its chest was twice as wide as it should be, and worst of all, the energy center in its middle—its stomach—was made up of three separate compartments where there should only be one.

I stood still, not able to breathe. Not able to run or even collapse into a ball on the ground. I watched as it ripped the arm open, savagely, but not destructively. It pulled out four intertwined cables from the inside and began fastening them to its own. I immediately recognized what it was doing. It was making itself stronger. It was growing. And it was ripping others apart to do it.

How human of it.

The titan began to turn around; the movement resurrected my survival instincts. I bolted down the ramp and for the exit before it could see me. Of course, it was far too late for that. Emerging onto the street, I stumbled over the fallen gate in my fear. My boot caught on the metal, and I struggled to free myself.

The Frankenzot burst from the upper level of the garage. It landed hard in front of me, pulverizing the pavement under its weight. Joyce looked at me with her yellow eyes and smiled. This was it. The end. I looked at my executioner dead on. I was ready.

It stared at me too. Calm, like it was sizing me up. A chill went through my entire body; I felt like it was thinking about what to do with me. A creature caught in the rubble, and it was just blankly watching me suffer.

Then came the rain.

I felt the cool wet on my face for the first time in what seemed like years. It came hard and fast, clouding over the sky and blocking the sun in mere seconds. I couldn't help but smile at the divine timing of it. The Zot before me looked up at the sky and contemplated. I couldn't be sure, but I thought for a moment it looked to be enjoying it as much as I was.

Soon, both me and the maneater were drenched. I shuttered. It sparked.

From the joint where its metal pelvis met the leg, it sparked.

Memories of Joyce screaming as her first leg was torn and broken, and then the other. Me grabbing the only thing I could find. A spade. Hacking at it while it was busy carving its meal. Slicing through a cable and watching the blood on it spit and sizzle. Taking one last look at Joyce's face. Running.

I ripped off my shoe and ran again, conjuring up all the will I had left in me. The beast took off after me with a giant leaping stride. I dodged and zigzagged around cars, just barely turning out of its grasp every time it reached out to seize me. I ran not from the monster behind me, but from the memories, and I have never run so fast in all my life.

The rain poured down so hard, I couldn't see more than a few hundred feet ahead. Out of nowhere, another Zot charged at me from the left, and I skidded to a stop. It circled back, looked at the Frankenzot behind me, and turned to run too late. He grabbed it and ripped it to shreds in an instant. I didn't wait around to see what happened this time. I took off again. I glanced behind me only once to see it staring after me. Still and thoughtful.

I think I sprinted for about a mile, then jogged at least three after that. Then I walked until I collapsed to the ground. My chest felt like it was being crushed, and my legs melted into the pavement. My one bootless foot no longer had much skin left. I didn't know how, but I had to go on. I knew that thing would follow me. It was going to hunt me down and live on my flesh. Only hours before, I had wanted to kill myself. But now I knew if I let that thing do it, I would be doomed to see

Joyce's demented face for all eternity.

The rain stopped when the sun went down, and I finally found the wherewithal to stand again. I continued down the road until I saw baseball diamonds with a covered complex at the center. I needed to rest and this place was as good a shelter as I was gonna find.

As soon as I got on the field, I saw him. Todd leaned against the wall of the pavilion and nodded to me like we were supposed to meet here all along. When I got close, he motioned another man to take me under the arm and lead me inside. Several people were camped out on the floor.

I remember my eyes falling on a boy and his limping fox just before I fell asleep.

When I awoke, a woman about as pretty as a sunstroked pig was mending my foot. I kicked out and she leaped back, packing up her gauze and scurrying away without a word. My hand on the wall beside me, I hauled my old, rusty body off the floor and went in search of Todd. I needed to tell him what was coming. I needed to get him out of here. We had all been lucky up to this point, but I knew that luck was about to run out for everyone.

I had no idea how long I had been out, but the sun was hanging high in the sky. In my imagination, the Frankenzot had picked up my trail and was coming for me. Maybe it was already here, watching from some hiding spot, just waiting for the right time to pick everyone off.

At last, I found Todd among a group of people huddled around an old map of Nevada discussing the best plan of action. A tall middle-aged Hispanic man was determined to go back south into the heart of Reno. Now that the Zots had moved passed, maybe they could set up a stronghold somewhere. To do what? Was beyond me. I guess to live out the remainder of humanity's dominion over the world in a puddle of their own sweat.

Others spouted off equally bad ideas, all the while Todd stood in silence on the outskirts with a sparkle in his eye that said he knew the best place to go, but he never did reveal its location.

I hobbled to his side and pulled him close. I rambled off my concerns so wildly that Todd just stared at me with pursed lips and a flying eyebrow. When I was done, he waited for me to take a few breaths before returning a chuckling 'huh?'

Frustrated, I grabbed him by the shoulder and away from the group, whose narrowed eyes I could feel all over me. I asked him what had happened with the horde. Not much. He told me how when it finally reached them, it was moving considerably faster than when it had come upon us at the Eldorado. Assumably, because by that time, most of the weak had been culled from the herd. Todd and the group ran for the baseball diamond, expecting to be sought out and taken out, but the horde just whizzed by them. Lucky again.

But it wasn't luck, was it? The Zots back in the casino were desperate alright, and they were ravenously scrambling for any amount of energy. But it wasn't for the reasons we thought. I knew, after witnessing the apparent fear in the Zot trying to escape the mutated beast, that they were desperate to escape. Just like millions of people before them in those last ten years.

It sent shivers down my spine thinking that this whole time the Zots weren't merely mindless killing machines—robotic zombies looking for their next brain to eat. They knew enough to be scared. They were aware enough to understand the need for survival on a level I didn't think possible. I suppose the AI was doing exactly what it was supposed to. Evolving.

I begged Todd to go with me. When the thing you fear runs scared, it's probably a good idea to run with it. But now it was Todd's turn to look at me like I was touched. I'll fully admit I sounded like an old man who had lost his vertical hold. Everything that had happened the day before felt like a fevered nightmare. The way the Frankenzot looked at me like it remembered me, the way it contemplated the rain, the noise the other Zot's arm made when it was wrenched from the socket...

Todd refused to leave. He dropped his arms to his side and put on the most serious demeanor I had seen from him yet. If the rest of these nomads were in danger, he couldn't in good conscience leave them, though I got the feeling he just plain didn't believe me. I couldn't understand it at the time. Why should he care what happened to those people who he had no connection with, nothing in common beyond having made it this far?

I thought about leaving without him again, though the times before hadn't worked out so good for me. I hated the idea of needing anyone, but I accepted that I'd grown to need Todd in the short time that I knew him.

I'd have to stay, and if saving Todd meant saving all those other assholes too, I would do it.

The night fell hard and hot as usual. The day before's showers were already a vague memory. I perched myself next to the fence that gave me the best vantage point of the south and kept vigil through the whole night. My body ached from my injuries and my mad dash. If Frankenzot did come around, I don't know how much good I would have been. I was so stiff I might have just snapped like a dry old twig. But he never showed that night or the next day. Or the ones after that. I spent the days sleeping and the nights back in my spot alone. Often, Todd would come down from the pavilion and sit with me, telling me stories of life before and after the world ended. Although I tried hard to remain serious and watchful, I'd more often than not forget about my self-assigned duties after a few minutes talking. Most of the time we'd end up next to tears laughing as the night grew late and the conversation would turn absurd in our exhaustion. I never talked to the others, and they never tried me. My disdain stayed plastered over my face, and it kept them well away.

Coming up on a week, the group was ready to leave. Todd must have told them my concerns because they chose to set out east and north in search of workable prairie land. Someplace they could settle and build a 'community.'

I don't think I have to tell you what I thought of that idea.

It was on that fateful day that my worst fears were realized. Like Lee Van Cleef making his entrance screen right, a sinister air blew over the ball diamonds, and weeds tumbled across the fields. I poked my head up to sniff the air for signs of predators and immediately focused my sights on the sun's bright glare off his metal body.

Zots can move quite stealthily when they need to. But once they spot you, they're quick and graceless. It's not pretty, but they're effective.

I could have sworn he was looking right at me, but he walked toward me with a gawking gait. Steady, and never once breaking his even stride. He'd grown since I'd seen him last. His new arm was accompanied by a large shoulder plate that peaked up past his head in a horrible spike.

I forgot myself and watched him in silence, a cocktail of

adrenaline, hate, and fear injected into my veins, and I shook from the load of it. At some point, the others took notice of him and scattered, their horrified faces made the shapes of screams and wails, but their instincts wouldn't let them make a sound.

Joyce screamed for them. So high pitched it was no longer human, but the sound of metal violently scraping against metal.

Todd grabbed me by the shoulders and shook me hard. I blinked my vapid eyes a few times before realizing who he was. We ran together, but there weren't too many places to hide, and every spot we came upon was already filled to capacity.

And then we saw him. The boy stood paralyzed on home base; his scruffy little friend stood before him panicked and makin' an awful sound like the scream an old woman might make falling down the stairs.

Frankenzot made his way toward him cautiously but amused. The way a pup plays with a frog or a snake. For the first time since I'd met him, I saw real fear in Todd's eyes, revealing a pain that I knew had to be there but that he'd kept so well hidden away. The pain that only a father who'd lost his boy would recognize. Nothing broke my heart more than that look. It shattered an image I'd made of Todd as a fun, strong, and angelic figure—smashed down in an instant. He became as human as you or I, and at that moment I loved him for it. I knew what I had to do.

I ran for the boy, touching down with my bad foot and leaping strides long enough to make up the difference with the other. I wasn't quick enough to save the fox that unfailingly fought for its friend. The Mega Zot, tired of playing with the creature, scooped it up in one fluid and lightning-fast motion.

Its grip around the animal's small body tightened, crushing it, then it stuffed it into the rear chamber of its stomach.

Tears flowed from the boy's eyes in cartoonish squirts, and his chest heaved as he struggled to catch his small breath. Frankenzot crouched in front of him, bringing itself to the child's level. I reached them before its knee hit the ground and pushed the boy hard. He flew a few feet before landing with a thud on the red earth. The violence of it put a fire under him, and he ran for the dugout; from the corner of my eye, I saw Todd scoop him up and disappear.

The Zot rose slowly, never taking its mechanical gaze off me. The space between us grew as it stood, and I felt small. We stared at each other. This time I knew he recognized me. And he understood the hate I held for him. I didn't lose my resolve. For once, my feet were planted in place. I wasn't going to run no more.

Joyce appeared before me. She had the dark tan of long days spent in the garden; her gray hair still highlighted with gold. She looked as resolute as I felt.

"Kill him, Hap."

I drove my fist into his middle and grabbed hold of the cables leading from the decomposition cavity to his chest. I didn't pull them out, but held my hand there and looked into my enemy's eyes. It peered down at my arm and cocked its head to the side. I twisted my hand and wrapped the cable around my wrist.

The machine seemed to grow irritated and grabbed my arm to pull it out, the force of it snapped my elbow. I screamed in pain, but the cable around my wrist kept me attached to him. He wrenched my arm to remove my hand, but the twisting in its gut gave it pause. The lights that lit up its makeshift face flickered.

My arm gushed blood. I couldn't even be sure that it was still attached to my body. The blood poured down over the Zot's pelvis, and I once again heard the sputter of its bare wires.

A loud clang came from behind the monster, followed by another.

The Zot lurched forward and stumbled, his heavy body pressing down on me. I tried to focus my spotted vision but could not. I heard shouting and more clanging.

"Kill him now!"

I reached up with my good arm as far as I could and grabbed its spiked shoulder. With all my might, I yanked. It wrenched off, taking a square plate of shoulder with it. I ripped my arm free of the cable. The flesh on my hand tore. I was quickly losing blood. I tried to scurry out from under him, but couldn't find the strength.

Frankenzot writhed on top of me, trying to find something to grasp, but we both slipped against the ground and each other, slick with my blood. Many arms I couldn't see gripped me under the shoulders and pulled me out into the cold air. The sudden weight off my chest and the chill of air in my lungs brought with it a clarity of mind I hadn't felt before. Spike in hand, I threw myself at my wife's murderer and forced its own shoulder into the small of its back.

Frankenzot buzzed as he powered down, and then there was silence. He toppled at the feet of the human circle that surrounded him. I swayed. Todd smiled, and I fell.

The world switched from day to night as I lay there, breathing through labored snorts and wheezes. I saw Todd's face appear above me, and I gargled a wet cackle.

"You knew . . . this was gonna end like this . . . all along, didn't you?" I coughed out the last of those words as blood from my throat. Todd wiped my mouth and put his backpack under my head. Others murmured around me, some grabbing at me and pulling on my clothes.

Someone somewhere said it was going to be okay.

"Yeah . . . it is." I let myself slide out again, closing my eyes to focus on the slowing of my awful heart when Todd sat down beside me and looked out to the far end of the field. Then he said the words that I will never forget in all my remaining time on earth.

"When we've got nothing left you can end the game. Or, I guess keep playing, keep fighting even when you're sure you're beat. It's always gonna be the same game, but you can make different choices. We can't ever forget the people we lost, and we can't bring them back either. We failed them. You and me. And they suffered because of it . . . though it wasn't for lack of trying. We can live haunted by that fact forever, or we can find peace in it, let go of the guilt. End our own suffering."

He looked me in the eye, his face slowly fading to black. "Let go of it, Hap."

I closed my eyes and Todd was gone.

Joyce's beautiful face smiled at me as she trimmed the roses in the front yard, the sun catching the dust in the air and making it sparkle.

When I awoke next, I was inside a canvas tent dim with the pale light of morning. I instinctively lifted my arm to inspect the damage and was pained but not surprised to see that most of it was missing. Groaning, I rubbed at my face, thick with straggly facial hair. I had been asleep for some time it would seem.

I turned my head to see a tiny face. It was gone in a flash as the little boy ran out of the tent and started yelling something. A few moments later, a young man came in. He told me his name was Gabriel, and he was a doctor. He had sewn me up as best he could, though it was obvious to him right away that the arm would have to go. That was fine because, for the first time in my life, I was happy just to be alive.

I asked to see Todd. Gabriel told me Todd had left as soon as he was sure that I was going to be okay. He headed north.

I was disappointed of course, but I understood. Canada is cold, he needed to be gone and on his way before the winter hit.

Something tells me, someday, I will see Todd again. I keep hope alive. Whatever he is doing, I hope he is not suffering. I hope he found home.

Dictator Dome
J . P . W I T H E R S

Welcome to the Elon Musk stadium for the 2092 TelePull Dictator Dome. It is a beautiful afternoon here on Earth C16, and we are moments away. So, John, while we wait, why don't you tell us a little about this year's players?

> Happy to, Mike. As usual, we have three teams competing. First on the roster for the Fascists, and back by popular demand, are past Dictator Dome champions, Adolf Hitler and Benito Mussolini, but with new addition, Francisco Franco, which should be interesting.

It should be, John. Hitler and Mussolini are a consistently strong team, but last year they had a rough go of it. Later in interviews, Hilter made some pretty critical comments of their then-teammate, Austrian Chancellor, Engelbert Dollfuss. So hopefully, Franco is a better fit and can keep up with the infamous pair.

> Only time will tell.

They will have some stiff competition with the Communists, John.

Yes. What a team this year! Of course, their captain is last year's champion, Joseph Stalin. He's playing with former competitor, twentieth-century Romanian president, Nicolae Ceauşescu, and new addition, Kim Jong-Un.

There's another interesting first-time player, as Kim only came up second in the polls, behind Mao Zedong, who was supposed to take his place on the team.

Well, something not all fans realize is how much work TelePull puts into these guys to get them ready for this event. And you know, some just can't make the cut in the end. These events are physically taxing, and as much as fans might want to see a certain dictator compete, not all have the heart for it.

I don't see Kim as a disappointment though. He was a star in training, and might just be the breakout champ we didn't see coming. So who do we have on our wildcard team this year, John?

Oh, this team is very exciting. We have Dictator Dome veterans, Saddam Hussein, and Muammar al-Gaddafi.

Those two are always a pair to look out for. They are true to the team name; you just never know what they're going to do. Full of surprises!

Indeed, Mike. Throughout training, they've kept a tight lid on their strategy for this year. Rumor has it, Saddam's got a trick up his sleeve—something that will *really* give him an edge. That will be exciting to see.

There is a newcomer to this team too, isn't there, John?

> That's right. With an unprecedented 100% of the vote in his category, Vladimir Putin joins the Wildcards this season. And I gotta say, he is made for this competition. He is more physically fit than any other player here so that does push the odds in his favor.

It is really building up to be a thrilling competition this year, John. The competitors are making their way onto the field. Only a few more minutes until we're off. But first, a quick message from our sponsor, and we will be right back for the 2092 TelePull Dictator Dome.

***

> Our organization started as a small group of scientists looking for a way to transcend space and time and has now grown into the largest time pull company in the multiverse, aiding governments, healthcare, and education. We can now bring you quality entertainment with programs like *Dancing with the Past, Rolling in their Graves Stand Up Comedy,* and *Dictator Dome.*

> You, our viewers, have loyally supported us for all these years, and now it is our turn to give back.

> Introducing Time Warp. The first inter-

dimensional cruise where guests can interact with all their favorite figures from the past, face-to-face. To help launch this historic opportunity, we are inviting thirty lucky viewers to join as for an all-expenses-paid cruise around sixteen Earths. Each of our winners will get the once in a lifetime chance to dine with their favorite historical figure.

So keep watching for more information and to learn how you can enter to win.

TelePull. *Out of time, just in time.*

***

Aaand we're back. Now seconds away from hearing that starting pistol.

The first event is the relay where team members race to complete a task before the next teammate is allowed to move on. The first leg of the race today is the *Peace Summit!* Each dictator must climb to the top of a steep, muddy hill and grab their team flag. They will need to watch out for those heavy boulders with the green question marks on them though.

That's right, John, along the way they will be bombarded with those boulders, dropped by our 'Human Rights Delegation,' waiting at the top of the hill. Our dictators will have to expertly dodge those questions if they want to make it to the top first.

And looks like we have the team captains, Stalin,
Hitler, and Hussein, on their marks . . . the pistol is up
and . . . They're off!

Hilter takes an early lead—he's at the hill, but I don't
think he's realized just how muddy that slope is today.
He seems to be struggling with his footing there, John.

He sure is. That starting lead is all but gone now, and
Hussein is on his heels, just tearing up that hill!

Stalin is not far behind either, though he is taking a
cautious approach, treading up nice and steady.

Alright, here comes the first question . . . and—Oh!
Hussein took that one head on! That boulder sent
him right back to where he started. He is well behind
now.

You can't underestimate the power behind these
boulders, John. Our delegates are androids that have
been programmed to give these guys a beating.

Yes, Mike. They are so human-like, it's hard to
remember how dangerous they can be.

Hitler has reclaimed his footing and is just about
neck-and-neck with Stalin.

Here come two more questions, and my oh my, did
those men dodge them beautifully!

You wouldn't think it to look at him, but that Stalin
can move like a butterfly when he needs to.

Hussein is back up and gaining quickly. If he can stay
safe now, he might have a chance to keep up.

The questions are coming at them fast and hard ...
Stalin and Hilter are almost at the top—Oh no! Hitler
has stumbled.

That hill sure is steep, Mike.

Stalin is yards away from his flag, but I don't think he
sees that boulder on his left, John.

You're absolutely right. He's going to be blindsided
by that question. He—He's down! That must be so
upsetting for him!

He's out cold, John. His teammates are just looking in,
not sure what to do.

I don't know, but the way that boulder hit him, he
just might be dead. He doesn't seem to be moving at
all. Ceauşescu and Kim have to go and check on their
teammate.

The Communists appear to be arguing over who will
tend to him. And I think that person will be ... Nope!
They've scattered. Looks like Stalin will be staying
right where he is.

In the meantime, Hitler has made it to the top first.
Hussein is just seconds behind.

The Fascists and Wildcards are onto the next leg of
the race!

Stalin hasn't finished, but it looks like Kim is going
to start his portion of the relay anyway, so he is in the
lead, followed by Mussolini and Putin in the back.

Now we move on to *Rein in the Media*, where our
dictators will have to enter the pen, wrangle, and
hogtie each of our journalist-droids before tagging in
the final members of their team.

Kim is already in the pen and seems to be unsure
of what to do. Those journalists are taunting him
something fierce, and he's taking their insults pretty
hard.

Yes, John, it's a slow start, but I think if he can get a
handle on his feelings, focus on getting under them,
and tripping them up, he might be all right.

We'll check back in on him in a minute. Mussolini is
doing really well over in his pen.

He is so efficient in taking each of his journalists down.
But we have to remember that he is a seasoned veteran
in this event, plus he is up against two novices which
gives him another advantage here.

Speaking of our new competitors, let's take it over to
Putin, who doesn't appear to be doing anything at all.

Well, no. He's going over to talk with one of the
journalists, John.

Not sure what his strategy could possibly be here,
Mike.

Whatever they're talking about, it appears to be pleasant . . . Wait. Hold on. What's happening?

No! This can't be! That journalist is getting on the ground and *letting* Putin tie him up. Never in all my years have I seen anything like this!

I can't believe it! The other journalists are doing the same.

Incredible! Just incredible!

A truly astonishing turn of events. Move over Mussolini, there is a new media wrangling champion in town.

Look, he's already done and leaving the pen, and they are smiling. They are smiling at him. The media love him!

Well, I'll be damned.

Mussolini is nearly finished up, only two more to go. You know Kim isn't doing a half-bad job himself now that he's pulled it together. Not bad at all.

Not bad maybe, but he is no Putin! Putin has blown his competitors out of the water. He is passing it over to Gaddafi now. It's looking really good for the Wildcards this year, John.

And that is why I love this team, Mike. You never know what to expect.

I don't think anyone was expecting what we just saw in that pen.

Let's quickly check in with Sarah who's got Putin
down on the field.

***

"How confident were you about your strategy
going in?"

"I felt good. Media is predictable. I know I
could win them over—they're docile like
polar bear, yes? Ha Ha Ha."

***

Well, there you have it. I knew he was going to be a
contender.

Yes, he really has proven his mettle, Mike. But let's
check back in on the players.

We've made it to the last leg of the relay, *Dissent Blaster*.
Here our dictators will need to use the fire hose to
push our oncoming protestor-droids back a hundred
yards behind the red line.

And they better not let the protestors get to them,
because they look angry, Mike.

Oh, they are, John. This has always been one of the
more dangerous events. The competitors really have
to keep their streams on target.

Gaddafi is well ahead and already blasting his
dissenters.

Well, he's been our golden boy with this event in
previous years.

And he is really giving those protestors a shower today.

Finally, here comes Franco with his hose. He's going to
have to blast these protestors away quickly and make
a run for the finish line if the Fascists are to win this,
John.

Like a racehorse, Mike. The Fascists haven't played as
well as they would have liked so far. Hopefully, Franco
is able to make up the time here.

I see Kim is finished with the media now. He is ready
to tag in his teammate, but Ceauşescu is nowhere to
be seen.

He just disappeared, Mike. I guess the death of Stalin
freaked him out more than we thought.

It looks like Kim is a one-man team now, and he's
going to complete this leg of the race himself.

He's a ways behind, but you have to admire his drive
and perseverance.

Absolutely, John.

Kim has picked up the hose and is blasting his
dissenters and Wow. Wow wow wow. Look at him go!
He's not gonna let those protestors get anywhere near
him.

This is his kind of contest. In this leg of the race you

really need to rely on your uh, how do you say . . . ?
Your innate . . . sense of self-importance. But those
protestors move fast. You can't get too cocky.

> Well, Kim is not that. He is really focused here and
> getting some good distance with that hose.

Yes. Just look at the arch on that stream. But uh oh,
John. There appears to be trouble for his competitors.
Gaddafi and Franco have accidentally crossed streams.
How embarrassing for them.

> Franco's recovered but Gaddafi is struggling to put the
> pressure on his dissenters. They are gaining on him
> fast.

He just doesn't have the time—

> Oh! That is not pretty. There is no coming back
> from that, Mike.

There is a reason this event doesn't air on prime-time
television, John. Sometimes it just gets too gruesome
for the kids.

> Everyone at home is clenching in their seats tonight.
> I know I am.

The distraction from Gaddafi is just what the other
two needed though, and both Franco and Kim have
pushed their protestors back and are making the final
sprint to the finish line.

> Incredible—the one-man army, Kim Jung-Un of the
> Communists has slid into first place! The Fascists

are at a close second, and the Wildcards have fallen into last. And considering the strong start made by Hussein, and the amazing show put on by Putin, this has to be a hard blow for them.

They still have a chance to take back the lead in the next round, John, but it will be difficult without Gaddafi.

Though we have yet to see Saddam's secret weapon, maybe it will be just what they need to win them the title this year.

Kim is going to have the toughest time moving forward, but I think after what we've seen from him in the last event, he can't be underestimated.

The Fascists have the biggest advantage going into this for sure, still having all their players. And Franco has proven himself a solid addition to the team.

Looks like they are ready to go, John, so let's review the rules of our main event.

Yes, yes. Alright! Up next is the *Purge*. Our teams must eliminate the other players who do not share their politics. They have the entire field to play, and we've set up obstacles and strategic cover to use however they need.

As usual, the *Purge* is played by historic dodgeball rules. If you're hit, you're out. Except instead of balls lined up in the center of the field, we have provided the players with an array of weapons from knives to assault rifles.

This event usually ends up being a Fascists vs.
Communists firefight. But it'll be interesting to see
how it shakes up considering the losses on two of the
teams already.

It would be a smart strategy for Kim, Hussein, and
Putin to work together, at least in the beginning.

Yes, but with the Wildcards as they are—you never
know where their loyalties are going to fall.

So true, John.

Alright. The dictators are ready to go, and they are off!

The Fascists are moving quick, and all three of them
have picked up semi-automatics. Shots are being fired!

Kim is deciding not to head for the center right away.
Instead, he's dodging from cover to cover, slowly
making his way to the middle, trying not to draw any
attention to himself.

Hussein has grabbed a sword, but I don't think it's
going to help him right now. Hitler and Mussolini are
coming for him, two on one!

Now would be a great time for Hussein to pull out that
secret weapon of his—

Oh my! Saddam Hussein has been shot in the chest!
What a disappointment.

I guess that rumor was false after all, Mike.

What a shame for the Wildcards.

It looks like the Fascists have this in the bag. Franco's pursuing Putin. So far he has been unable to land a single shot. But Hilter and Mussolini are coming to join him now. Hmm, Hitler is calling Mussolini over to him, I suppose to plan the next attack—Oh my god! Hitler just shot Mussolini point-blank!

What a move! I can't believe it. Hitler has shot his own teammate!

Makes you wonder what could have possibly happened between them. Hilter has always looked up to the Dictator Dome veteran. This could not have been more unexpected!

Franco has seen the whole thing and is taking cover now.

Smart move. He can only assume Hitler will be coming for him next.

That leaves Putin free. He is so calm out there, John. He's picked up a pistol and doesn't look worried in the least.

Hitler has his sights on him. He means business.

He's got his rifle up, and at that distance, Hitler should easily be able to make that shot.

Putin isn't moving an inch.

Wait a second, here comes Kim!

He's right in front of him, but Hilter can't even see

him coming; he's looking up at Putin. And Kim just
barely slices his thigh with a steak knife.

And Hitler is out!

The German is not happy about that, Mike. He's
throwing a full tantrum out there.

He's yelling at the referee now, but there is no arguing
this one, he is definitely done for today. He's stamping
off the field, leaving Franco as the Fascist's last hope.

I bet Hitler is regretting his move against Mussolini
now.

Kim is hiding again, waiting for his chance to pounce,
and Putin has spotted Franco behind the left pillar.
The way he is calmly walking over to him reminds
me of the villain in a horror movie. Franco must be
wetting his pants right now.

I know I would be, Mike.

Oh my god! What is this? Ceaușescu has come out of
nowhere and is barreling for Putin. Can he...? Oh no!
Putin just shot him in the face! Not even a twitch from
Putin. Incredible!

I don't know where Ceaușescu was hiding, but he
should have stayed there. That was an execution!

Hold up, hold up. Franco is putting down his weapon.
He's stepping out from behind the pillar with his
hands up.

He's conceding to Putin! Unbelievable.

Here comes Kim. He's dropped his knife and is doing the same. Both men have surrendered!

Never in my twenty years commentating for Dictator Dome have I *ever* seen anything like this! What an upset!

I can only imagine what these leaders are thinking. It's like they have resigned themselves to the fact that Putin is simply the stronger player. Inconceivable! Just insane!

Look at that. Putin's taking off his shirt. The crowd is going wild!

I think Sarah just fainted down there.

Ha! Someone get that man a horse for a victory lap.

What a shocking end to a very exciting game. Vladimir Putin is the 2092 Dictator Dome Champion by default!

From all of us here at the Elon Musk Stadium on Earth C16, I'm John Cherno.

And I'm Mike Valencia. Thank you for joining us for the 2092 Dictator Dome, brought to you by TelePull. Out of time, just in time.

***

This year's Dictator Dome champion needs worthy opponents for 2093. Dictators are waiting for their chance to be pulled out of time. Cast your ballot before December 15th at:

telepull.com/dictatordome2093/vote.

***

WHEN WILL IT END?

4

From Light

NICK NIKOLOV

Metal and glass pierced my flesh. That was the last thing I felt.
A moment of blackness later, the world stops spinning and my
car disappears. It was day before, now everything around me
is dark. Blinking my eyes, I see buildings with lights in their
windows. I feel light on my back as well. I try to step forward
but trip and fall to my knees, the shift from moving to still
images makes me gag. Vomit burns my throat, and I hunch
forward to spew it out.

"What . . . *is this?*"

My voice is normal; I sound like myself. I have cognition it
seems, but the scenery has changed. Behind me, stands a giant
black monolith, an obelisk jutting from the ground, its surface
shining against the night sky in a color darker than black.

The edges of a carved doorway at the obelisk's base gives
way to a thick tangle of light, streaming down like a waterfall.
Around the doorway is a frame of dark, ancient-looking
material. I try to move to the side but the light begins to churn
wildly like a violent tide. Something appears inside the light,
moves forward, and begins to take shape.

I stumble back, knowing by instinct that the tempest in
front of me is dangerous. The storm of light takes human
form and a moment later there it is. A human! I scrape along

the ground trying to get farther back, the light cast by the doorway only covering half of my body now. The skin on the parts of me shrouded in darkness begins to crawl, and I am physically repulsed. I draw myself back inside the safety of the light.

Think. This isn't possible, I should be dead. Why am I alive?

The person that materialized, a woman, has a moment of confusion run through her features before she calmly takes a step forward without looking down at me. She stops at the very edge of the light. Beyond the tips of her toes, the night takes claim to everything.

Trying to stand, my right foot buckles and hits the pavement. I feel pain, normal pain. Shaking my head, I focus then slowly lift myself up and walk over to her.

"Hello, miss? My name is Daniel Vesta. I'm a Doctor."

The woman fixes her gaze on me for a second then continues to stare beyond the light. Her features are locked as if she were a marble statue.

As I study her, a loud crash shakes the ground beneath my feet, and I fall to the pavement yet again. Looking over my shoulder, I see that another obelisk, identical to the first, has appeared just a few feet away from us.

More crashes follow. Obelisk after obelisk fall to the street, never hitting cars or property, just landing perfectly where there is space for their bulk and for the protective light they're casting.

How do I know the light protects? I just do.

As I get back to my feet, the energy coming from the doorways of the obelisks begins to storm into more human shapes. Every structure produces a person at the exact same time. Every shape that comes out walks to the edge of the light and freezes there, staring out into nothing.

No obvious signs of cognition, except for myself. Why is that? I turn around and gingerly step out of the daylight being cast down by my obelisk. The previous terrible feeling of dread, almost to the point of pain, is gone. We now have three total new arrivals, all standing in a perfect line at the edge of our bright havens. I walk back over to the first woman who came from the light.

"I just want to perform some rudimentary tests if I may."

The woman does not respond, her eyes don't even focus on me, she just stares outward. I try a few more times to get her attention with no luck. Grabbing her arm, I place my right index finger on a vein. As her arm moves into shadow, an emotion flows over her face, something akin to fright and not quite a wince. A moment later the emotion is gone, and the woman's face returns to its blank expression. Her pulse is normal, so I let go of her arm, grab her shoulders, and gently twist her upper body to the side, toward the light. Doing this a few times for each side, I'm confident her pupils are dilating properly, but the woman still makes no indication that she's even aware I am in front of her. Gritting my teeth, I step back farther into the night and cross my arms. Ideas flood my head.

I take a deep breath and steady my mind. Think logically, what could be happening here? I gaze at the forming shapes and ponder. I should be dead, rather I *did* die. I remember the terrible weight of the pieces of car that ripped through my torso, the glass in my face and eyes, then darkness. Remembering the black abyss that followed makes me shiver, the pain and terror from the car crash seem insignificant next to that all-devouring void. My hands begin to tremble, and I have to plunge them beneath my armpits to regain control.

So it must have been cerebral death then, no feeling, no perception, only nothingness. What I wouldn't give to see my MRI right now. I sigh and plop down on the ground. The government should be here to collect us soon. Whatever is happening, I seem to be the only one acting differently so they'll want to contain me somewhere, that's just standard biohazard procedure. I look around and notice the buildings are all familiar. The street remarkably resembles Main Street of the town I live in. *Lived in?*

The buildings match store placement and color palettes. This could be a simulation, if my brain were preserved after the crash, I could be in some kind of experiment. Nodding to myself, I stand and head to the nearest building to touch its wall. It feels real. Of course it does. I shake my head and return to my obelisk, running my hands along the smooth texture of its black exterior. The other alternative, which is even less likely, is that this is some kind of alien technology. But why would an advanced alien race bother with Earth, more importantly, Earth's dead? Deep in thought, I hear tires screech behind me. Turning, I see a dozen cars stop half a mile down the road.

"Finally."

I watch as men clad in black file out onto the street. I kneel on the ground and lock my fingers behind my head. The men set up barricades in front of their cars, and others, dressed in bright yellow suits, gather behind them. Two men, one in yellow the other in black, begin discussing something, and once done, the man in yellow signals his fellows, and they begin moving. When they get close, I notice that some of the new arrivals have weapons in their hands while the others hold a kind of device. Judging by the sounds they make, these instruments are Geiger counters. Three men make a circle around me, their weapons at the ready. The ones with counters begin moving through the people. As they come closer to me, their devices start to shriek.

Not good. I let my head fall, and the men with weapons take a half-step back, guns raised.

"Sorry, sorry," I apologize. "I won't move anymore; can we just speed this along please?"

A man without a weapon steps to the side and waves a few people over to us. When they come, they speak amongst themselves. I cannot hear their words but it is obvious by their sideways glances that I am the topic of discussion. This lasts roughly twenty minutes by my estimates. My knees started hurting fifteen minutes ago.

"Look guys," I say and sway my hands non-threateningly. "I'll just sit down because this position is killing me."

Without waiting for permission, I sit, cross my legs, and lean forward, placing my palms on my knees. I want to voice my joy at the comfort but decide against it as the men around me seem increasingly twitchy. They remain alert and on edge for the next few minutes while their superiors no doubt confer on what to do with me. Eventually, the man in front of me raises his hand to his ear and nods to the air.

"You," he barks and gestures with his finger for me to get up.

"Can you please take me away to some sort of containment." I stand and comply, my hands up. "I'm obviously different in some way, judging by the others who came from the structures."

The men do not move or say anything. I shake my head and sigh. "Listen, I know what I'm talking about, I was a professor of Neurology before . . . What date is it anyway?"

The men are not impressed by my vocation, nor do they answer my question. The man giving the orders gestures to someone behind me. "Containment is on its way. We'll be taking you away momentarily, *Professor*."

Just as he finishes speaking, I see men appear from behind the barricade. They hold long metal bars that end with manacles as wide as a man's neck. I gulp.

"Please, there's no need for those." I point toward the medieval-looking equipment. "I'll cooperate."

I make the mistake of stepping forward to plead my case and hear the click of multiple guns readying to kill. I freeze.

The men with lengthened manacles come closer. They lunge their devices at my neck. First, a metal ring hits the right side of my throat, snapping into place; the left side experiences the same a moment later. I am now safely immobilized from both sides. The men holding guns visibly relax but do not move away or lower their weapons.

Fair enough. I stare out into the barricades where a line has formed. The people who had appeared from the obelisks after me are being measured for radiation then guided gently through a pathway leading beyond. To freedom?

I sigh and close my eyes. When I reopen them, the men surrounding me are standing with different postures and without their previous killing intent. They seem like entirely different people. Looking around, I see the man in charge, standing a good distance away now. He raises his hand toward the barricade.

"Next ones up. On the double!" His powerful voice echoes off the buildings.

Six men appear from the barricade and jog over to us. Each

new man takes up position behind my guards, and when the new arrival's weapons are trained on me, they tap their fellow soldiers on the shoulders. The first team lower their guns, step back, and walk away.

As I am about to ask what is going on, a black truck appears in the distance and slowly backs toward us. One man is guiding the driver with his hands, and when the truck is close enough he motions for him to stop. There are yellow and black signs pasted onto both back doors that warn of radioactive danger. The doors swing open.

The man in charge stands next to the dark opening.

"After you, Professor," he says with steel in his voice and gestures for my handlers to bring me closer.

Before they are able to, I take the man's invitation and stride up into the truck. The manacles around my neck release, and I turn around.

"Close it up," the man in charge says, and the doors to the outside slam shut. Two loud bangs on the side of the truck follow, and we are on our way.

The inside is unilluminated and there are no benches to sit on. After all, why would hazardous material need comfort? As the truck picks up speed, I inch forward toward the door, lean back on it, and slide down to the floor. The rhythmic vibration of the radioactively-shielded plating rocks me to sleep.

I don't know how long the transport takes, but it's long enough that I am able to fall asleep a few more times from boredom. Good. The farther away I am from people the better. Whatever happens to me doesn't matter as long as my family is safe. Remembering my wife and kids puts a smile on my face despite the situation. The sensation of smiling gives me pause for some reason. Why do we smile in the first place?

The truck stops, and I stand up and move away from the door. I raise my hands, palms facing out, and wait.

The doors open. Light floods in, destroying the darkness and enveloping me almost compassionately. It chases away my concerns, and I just feel right. My eyes focus, and I see four men, holding weapons of course, in hazmat suits who wince back as if they had just opened an oven door.

"Out please," a fifth man who stands a few feet behind the others says while gesturing with his hand for me to come down.

I step out into noticeably cooler air; there is at least a fifteen to twenty-five-degree difference. Before I have time to ponder the cause, the man in the back speaks.

"Move forward to the entrance of the building. Once inside you will take the elevator to the bottom floor then follow directions to holding. Is that understood?"

"Understood." I nod and make my way to the concrete building at the end of the path. Inside, I take the elevator to the bottom level and follow arrows leading down corridors going only one way. Deep underground.

I reach a room, and as I get close, its doors open. Inside there is a chair, a table, and a white wall with a giant TV screen. Opposite the screen is a very solid-looking white door. It opens as well, and a disembodied female voice urges me to enter. This room is similar to the last with only the addition of a washbasin and bed—which looks more like a cot. There is no TV screen in this room, so it appears my boredom will be prolonged. I sit down on the chair, and the door to the outside closes and locks itself.

"This is it then." I take a deep breath and look up.

The walls, door, and ceiling blend into each other making

me feel like I have been put inside an aluminum cube, one able to withstand some punishment by the looks of it. The only difference between the walls and ceiling is a slight sheen. I have to narrow my eyes, but I see the distinction. The level of detail I am able to distinguish amazes me. My eyesight was never bad, but I couldn't see this well at any point in my life.

I continue to survey the room. There are no visible cameras, but I'm sure I am being surveilled. I can feel the people looking at me as if they are sitting in the room. Nonsense. I shake my head.

My surroundings are boring me, so I closed my eyes and wait. After a while, something is thrown into the room. I almost fall out of my chair from the sound. Standing up, I look back over my shoulder and see a tray of food on the floor. My gaze shifts up to a small opening in the door as it snaps shut. I walk over, grab the tray, and sit back down at the table.

A faint sizzle comes from the covered tray. I'm impressed that the food provided to me is still hot until I lift my hand to find holes in the foil.

No, not holes, but scorch marks. Did my fingers do that? I move a finger to the middle of the tray and push into the foil. Sure enough, it burns away beneath my touch.

"Not good," I remark to the hidden surveillance as I tear the foil away and begin eating.

Maybe this is some sort of hallucination. A withdrawal from reality? The mind making an effort to protect itself. Without any data, I can't be sure, so this is just idle speculation which can be dangerous—I take a look around—for a confined individual.

These revelations should unnerve me, make me frantic to find out what's going on, get some answers. Yet I sit here and don't feel any anxiety, no panic at the thought that I am a prisoner. All that I am capable of right now seems to be cold rationalization. Though this doesn't surprise me either because, during my years of practice, I'd developed a way to detach myself from a situation, from the feelings I have for an individual that I'm treating. But with each moment that passes since my return from the dead, I feel more emotionally distant.

The first moments of consciousness on the street were like a whirlwind in my head. Now my emotions are like a calm breeze, like something that can be safely ignored. I don't care about my wellbeing, I don't care that something is obviously wrong with my body. My last strong link to humanity appears to be my family. I care very much about being put in this cell and ensuring that whatever affliction I have doesn't reach them. This realization should hurt me deeply, it should threaten to shatter my soul, to destabilize my mind, it should feel different! Absolutely not like this. This is what something fashioned to resemble a human would feel. A poor replica of the complexity that each individual is comprised of.

I am falling apart.

Not even this deepest truth makes my heart ache. I am alive but not like before.

This train of thought has run its course, so I think of my family again, their bright eyes and shining smiles. I am happy, I suppose. I have a smile on my face, but its presence doesn't signify anything. Why should a physical change in my face make me feel better?

I lean back into the chair and fix my gaze on the room's door. Sitting and watching for a few moments, I blink; another tray of food slides on the floor next to the door.

What's happening? I stand and walk over to the tray. I just ate, why are they giving me more food? Looking around the room I try to gauge how much time has passed, but the artificial light remains constant, and everything else is the same as before.

I kneel down picking up the tray then walk back to the table where I eat unenthusiastically. As I am finishing, something catches my attention. A black screen descends mechanically from the ceiling. When it stops, letters appear on the screen.

"Food hatch will open in sixty seconds, push both trays out of the room," I read out loud then run my thumb over the side of my nose. "Easy enough."

The letters change and something else is written.

"First interview will begin in six hours. . . ."

The small rectangular hatch on the door opens with a metallic clank. I pick both trays up off the table and push them out through the hatch. With that done, I go back to the table, move my chair to face the screen and stare. Then blink.

The picture on the screen is different now. Instead of letters, it displays the identical room next door. The interview isn't supposed to be for six hours yet.

The screen relays sound to me, and I hear someone walking. A woman in a black work dress appears inside the frame and takes a seat on a chair identical to mine. The woman is in her early thirties, her hair is short and dark blonde. I think people call it sandy. Her eyes are blue, and her demeanor is formal. I realize we aren't facing each other. Just on the other side of the door behind me, the woman is sitting with her back to the door as well.

"Hello, Professor Vesta," the woman says in a pleasant and practiced voice. "My name is Felicia Rousseau, I've been assigned to lead these interviews." A small smile tugs on her lips, marking the end of her introduction.

"I can't say it's a pleasure to meet you"—I raise my arms up in an encompassing gesture—"under the circumstances. But I can assure you I will fully cooperate. The last thing I want is to be a danger to anyone."

Felicia closes her eyes and nods in agreement or affirmation, I'm not sure.

"Thank you for your candor, Professor Vesta."

"Please call me Daniel."

"As you wish." Felicia opens a folder and continues speaking. "I will now ask you some questions to determine the validity of your alleged identity."

"Alleged . . . what?" I shake my head and scoff.

"Please, Daniel, you said you would cooperate." Felicia's expression and tone convey her disappointment.

She looks like a school teacher about to give me a bad grade. I swallow my pride and nod silently. Felicia acknowledges me with a satisfied nod of her own.

"Where did you take your wife on your first date?"

"Small Italian restaurant close to my dorm, it was three blocks down and had the best quality to price ratio. The date was the 25th of May, 2005." As soon as I finish, Felicia scribbles something in the file before her.

"What was the name of your first pet?"

"Whiskers. Black and white spotted cat."

"What happened to that pet?" Felicia narrows her eyes at me and adds, "What really happened?"

"I told my parents that he ran away, but the truth was one of my friends pressured me into putting him in a box to see how long he could stay there without air. I went along with it, and we kept him inside until the box started jumping from Whiskers's violent attempts to get out. I went to help him, but my friend grabbed me and only let me go once the shaking had stopped." I pause to study her. No emotion shows on her face, no judgment, she just takes more notes.

"Thank you," Felicia says, scribbling something. "Next question. What happened at your Neurology conference in the year 2013?"

This is the second question that has an "official" statement that I had given to others and a truth told only to my wife. I realized that's who they must be getting their information from.

"I couldn't attend it because I had a very bad stomach flu."

Felicia writes that down then stares at her notes. After a few moments of silence, she begins to tap the page with the ballpoint of her pen. I don't say anything.

She looks up.

"Daniel, we are trying to establish what happened and if we can help"—her index finger uncoils in my direction—"you. But as I said before, cooperation is key, as is honesty. Currently, we are both aware that what you just said is not what really happened."

She leans back in her chair and pointedly crosses her arms. I notice that the chest of her dress is embroidered with flowers, they are deep blue in color and only intimate proximity would allow someone to see them. This is hardly a work dress, it looks like she was brought here from a party.

"I was supposed to headline our panel for the conference, but a colleague of mine who wasn't as . . . let's say, mentally capable, was appointed the task a few weeks before the event."

Felicia leans forward and continues to write, making no

comment.

"I tried my best to reverse this, but my colleague had academic friends in the right places, so ultimately I wasn't able to. I faked the flu, because I physically, at that point in time, couldn't stand that slimy, little bastard. Pardon the language."

Felicia raises her palm and waves dismissively without looking up. I hope my explanation doesn't make me come off as petty, even though that is exactly what I was. The sting from those memories is gone, however. Before today, remembering the incident made my stomach fill with anger like molten rock. It made me so mad I couldn't think straight, and that's why I decided to fake the illness. Right now I don't feel even an ember of that fire, it's almost like it happened to another person. Could this be tied to my condition? I manage to crack a smile. *Condition.* That is exactly how they see it, Felicia and her superiors. And why not? I am suffering from something, but we just don't know what that is yet.

"Shortly before your, uh . . . departure, you and your wife had a fight inside your bedroom. Could you please tell me what the nature of that argument was?"

"The argument was about my hours spent working. I tend to get lost in my research and lose track of time." I lean forward in my chair. "I just want to point out that I'm not some harebrained scientist who neglects his family for his research. I was on the cusp of something great, world-changing even!"

I get a rush of exhilaration when talking about the potential of my work—allowing mankind to leap a thousand-year technological gap in just a single generation. Unleashing the full potential of the human brain. The possibilities!

"I'm sure all scientists feel that way, Daniel. But please finish your explanation." Felicia's tone is cold, almost bitter.

She skews her face for a moment; the expression disappears as she swallows hard. Perhaps the topic is hitting a bit too close to home for her. Then again, it could just be my imagination. Either way, I know she's serious because she has unglued her writing hand from the desk and is gesturing with it for me to continue.

I fake a cough to regain composure and continue my story. "My wife thought, some would argue rightly so"—I throw a glance at Felicia, but she doesn't catch it—"that I was neglecting my family. The day before the argument I had missed my son's science fair, and the week before that I wasn't able to make an appearance at my daughter's career week. As I said, my research . . ."

Felicia raises her writing hand again to cut me off. "Next question."

She looks very pleased with herself. I should be mad, retaliate somehow, but the will for that no longer resides in me. It is as if the burst of emotion I felt a minute ago had burned away everything around it, leaving me with a lens of frosty calculation once more. Thinking about it now, that could be another side-effect of my resurrection. Maybe I came back wrong somehow. Not myself, but an almost perfect copy. Following that logic, I am not Daniel Vesta. Daniel Vesta is dead, and I am his imitation.

"Daniel!"

Felicia is yelling. I blink once and focus on her image.

"Yes?"

"I asked you what you say to your kids before bed."

"Right—uh, I tell them that I'm sorry I couldn't be here for you today kids, I'm doing something very important that will help everyone someday. You'll be proud of me, I promise."

I stop speaking and watch my interrogator. She finishes writing and locks eyes with me through the television.

"Thank you. That will be all for now. I'll see you in six hours."

I hear her chair scrape along the floor, and she walks off the screen without giving me the chance to say anything.

I expel a great billow of tension from my lungs and lean back into my chair. The giant TV screen ascends up into the ceiling and vanishes. I watch the whiteness of the wall until my eyes start to hurt.

I blink.

A sound comes from behind. I turn around to find another tray of food has made its way inside the room. I get the tray and set it on the table. I'm not hungry at all, but I have to eat.

Or do I?

I slide the tray to the side using my left index finger. The wrapping burns at my touch once again, but this time it shies away faster, more eagerly. My internal temperature is rising. With the added loss of appetite and the emotional detachment, I presume I am not going to be among the living for long.

The door slot behind me opens and breaks me out of my thoughts. I take food from the table and slide it outside. As I get back in my chair, the TV descends again. Felicia appears on the screen. This time her dress has no decoration on it, it's just black.

"Hello again, Daniel."

"Hello?"

"The answers you provided were very insightful, and I was given the go-ahead to continue on with the next phase of our interview."

"I see. . . . And what would that entail?"

"Since you seem to be Daniel Vesta, I will now ask you some questions regarding what you've experienced."

"Of course." I nod and cross my arms over my chest. "Just a heads up though, I don't remember much, and I don't think I'll be of any help. But, go ahead."

"Thank you. Firstly, you were returned approximately twenty-three hours ago."

Returned. Yes, very apt. I marvel at the word while Felicia continues to speak. Wait! Did she say twenty-three hours ago? That's impossible.

"Sorry." I raise my hand like I'm in high school again. "I can't tell the time in here, but surely no more than twelve hours have passed."

Felicia sizes me up with her gaze for a long time before she answers, "Twenty-three hours is correct, yes. After your last meal you spent approximately five hours, fifty-nine minutes and thirty seconds staring at the wall." She pauses to study my expression.

"Show him the footage," she says at last, and the screen's image changes a few moments later.

I see myself from a left angle, sitting in the same chair, but this time facing the door. The timestamp on the bottom of the screen says 11:00:00 AM. The footage speeds up, but my body doesn't move. One hour passes, then two, then three. I just keep staring at the door. Once the promised six hours have passed, only then do I stir. The TV screen comes down and the timestamp slows. I raise one arm and see it rise on the screen as well. The footage is cut and Felicia reappears.

"As you saw, you were in some sort of catatonic state until quite recently. Your first six hours in holding were identical,

I don't have to show you that footage as well, do I?" Felicia arches her eyebrow.

"No, no. I'll take your word for it. Please continue with your questions." I slump further into my chair.

"Thank you," Felicia says in a tone dangerously close to ironic. "So, after you were returned, the retrieval team secured and transported you to holding. And here we are now." Felicia leaves the folder on the table, clasps her hands and leans into the screen. "What I want to know is, what do you remember?" both of her index fingers extend to point at me. "Any information you can give us would be vital."

Vital? That must mean no other subjects are as responsive as I am, or at least as willing to cooperate. The blank faces of all the other returnees flash in my brain. No wonder she's willing to come interview me every six hours.

"What I remember is suddenly *being* again. I can't quite explain it. I remember the crash, a tumbling sensation, sharp things cutting my face and body, the horizon swirling then . . ." I pause as a chill runs down my spine ". . . darkness. Nothingness. Until I stepped onto solid ground again."

I cup my hands together and set them on the table. The gesture is meant to give me time to compose myself, but the memory of the cold darkness scratches at the back of my mind, and I realize I am pushing my fingernails into the skin of my palm. Oblivion isn't a pleasant thing to think about, especially when one has experienced it firsthand.

I take a deep breath and steady my thoughts. This memory triggers an emotional response, as so few things do now. I am glad for the feeling, even if it is a deep, bone-chilling fear. It is something.

"No one else who came from the structures was responsive,"

I recount. "I tried to talk to a few others, but they didn't acknowledge me at all. They all stood at the edge of the light cast from the obelisks, no one besides myself crossed over. Once I saw I was the only one displaying different characteristics, I stood in place and waited for someone to contain me."

She nods and says, "I see. Then can you tell me anything about how you were sent here, from where? Do you have any recollections before being returned?"

"I'm afraid not. I don't remember anything except a vague floating feeling, but that was only for a moment after I returned. Now it seems not like a memory, but rather a dream."

"Well then"—Felicia gathers up her folder and stands— "if that's all you remember, I'll see you in six hours."

"Wait." I shoot my hand toward the screen.

Felicia is gone.

I slump back into the chair and stare at the wall that was a video screen moments ago. The hatch on the door opens and yet another tray is pushed inside. I don't bother getting up this time.

Before I know it, the screen in the room is lowered back down and Felicia reappears. She asks all the same questions. From where was I returned? How was that managed? Did I remember anything? I always give the same answers. I don't know. That's not enough however, because the same questions follow each time, and each time I give the same answers.

The trays that slide inside the room start to pile up behind me. I do nothing at all besides sit and think about my condition. How am I even alive? I'm not eating, I'm not sleeping, I don't seem to have the need for any bodily functions. These thoughts are the only thing keeping me lucid, or what passes for lucid in my white, timeless prison cell.

The interviews continue, sometimes Felicia isn't available so another woman steps in to take her place. I don't bother remembering her name, but what strikes me about her is that she is exceptionally jumpy whenever we speak. I'm not sure why that is, but it can't be good.

The next scheduled interview confirms my suspicions as Felicia comes into view, but this time she isn't seated in the adjacent room. The décor has changed drastically from the stark white background I am accustomed to seeing.

"Hello, Daniel," Felicia seems somewhat unnerved. "As you can tell, I'm not currently present at your holding facility due to safety measures."

I simply nod but say nothing. If she has been transferred somewhere safer, that means my condition has deteriorated to the point it is no longer manageable enough to allow people in close proximity.

"What we have concluded from our interviews so far, is that you are indeed Daniel Vesta, a professor of neurology who died approximately six months and twenty-one days ago."

The time Felicia specifies should shock me, but it does not. There is nothing to say.

Felicia continues, "You have been in our protective custody for nine days, during which your body temperature has risen by nearly 100 degrees Fahrenheit. Currently, we are unable to determine what has caused this or if there is a way to reverse it."

Felicia looks displeased at sharing this information, or perhaps just with her team's inability to establish the cause of my condition.

"In light of that, I have been given permission to relay some classified information to you."

I nod again.

"We are hoping you can provide some insight into what's happening."

I simply shrug.

"Right then." Felicia purses her lips, making her look like a tuna fish, then continues, "what we've managed to establish so far regarding the subjects returned from the structures, which we've codenamed—revenant gates; is that they all seem to be absolute experts in their respective fields. Engineering, biochemistry, zero-gravity welding, astronomy, hazardous material mitigation, the list goes on. All of them follow a set pattern, they sleep for seven hours and thirty minutes, get up, eat, then sit in place, unless prompted into movement by someone else."

The picture on the screen changes to a man sitting in a barren, not much different than my own, room. A tray of food is brought by someone who helps the man get up and go to the table. The man begins to eat and when done, he is motionless again. The footage speeds up and more food is brought. The sequence is repeated once more, but this time the person who brings the food also helps the man to the toilet then to his bed. According to the timestamp on the bottom right of the screen, I have watched an entire day pass in this man's life.

The footage disappears and Felicia returns.

"We have discovered that bringing stimulus related to the revenant's previous occupation pulls them from their stupor, and they begin to work."

The screen changes again, this time to the image of a woman standing in front of a table covered in a vast array of electronic devices and parts. She gathers the devices and fidgets with them, using tools set beside her on another table, she disassembles something. When this is done, she begins to construct something new.

I hear Felicia's voice over the footage. "Additionally, we have discovered that by pairing some individuals, they begin to work toward a common goal. What that goal is and why they are doing it is precisely the question I would like to ask you, as you are the single responsive revenant we have. No one else talks about anything besides what materials they need, or to confer with their partners about the next steps toward their ultimate goal. And that is a direct quote from them—*ultimate goal*. That's what they call their projects. Some are harmless, as far as our scientists have established, like deep space object detection. The others are . . ."

Felicia obviously doesn't want to go on. She looks to the side for a moment then continues, "The most dangerous project we've encountered yet is—again, as far as we can tell—an orbital geo-synchronous device that seems to be capable of creating a pin-point heat burst beam which could, hypothetically, put holes in the Moon."

I open my mouth to speak, but for a moment I can't remember how. I let out an unintelligible noise, and cough into my hand before responding. "Thank you for sharing that information with me, but I simply don't know anything beyond what we've already discussed. I have no insight into what's happening, I was just dead and then . . . I wasn't. Those are my truthful and best recollections. I have nothing else to give you."

Felicia studies my face for a while. It doesn't seem to reveal anything to her so she exhales loudly. I watch her and wait for another barrage of questions.

"I see. Thank you, Professor Vesta." Her eyes sparkle for

a moment as her usual cold demeanor melts. "I am sorry to inform you that this will be our last face to face interview. From now on we only ask that you provide a blood sample each time you receive your meals. The sample is for, uh . . . future reference. Unfortunately, no one will be able to help you with that as your living quarters have become inhospitable to . . ."

"Humans," I finish for her.

The irony is able to force me out of my numbness for a moment, and I give her a sad, knowing smile. "It's quite alright, Miss Rousseau, I don't want to endanger anyone anyway. I'll provide all that you need."

She gives me a nod, and after a few moments of silence adds, "Farewell, Daniel."

The picture turns black, and the screen rises up into the ceiling for probably the last time.

That's that then, I am going to die soon. Or at least that's what they expect. Hell, I expect it too, but it doesn't seem to be coming for some reason. Right now, if I push my fingers into an object, it starts to sizzle and burn. I move my right index finger over the table, extend it down, and let it rest on the surface. A few seconds later the table begins to smoke. Moving my finger down, I write the letter D.

As I finish, I notice the inside of my sleeve is smoking. I rip off all my clothes and throw them in the corner. At least since the interviews are over, I won't have to talk to Felicia in the nude. The thought comes to me by pure reflex. Reflecting on it now, I don't care whether I am clothed or not, fed or not—alive . . . or not.

The slot behind me opens, and food is pushed inside along with a blood kit. I grab the kit and work fast, trying not to be in contact with the tools for too long. Moments after I am done taking my sample, the slot opens again and stays that way. I slide the sample out.

"Don't bother with the food," I say and push the meal that had come in out as well.

The slot clinks shut without a comment. I go over to my chair. The slot opens up behind me again, just moments after I sit down. Another blood demand. I comply and give the sample back again along with the food I specifically asked not to receive. This time I don't bother to sit, but pace instead. As soon as I have made two steps, the tray appears. I repeat the process again and again, every two steps yielding another request for blood. Soon all the world turns to blood and food, blood and food every six hours if the pattern has remained the same. After a few meal and blood kits of time have passed, I can no longer hold the instruments without them melting in my hands. Only trays of food continue to be pushed inside, marking the passage time.

Five or six repetitions later, I decide to sit. The chair beneath me begins to sizzle. Before I am able to stand, half the seat has melted away. The residual heat works its way down, and thick black smoke moves up into the room's invisible ventilation ducts. The four legs clatter to the ground. The loss of the chair moves me to the wall opposite the door where I lean my back and tilt my head up, watching the ceiling as days continue to pass around me like a calm stream of water.

Suddenly, I feel it is time. I don't know how I know, or what the time has come for, but it has arrived. Death perhaps, or whatever state follows my current one. The darkness I experienced before? Nothingness? It doesn't matter, or at least it doesn't matter to me.

"I want . . ." my voice sounds so foreign to me. "I want to see my family. I need to see them just for a moment, please."

I walk over to the door, as far as I can get from the screen, which is down a blink later. The screen says "Standby" and I do.

From black comes color. A living room. A woman is setting the table as a boy and girl run around her. The woman says something to the children, and they both take their seats. Finally done, she herself sits down. The small boy pesters his sister while they eat. I watch as my family enjoys their meal. They seem happy. I search inside myself, trying to find something, trying to feel something, but there is nothing. All I can focus on is how their appearance has changed, the position of the room's appliances, and the fade on the wallpaper. I see everything, analyze everything, but feel no empathy. I see only a woman caring for her children.

A crack appears in the picture, rapidly spreading to the ends of the screen. The woman and children disappear, my humanity seeping through the jagged lines on the glass. Then the darkness on the screen jumps out of its confines, it begins to crawl along the walls of the room until it envelops everything and I am left in a void. Again.

A breath later, brilliant colors emerge. They come close and grip me as if in a giant hand, trying to pull me up to somewhere else. The colors permeate into my mind, pulling me by the atoms.

Then, unspeakable pain.

I have never even considered there could be such depths of agony. My mouth opens, and I scream, my voice coming out as color. This new color, my color, spreads forward, pushing the others back. And, to my surprise, they relent instantly, apologetically. The goal of the invading colors changes and instead of grasping me, they drift to my head, flowing directly into my mind until they are gone.

I am forced to close my eyes at the endless amount of information now being forced inside my brain. Once I am able to open them again, the world has returned, but different somehow. Or rather, I am different, because I know. I know what is happening and what I need to do.

I walk over to my bed and place my hand on the wall. After closing my eyes and straining to concentrate, I make it happen. The metal wall is gone, only the concrete keeping the dirt at bay remains. After a nod to myself, I head for the door.

"I need to leave. Open the door. Whoever is listening, order the people guarding me to stand down. I have something important to do and do not wish to hurt anyone."

The door to my cell doesn't open. Placing my hand upon it, I don't even need to concentrate this time to vaporize it.

I take a single step yet find myself outside the entrance to the compound. Fifty armed soldiers are waiting in a half-circle around me. I move forward, and they open fire. Hundreds of bullets hit my skin, but none of them make it through. As soon as they touch me they disintegrate. I withstand the barrage of lead. When all firing ceases, I try to take a step forward but realize that that single motion would mean the deaths of all these people. My presence would disrupt their atomic structure, turning them into free-roaming cosmic winds. I turn around.

I have a very clear destination. I don't know where it is but I know how to get there. Colors move around me; my mind understands what they mean, but my optical organs can't make sense of the information. Then, in what feels like only moments later, I arrive.

The black obelisk, the revenant gate I was returned from, stands but a few feet away. Men with guns shout something behind me then open fire. Their bullets are powerless as well, they don't bother me while I watch the amazing shimmer of light in front of me. I'm delighted by its sparkling array in all shades of gold. Finally, I raise my hand and reach for my halcyon gate.

"Daniel, stop!"

Felicia. She isn't here of course, but her voice is.

"If a revenant crosses the gate's threshold, they cannot come back. Whatever appendage is plunged into the light cannot be returned here. If you put your arm inside it, it will be gone!"

I smile at the irony and step into the light.

Everything changes inside. My mind, my body—all remade so that I can survive in this space. I understand this.

Looking down at myself, or as is the case, becoming aware of myself, I discover I am no longer made of flesh. I no longer see as I had before. For if I had regular human eyes here, I'd be able to see nothing.

Human eyes.

Clearly, I am no longer human. The question now is, what am I?

"You are changed," something close to me says. It doesn't really speak as humans understand it, but it communicates with me all the same.

"No longer human, but not quite us either," says another being that exists close to the first.

Close, in this case, is not the correct term. I find it hard to judge distances as everything seems to be just floating energy—like I am inside a half-done oil painting. There is no perspective, only an awareness of whatever is around. The speaking shapes, however, are easy to distinguish. They are so powerful that all other energy drifts toward and around them. I understand this as well. I myself am a being much like them, but on a scale of gods and men, I occupy a small space only a fraction above men.

"Soon enough you will understand what your purpose is and why you are here," the first being speaks again. It is light blue; beautiful red shades of energy drift behind it almost like a cloak.

Both figures transmit themselves closer to me, and I feel my form grow and strengthen. I am now fully conscious of my surroundings. I understand how they work but still lack the mental capacity to behold them in their entirety.

"You are rebuilt," the second being says, purple in color, a golden green halo adorning its upper half.

"Now that you are capable, we will give you the information you'll need when you go back," the cloaked being says.

"Go back?" I ask. "But why?"

"You were chosen out of all the remade as the single person capable of surviving the transformation to the form you are inhabiting now," the crowned being says. "The work you poured your soul into, the concepts you were developing. How close you came to unlocking the power of your human mind made you the only viable candidate."

The cloaked figure drifts closer. "However, the change will not hold if you return through the gateway again. We can imbue you with enough power to last a few moments, otherwise, you will destroy your planet and the system it resides in."

Immediately after these words, I feel power surge through

me.

"Once you have imparted the necessary information to the human race, we will make sure your new form is returned to us." The crowned figure draws closer as well.

"Your consciousness will be fragmented after this journey, you must be aware of this and choose to step back of your own volition," the cloaked figure says and imbues me with more power.

"You will not die as humans die; you will simply slumber with us, as we guard and nurture you back to cognition." The crowned figure then embraces me.

The tenderness of the gesture sparks memories of my mother hugging me when I was small. I'm at peace.

"He is ready," the cloaked figure announces.

Information streams into me. Like the last time, colors penetrate my mind. And with them, knowledge spreads through the blank canvas that is my consciousness.

Trajectories, dates, cosmic speeds, possible counter-measures, and everything else I need to impart to the rest of humanity. The information is so overwhelming that I fall to my knees, or the equivalent of that, which in this space is akin to fading into surrounding colors. Once the transfer is complete, I compose myself, concentrating my being into a single form out of the colorful storm of energies around me.

"You are complete," the crowned figure says, and I feel it draw back.

"The decision to go back is yours and yours alone," the cloaked figure says, pointing at me.

"You are the only bridge between us and the humans, you are the only one capable of returning and giving them the information they need," the crowned figure continues.

"Decide!" both figures boom in unison.

I gaze at them for a moment, then turn around and move to the riven in space that led me here.

"Why are you helping? Why even bother?" I ask before the exit.

"If your family were in danger though very, very far away, would you still not help them?" the crowned figure replies.

I like that answer. It makes my will resolute. I will save my family and all the others I can. Readying myself for my doom, I slip through the shining laceration in space.

I am flesh again. It feels small, constraining. My mind is so slow it's laughable. Looking down at my hands I see the skin and tissue slowly fade away into pure light. My true form is breaking through the previous one. My fingers are light that bleeds fine gold dust which is eagerly sucked into the shimmering gate behind me. Looking up, I see people coming. Once they are in hearing range, I extend my arm and a part of me drifts up and into a device a man wears on his vest. As more people come, I give more of myself to them. The information I'd received is being transmitted to any device capable of storage. It just might be enough, I calculate as my lower body disperses.

"Look toward Orion," I say, though the words come hard to me. Language is unnecessary and simple. "Falling fire in five years. Gather the remade we've sent back, for they need to build a shield of light to protect the planet. We have given them the knowledge."

After I utter those words, a mist of color explodes as my torso and upper arms stream into more devices, becoming a hope for the future.

The transference is only seen by me, and the added strain

drains my body even faster. I am just a glimmer now. The gate behind me beckons, like a warm blanket on a rainy night. My face is the last thing remaining in the corporeal world.

"Light will save you," I manage to say just as my mouth becomes radiance.

Energy returns to energy. The last of the light that had been Daniel Vesta merges with the revenant gate and it too disappears, leaving only a hollowed-out rectangle at the base of a black edifice.

The Zero

GEORGE SANDIFER-SMITH

I

Landing could be tricky, I thought, watching the frozen blast of a geyser break the atmosphere. We sat just above the moon, and if planetfall was off, we'd be pelted back into space with half the walls missing. I looked at the instruments, assessing an algorithm simulating the geyser blasts.

"How's it looking?" asked Poul, turning in his chair.

"Still calculating," I said. In an ideal universe, we'd park the ship here and teleport down to the surface. A lot of people don't like teleports. But I've always maintained that the self is more than the physical body, so the idea that the you who turns up in the next place is completely new doesn't worry me.

But getting down to Enceladus with the current breed of teleporter would be too difficult. The geysers were doing funny things to the atmosphere; the teleporter's safety settings might panic and try to return you to the ship. And if the ship had moved even a fraction, you could find yourself scattered into the stars like dust on the wind.

"They should have spent more time maintaining those terraforming units," I said. The calculations were still incomplete.

"It wasn't time they ran out of," said Poul, "it was money. Plenty of time, no money."

"That and the war," said Nia, entering the bridge. "Abi, how are we doing?"

All of our screens were compatible. She could have looked it up on her own device, but Nia—as the youngest—liked to keep the humany stuff going. "Shouldn't be long now. Probably best to strap yourself in. Is Carlos joining us?"

"Hang on." Nia pushed the button on the nearest comms unit. "Carlos, Abi's saying we'll probably be starting our descent soon. Will you be joining us on the bridge or clinging on for dear life down there?"

Carlos's voice had the echo of the stores as it filtered back through. "Clinging, of course," he said. "I'm not anticipating too much of a bumpy landing."

"Carlos, you're not a member of the corps," I said.

Nia stifled a giggle.

"So?" said Carlos's disembodied voice.

"So you let us judge whether or not it'll be a bumpy landing," called Poul from the front.

"Fine," said Carlos, sounding annoyed. "Will it be a difficult one?"

"The algorithm—which, by the way, *you* re-designed—is taking a while to tell us," I said, "so it's more of a yes than a no at this juncture."

"I'll belt up in my cabin then." The comms unit gave an abrupt click to indicate Carlos had ended the conversation.

"You know, I never like only having three of the four crew actually on the bridge," said Nia. "It feels like bad luck."

"I make myself feel better about it by reminding myself Carlos isn't crew," said Poul. "Not that he would have made it.

Far too insubordinate." As our commanding officer, Poul had only the smallest fixation on the chain of command. It didn't come up much, but when it did, you could tell.

"I wish we hadn't had to invite him," I said. "Sorry, is that awful to say? Just, you know, if we were going to invite civilians along, I'd rather have brought my wife."

Poul chuckled. "I'd rather have brought mine too. Carlos may not be in the corps, but they're paying him a ton to be here."

"On a rescue mission?" asked Nia.

"Got to wonder why we've been sent to pick up these nuns now?" I said. "Come on. They've been trapped down there for years."

"I assumed it was the Ice Pirates they were tracking. Like the report says, they were last seen here." She looked at me sternly.

"But why wait a year?" I said. "The Ice Pirates probably crashed. Or the nuns took care of them."

Nia laughed, letting me know she wasn't entirely annoyed with me. "Nuns, really! Fighting off a bunch of Ice Pirates!"

"Hey, some of our highest-ranking officers became nuns," said Poul. "Mind you, you'd have to find a pretty old nun now that hadn't been bred into it."

"I always thought that was weird," I said, "being bred into it. Raised that way. Takes away the spiritual element of it. Surely faith is a matter of choice?"

"Depends on the faith," said Nia.

The comms unit bleeped. "Are we going to land anytime soon? Only, I've been strapped into this bunk for a while now, and I'd like to get on with my work."

"Sorry, Carlos," I said, "we got a little distracted up here.

Crisis of faith."

He laughed, like shifting leaves. It wasn't a warm laugh. "Nuns, eh? Let's just get down there and herd any of them still breathing onto the ship. Then I can crack on." The unit clicked off again.

"Any of them still breathing?" Nia cringed. "Charming."

"I bet he tells people he's got no sense of compassion because he's a scientist," I said.

"My wife's a scientist," said Poul, "and she's the most compassionate person I know. What Carlos is . . . is, well—"

"Sorry to cut you off, Poul, though I'm sure you were about to say something very professional." I smirked. "The readouts have come through. Ready when you are to begin countdown to planetfall."

The ship's legs deployed with plenty of time, and the system put us down in a ravine. The oxygen was lower than the most recent survey said it would be, but then, the last survey of Enceladus had been taken years ago. I'd always assumed that when the terraforming gear had been deployed, the ecosystem was altered for good—that the human way had scarred the planet forever, Earth-izing it. But Enceladus, in a remarkably short span of time, had made leaps and bounds on its way back to being only pseudo-habitable.

I watched the computer interface on the screen of my helmet. The full suit probably wasn't necessary, but I preferred the comfort of breathing in the oxygen we'd brought to the thin air outside.

"Beautiful, isn't it?" said Nia.

I turned to look at her. "You should put your helmet on."

"Oh, come on," she shot me a playful smile. "Space exploration. Pushing the boundaries of human endeavor.

Final frontier. We're all so blasé about it now. Standing on alien sands lightyears from Earth, watching strange birds wheel in the sky. I love all that."

"No birds here. The readout says they're all long gone." I frowned. "And, Nia, I thought you said you were from Io. Have you even been to Earth?"

"I've always meant to," she said, sheepishly. "Just, you know . . . finding the time and the money."

"Earth? Don't talk to me about Earth." Carlos pushed past me.

"Not a fan of the cradle of civilization, then, Carlos?" I moved to catch up with him. He strode with purpose, which worried me for reasons I couldn't put my finger on.

He swung round to look at me. "If Earth were so great, our species would have stuck around there." He shrugged. "Instead, we spread our seed throughout the Solar System. Beyond, now. Humanity couldn't wait to cast off the dirt of its birth and go ruin someone else's planet. Soon Io will be a heap, and they will have to abandon it too."

"Carlos, where's Poul?" Nia didn't bother masking the ice in her voice. I'd met plenty of cynical, brain-centric jerk-offs like Carlos in my time, but Nia was younger, and he found it very easy to irritate her.

"Final landing checks," he said, rolling his eyes. "Your boss is such a stickler."

"Our *captain*," I corrected him. "Ours. Yours too. Yours as long as the corps is paying you."

"Oh, of course. My paycheck. Yes. That's why I have to salute you all and tell you what heroes you are." Carlos looked to me and his tone weakened like he knew he'd gone too far. "Hey, how close is this complex?"

I welcomed the change in subject. "The nunnery is just over the ridge."

Carlos laughed and shook his head. "Man. Space nuns."

"They're just nuns," I scoffed. "We've been colonizing for centuries, let's not keep making a novelty of normal things by adding the prefix of 'space.'"

Nia came up from behind and patted my shoulder. "See, I'd like a little more of that."

"Shouldn't you have your helmet on?" asked Carlos.

"I'm breathing in the air of a strange world. Only people to have touched down here in years were those Ice Pirates. The moon has reclaimed the atmosphere. Come on, Carlos. You of all people can appreciate the beauty of this." Nia took a slow, deep breath. "Low oxygen, but it tastes like . . . snow. That's a holiday smell. But with something else. Something we don't get on the colonies."

"That'll be the microbes in the air that your body isn't adapted to." Carlos tapped the side of his helmet. "Put. On. Your. Helmet."

"Nia, he's right." Poul joined us. "I'm as much of a swashbuckling space adventurer as the next man—"

I chuckled. Poul was definitely no swashbuckler.

"Something funny, Abi?" he asked, raising an eyebrow.

"No, Poul, I'm sure you're right. I'm not getting anything on these readings to indicate that the atmosphere might contain anything harmful, but it's been a long time since the last survey."

"Exactly," rejoined Carlos. "The quality of those stats doesn't fill me with confidence. We're here to do our jobs, not die from some Enceladun disease."

"Our jobs?" I said. "Hold on. The report states that this is a simple rescue op."

"It didn't say simple," said Nia, whose helmet was sealing around her head and already carrying out its own med-check.

I rolled my eyes in her direction. "But Carlos, you said 'jobs,' like we have other reasons to be here."

"*You* don't have other reasons to be here," he said, "though I'd appreciate you keeping me safe while you're at it."

I nodded. "Ice Pirates."

"If you like." He shrugged. "I mean, I'm doing a little surveying on behalf of your corps. The environment might get hostile."

"Is this true?" I turned to my superior officer. I trusted Poul—it was weird that he'd left out this part of the mission. Weirder still that it hadn't even been in the report.

"I was given some very vague instructions regarding Carlos's presence here with us," said Poul. "Can't say I like vague instructions, particularly with recent developments in the war. But vague instructions are still instructions, and we need to follow them as much as we can. Carlos, we'll keep you safe . . . you're one of us.'

"Until I step out of line," muttered Carlos, turning to the ridge. "So, we heading over to that nunnery or what?"

"Well, no time like the present," said Nia. "Especially now I'm all suited up. Poul?"

"Okay," Poul kept his eyes on Carlos, who'd already started his march up the ridge. I noticed his hand hovering above the holster on his suit. "Let's go rescue those nuns."

II

The complex, or the nunnery of the Order of the Drowned Saint Govan, was a mix of classic Earth-style architecture with more modern colonial features. The central building, presumably including the living quarters and facilities for visitors, was a fortress, a reassuring rectangle set in the frozen dust. At one end, a tubular passage fed out to a small chapel, rendered in something that looked like stone with metal tubes feeding through its walls. At the other end, a similar tubular passage led to a transparent dome, where—with a little enhancement from my suit's display—I could see the shadowy outline of some sort of vegetation. "They've kept growing things."

"Not necessarily," said Carlos. "The trees at these level nines are augmented. They're self-maintaining, to a degree. One less thing for the residents to worry about, especially when it comes to oxygen levels."

"Do you think they're still growing anything else?" asked Nia.

"It's possible," I said. "If the water recycling units are still operational, and the trees are still alive and producing oxygen."

"Carlos." Poul hovered over the scientist, kneeling in the dust and inserting a probe into the ground. "What are you up to?"

"Just taking a reading here," he said. "We can collect it on the way back."

"Is that all you needed to do for your survey?" I asked. "We could have done that. You needn't have risked life and limb coming out here with us."

"The corps needn't have given you that big paycheck neither," Nia sneered. "You must have made one hell of a pitch."

Carlos smiled, and though it might have just been the half-light of the atmosphere or a reflection in his helmet, looked a little sad. It was the first time I'd seen him looking anything less than quietly angry. "Your corps gave me the pitch," he said.

"Well, you should have told them you didn't need to be here."

"It's not . . ." He exhaled and, for some reason, looked over his shoulder. "Never mind. There's a lot to do here; it's more than the probe. I have to make . . . observations."

"Look," said Poul, using his captain voice to address us. "Abi, Nia. The corps never do anything without a good reason. I'm sure Carlos knows what he's doing, though we could all do with him being a little less obtuse about it."

Carlos returned to looking annoyed, but not before glancing over his shoulder a second time. "Yes," he said, "I know what I'm doing. The corps wouldn't do anything without the right reasons. All hail the corps."

Carlos marched toward the complex before Poul could question him on his insubordination.

"He's got a lot of issues with the corps," said Nia.

I nodded. "You'd think he wouldn't want to work for them, big paycheck or otherwise."

There was a low rumble in the distance. Even through the temperature-controlled suit, I felt a cold gale blow in from the east. "Don't worry," said Poul, "just a geyser. The ship landed us far enough away from any so we wouldn't be at risk."

"You know, even back in the twenty-first century, they could see those geysers with cameras. From Earth." Nia was back on her space adventurer kick.

"The cameras weren't on Earth, Nia," I said. "They sent them out into space. Big probes with telescopes."

"Well, the geyser blasts were still visible from above the surface. That's why they colonized this place second, after Mars. Because of the water."

"Doesn't matter. It's not much of anything to anyone now." Poul said.

"Except the Order of the Drowned Saint Govan, and their miraculous healing springs" I smirked.

Poul shook his head. "Not a miracle. Just another thing for science to crack, given enough time."

The comms unit in our suits crackled. "Hello?" said Carlos. "I'm knocking on the front door. Hurry up and get here."

The 'front door,' the airlock on the side of the complex nearest to us, required a bit of fiddling with. I tried some of the old codes used by the corps, with no luck. "Nia, you're up."

She stepped past me and took a flimsy card out of a pocket on the leg of her suit.

I craned my head over her shoulder. "What is that?"

"Memory wafer from an antique store," she said, "I've adapted it to unlock unwilling doors from its own time period. Might be a bit early for this, but I imagine the nuns would have wanted some sort of compatibility slot just in case any of the old Brothers were visiting for a quick—aha!"

As soon as she inserted the wafer, the door started creaking open. Having the airlock wasn't entirely necessary, as the atmosphere was breathable in spite of its harshness, but it helped to de-pressurize before going in. Carlos was the first to take his helmet off once we were inside.

"Not so worried about the microbes in here, eh?" Nia

removed her helmet too.

"It should be fairly safe." He looked over at the captain. "Right, Poul?"

"Absolutely." The captain walked past him. "Well, I mean, affirmative. Should never speak in absolutes."

"There's something we can agree on," said Carlos. "I have to head to the greenhouse—"

"Hang on." Poul stepped up to block his path. "Rescue first, survey later. The nuns might be a bit jumpy, and potentially armed."

"The last thing we want is to be split up," I said. 'We reassure them first. Find out how many of them are still with us." I looked nervously at Carlos, thinking of what he'd said earlier. How many of them are still breathing?

"Honestly, I think I'll be okay," said Carlos, "I've just got to get to the greenhouse, then I'll be ready—"

"No." Poul's face hardened. "We stick together. You aren't a member of the corps, Carlos. So you're under the protection of me, Abi, and Nia. Whether you like it or not."

Carlos shrugged. "Whatever. Just as long as we don't leave without seeing that greenhouse. There's something down there the corps was particularly keen for me to survey."

"What, there's a new kind of cabbage the nuns have bred that'll feed the outer colonies?" said Nia.

Carlos snorted. "Please. My father came from the outer colonies. Like the corps cares about those planets. They're busy spending too much on this war."

"And you're happy to take their pay, even if you feel like that about them?" Nia laughed but stopped quickly when Carlos got in her face.

"Don't you dare laugh," he snarled.

There it was. That's what it took. I heard the safety click off on Poul's blaster. "Take a step back from her, Carlos." He was very calm. I realized that I'd wrapped my gloved fingers around a wrench I had attached to my suit.

Carlos looked at Poul, then me. Then Nia, who, in spite of the slight tremble of her lip, said, "Yeah. I can see right up your nose."

Carlos laughed. "Sorry. Guess we're all a bit tense. And why do I take pay from the corps?" He took the step back he'd been ordered to. "I have a husband and two beautiful daughters." He laughed again, but it sounded different. Nervous.

Poul's expression hadn't changed at all. Nor had he moved his finger off the trigger. "If you do something like that again, I might be forced to assume you've lost it," he said with a calm voice that reminded me of why he'd made it as a captain. "It's a barren outpost. Does things to the mind. Breaks you in such a way that I might be forced to take drastic measures to stop you hurting anyone else."

Carlos raised an eyebrow. "Do they teach you lines like that in officer training? I mean, is there a set of stock phrases that all begin with 'I might be forced to'?"

"Okay." I held a palm up in each man's direction. "I think we should stop this testosto-thon right here. Poul's in charge. Carlos, we'll do whatever we came here to do and get you back to your husband and daughters. Home in time for tea. Sound good?"

"Fine," said Carlos. "Come on. Central quarters." He tapped a sign on the wall indicating the left-hand corridor. "I mean, if that's where you think it might be best to start. Poul?"

Poul nodded. "At your own pace, Carlos. This is a rescue mission, not a military offensive."

Carlos set off first down the corridor, the halls motion sensors lighting up the path as we went. Nia pursed her lips and raised her brows before following close behind. I caught up to her. "Hey. You okay?"

"Fine," she said.

"Want to talk about it?"

"No." She looked down at her handset, at readings I knew were not very interesting at all. I let her take the lead by a few paces.

"Abi," called Poul, who had taken up the rear. "Thanks."

"No need," I said. "We know what Carlos is like from the trip over. I'm not sure your posturing is going to scare him."

"He just grinds my gears," he said. "I don't like having him here. He's not one of us."

"Command didn't give you any more info on him?" I asked. "None at all?"

"Well . . . " Poul glanced to the two ahead of us and slowed his pace to create a little more distance.

"What?" I slowed with him. "What is it? Come on, I'll keep it confidential."

"Okay," said Poul, "but this is for your ears only. Don't go telling Nia. Or anyone else in the corps."

"Promise."

"Carlos turned down this survey three times in the last year," he continued, "and—if my timings are right—we only got assigned the mission because he finally became available."

"So you think the survey is the primary mission? Not the rescue?"

He nodded. "Here's the thing: Carlos didn't clear his schedule. I think, from how he's been acting, he wouldn't have wanted to work for the corps. He's been outspoken about the war for years. No. The corps apparently seized some of his assets. That's why he's here."

"His assets?" I stared in disbelief. "Poul, this would have been really useful information a few days ago when we all first met him."

"I was waiting for him to bring it up, you know what he's like. But he hasn't. Maybe he thinks the corps are listening."

"They wouldn't do that . . . would they?" I thought about the corps-issued suits, the ship, and the communication technology advanced enough to reach across star systems. It wouldn't be beyond the abilities of the corps to eavesdrop on us. "Even if they did, it's not like it would matter. So Carlos loses some of his privileges, a research grant or two. He'd get back on his feet. I don't think he'd care."

"See, this is the thing—"

The sound of Nia's scream filled the corridor, bending around an upcoming corner.

"Nia!" I yelled, running ahead. "Nia! Are you okay? What's happening?" I could hear Carlos swearing, and I wondered— really wondered—how desperate he was. What working for an organization you blamed for all the atrocities of war might do . . .

"It's all right, Nia." Carlos had his arm around her. They were both crouching down. No. Carlos was holding her. Beyond them, I could see a pile of black cloths bundled on the ground. "Nia, come on. We're okay. Hey, who's the soldier, and who's the scientist who stays at home most days?"

"Thanks, Carlos," I said and meant it. I took his place and knelt by her side. "Nia. What is it?"

"Turn it over," she whispered.

"What, this?" I pointed to the bundle. She nodded. I

reached out to it, and even through my gloves, I felt my fingers beginning to chill. With a graceless shove, I flipped the bundle onto its side. It had been a short nun, middle-aged. Her face was totally white, her skin shimmering with ice crystals. Her open eyes were cracked, specks of blood-dust scattered on her cheeks.

"I was . . . it caught me by surprise." Nia stood and wiped her face. "See, I'm fine."

"I expected casualties," said Poul, who'd been keeping his distance. "Ice Pirates."

"She's freezing," said Carlos, his hand hovering above the corpse.

"Well, she's hardly likely to have that warm, healthy glow now, is she?" I said.

"That's not what I meant. The rest of the facility"—Carlos waved his arms around—"how does it feel to you? Temperature-wise?"

"Room temperature." Nia winced. "Average. Tepid. You know what I mean."

"So, she shouldn't be frozen like this," Carlos concluded. "It's not possible."

"Ice Pirates." repeated Poul.

"Were last spotted about a year ago," said Carlos. "I know, I read the report. But for her to still be this well-preserved, she'd have to have been killed recently. Or . . ." He scratched his head. "Nope. I'm stumped."

He didn't look stumped. He looked worried.

"So's she," said Nia, who had now fully composed herself and was moving the corpse's limbs around with a wrench.

"What do you mean?" Poul finally moved in close to join the rest of us.

"She's got no hands." Nia lifted the frozen left arm with the wrench and laughed nervously. "See? Stumped."

"Not appropriate." I nudged the back of Nia's shoulder. "Look, let's save ourselves the trouble of scaring any survivors. Nia, I know it's a pain, but can you patch our suits into the internal comms system? I don't want us to keep wandering into things like this." I looked at Poul. "I mean, sorry, I assume that's okay?"

"Just do it," muttered Poul, who was still staring at the corpse. "I've flown more dangerous missions than this. I could just do without the nonsense."

Carlos sighed. "Right. Now Poul's let us know he's still the manliest man on Enceladus, let's patch into that comms system."

Poul scowled but let the comment slide.

"Easier said than done," said Nia. "I'll need a bit of time."

The captain nodded. "You've got two hours."

III

We set up camp in the library. Entry to the door required a hand-scan—or one of Nia's augmented memory wafers, at least—so I thought that might explain why the dead nun in the corridor outside was missing hers. Nia used the library cataloging system as a 'back door' into the internal comms, though it took even longer because of the antiquated technology. "Look at the old comms boxes in the corner of each room," she said. "That is some retro space-age stuff right there."

"I always thought it was a very clunky aesthetic," I agreed, watching her work. "Like big puffy space suits."

"Is it going to be much longer?" Poul sat in the corner reading a hard copy of the Book of Govan, the nuns' holy text.

"It'll be as long as it is," said Nia. "The old comms boxes here only recognize the nuns. I'm having to break into the system so it'll recognize us too, then we'll be able to transmit from one of the boxes . . . in theory."

"This mission is certainly not shaping up to be the one we had in mind," I sighed and left Nia to her fiddling. "Just to let you know, Carlos," I shouted over the library stacks where he'd disappeared, sulking—back to normal, "this is not regular business for the corps!"

"Horror, death, lack of planning or coherence, seems normal to me!" he yelled back.

"I hate to break up an ethical debate about just wars before it really gets going," said Nia, "but I think I've got this working. Poul, would you like to do the honors?"

Poul stood and walked over to the comms box in the corner, passing me the Book of Govan on the way. "Attention," he said, stooping to level the external mic on his suit to the box's microphone. "Attention, attention."

"What a reassuring word," said Carlos, returning from his perch in the stacks.

"This is Poul Collins, captain of the Republic's corps," he said, "I'm sure you'll remember in the last transmissions—"

Poul turned red and swallowed hard. "I mean . . . well, we are the rescue team. If those among you to . . . that is to say, you are still . . . Would the remaining residents of the complex please make their way to the library, where we have stationed ourselves. We will be here for the next hour, then for the hour after that we will be carrying out valuable environmental survey work." He looked over at Carlos. "Thank you for, uh, your attention." Poul turned off the mic.

"So . . . you guys don't do a lot of rescue missions, huh?' said Carlos.

"Not a lot of call for them," said Poul, quickly and angrily. "Special case, this. Sorry if I didn't have time for the sort of PR training that your university doles out to its employees."

Carlos laughed. "Do I look like a guy who's had any PR training? Hey, I know you told those nuns that we'd wait an hour before carrying out the survey, but I think I'm going to head to the greenhouse to get that reading. It'll only take a second—"

"No!" Poul had his blaster out again. "I told you, no. We stick together."

"Poul." I took up mantle between them again. "Take it easy. I'm sure Carlos was only saying that to—"

"They really didn't tell you," Carlos scoffed. "They really didn't tell you what it is I'm here for?" He looked over his shoulder again.

"*You* tell us," said Nia.

"Nia." Poul didn't take his eyes from Carlos. "Don't encourage him. I'm sure whatever was classified was—"

"No." Nia came to join me. "I understand that instructions are instructions, but Carlos was barely phased by that corpse out there. I know he seems cold, but he's not that cold. He's so insistent about the greenhouse too, when there are plenty of other places to set up probes for the survey. So what is it, Carlos? Tell us now."

"Carlos?" I asked, turning to him. "It's okay. Nobody's

listening in."

He hesitated, shaking his head. "Look . . . I've got a husband. My kids. If there's even the slightest risk—"

"We have to know." I lowered my voice in an effort to calm the room. "This team is on the verge of falling apart, right now. Tell us, so that we can at least understand each other a little better."

"Fine." Carlos seemed to deflate. "But first, I want Poul to reassure me that he at least thinks we aren't being listened to."

Poul nodded, though reluctantly. "Even if the corps did bug our suits, the signal here would be too weak. The atmosphere does something to it. That's why the nuns found it so difficult to transmit messages before . . . well, whatever happened."

"Alright." Carlos sat down. "So. The *assets* the corps seized—and yes, I heard you—weren't anything to do with my research. It was my family. My husband, my daughters. My mother, too, even though she's so old and gaga she wouldn't recognize me on my birthday. I am getting paid, but it's shut-up money, and I'd turn it down if I could. To be honest, I'm contemplating taking it to move to one of the outer colonies when this is over. If we survive."

"We will," said Poul, with honest enthusiasm.

"The corps contacted me last year to tell me that they'd picked up on a transmission. Some nun, Sister Cornish, had managed to bounce a message off several satellites to get it to them. It contained data of interest to them regarding a project they'd abandoned a very long time ago. An energy signature that had particularly spiked in the greenhouse here. They'd called it the Zero, based on the previous research they'd had when there was a scientific residency here."

"Wait, there was a scientific residency here?" Poul

interrupted.

Carlos nodded. "They were the ones who discovered the healing effects of the springs. Of course, word got out, nuns got involved, gods ended up moving in, et cetera. Hard to keep the mystic powers of cellular regeneration a secret, right?"

"The springs didn't always work though, did they?" I said. "I mean, especially after a while. That's why the place was abandoned. They used up all the magic."

"That's not a very scientific term," said Carlos, smirking.

"You know what I mean."

Poul tapped the comms box. "Do you think the nuns would try to call us back on this thing?"

"To be honest"—Nia looked apologetic—"I'm just hoping the other boxes in the complex work. Just because I was able to get ours transmitting, doesn't mean all the other ones are receiving."

"Right," said Carlos, marching towards the door, "that settles it. We can't stay in here all day."

I watched Poul hesitantly glance at his blaster.

"What do you say, Captain?"

"I say Nia should have told us her doubts about the comms system here before we settled into this room." He sighed.

"I'm sorry," said Nia, "but you did insist. And, for the record, I made it very clear that I wasn't sure I'd even be able to get into the system."

Carlos stopped fiddling with the library door. "Well, let's all go to the greenhouse. We stick together, remember? Just send out a last transmission saying that's where we're going. I'm starting to doubt there are any survivors anyway."

Poul nodded. "Since you know so much about this place, I'll allow it. Let's move out." He joined Carlos by the door.

"Nia, would you open this up?"

She bit her lip. "Are we absolutely sure this is the best course of action?"

"Look." I laid a reassuring hand on her arm. "Why don't you stay here? Keep the transmissions going. You can still speak to us on our suit comms. Or the complex's comms boxes. If we come across anything else worrying, we'll let you know."

"Sure," she said, though she didn't sound like she was. "I'll hang back here. I might even be able to monitor the system from inside and let you know if anything unusual comes your way."

"Excellent." I joined Carlos and Poul at the door we'd come in through. "It's settled then. That work for you, Poul?"

"Whatever." Poul took his weapon in hand. "Let's set off."

IV

It was dark when we passed through the door. Except, this time, the lights didn't switch on as we progressed down the corridor.

"Darkness," said Carlos. "Why do you reckon that is?"

"Could be on a daily power save," I guessed. "Or certain sections had limited power, and we just happened to drain the last of it walking this way earlier."

"Now, wouldn't that be a coincidence?" said Poul.

"Stranger things have happened," said Carlos. "You'd be amazed how improbable the universe is sometimes."

"I don't like the improbable." Poul tightened his grip on the blaster. "Not at all. Which direction are we heading in for the greenhouse?"

"You're not going to like it," I said, looking at the display on my handheld unit.

"Past the sleeping nun?" said Carlos.

"Bingo." I took a step forward, cautious in the dark. "I'm sure I don't need to tell you, but watch your step. There might be more bodies on the floor."

We reached the nun with no hands, just about visible in the light filtering in through the windows. I crept around the side of her, my back against the wall. "Poul, you don't want to lead the way?"

"We're more likely to be attacked from the rear," came Poul's disembodied voice. "If those Ice Pirates are still around, I mean."

"They never left Enceladus," said Carlos. "But then, I don't suppose that means they're still around, either."

"Death by nun." I chuckled but kept my eye on the bundle on the floor. Something about it felt wrong. There was a crackling sound in the darkness.

"*Abi.*" My name creeped out of the shadows coated in distortion. I felt the nun curl something around my foot, and I fell screaming.

"*Abi.*"

"Get off me!" I yelled. "Get off me! Poul, damn it, blaster!"

He didn't need telling. The corridor lit up as the bolts sizzled and seared against the frozen flesh. A horrible smell of fresh death filled the air, like roasted meat and copper.

"Hey!" said Carlos, sounding far away. "It's okay! Abi, it's okay!"

I shuffled away from the corpse. "Are you kidding?"

"No. Shhh. Listen."

There it was again. "*Abi. Abi.*" The comms in my suit. It was

Nia. I could just about recognize her voice now that I'd calmed down. "*Abi, are you—?*" The sound was frazzled, garbled.

"She caught her leg on the robe."

I could barely make out Carlos in the dark, patting the outer rim of the corpse. I heard Poul exhaling loudly.

"Jesus, Nia," I said. There was a muffled response. "Nia, your suit comms have gone really patchy."

"*Ha . . . ng . . . on.*"

"You all right, Abi?" Poul had made his way around the corpse. I felt his hand on my shoulder and took it, letting him help me up. "Not a word, Carlos."

"I'm saying nothing."

"*Is that better?*" Nia's voice was clearer now, but it was coming from somewhere down the corridor as if she'd thrown it.

"Better, but not coming out of my suit," I said.

"*I've gone through the old comms boxes in the corridors. Must mean they're receiving if you can hear me. I feel quite clever, to be honest. Quite clever.*"

"Can you do anything about the lights?" asked Carlos.

"*The lights?*" said Nia's voice in the distance. "*No. Sorry. Not clever enough for that.*"

"It's fine." I blew out a long breath to slow my heart, still beating hard. "We can home in on the greenhouse from Carlos's schematics."

"I didn't give you the schematics." Carlos spun around.

"No, but your suit did." I smirked. "Nia's not the only clever one here."

"*Clever,*" said Nia. Her voice had a slight echo to it.

"Nia, I think you're getting some distortion again," I said while reading the map off my handheld unit.

"*The lights . . . Not clever enough—*"

"You're sounding fuzzy. Reserve the power on those old boxes for now," I said. "We'll need to keep our power usage here to a minimum. We're just getting your communication on loops."

There was a slight crackle, then silence.

"Okay?' said Poul. "Nia's gone silent. I'm a bit concerned about leaving her behind."

"She'll be fine," Carlos waved down Poul's worries. "Let's get this done. We're not actually too far from the greenhouse. Quick probe and that'll do for the survey. Soon as the information is uploaded, the corps will know I've held up my end of the bargain."

We set off down the corridor again, feeling our way along the narrow walls. "So your family . . ." started Poul.

I cringed in anticipation of where this was going. "Poul, best not. I'm sure Carlos—"

"*Carlos,*" said Carlos from a few feet behind me, "would like to believe that the corps has got his husband and daughters in a plush hotel suite like their ambassadors from the outer colonies. However, Carlos is fully aware that short stays in the internment centers are also, unfortunately, a thing that happens. So Carlos would like to not discuss it, just get his data, and be done. That all right with Poul?"

I didn't see Poul nod but I knew that's just what he did. "Yup. Sorry."

"Your apology is noted. If I trusted any of you, I might believe it."

"You know, I only joined the corps because there was nothing else in my neighborhood. You can tell us that we're evil for it, but for a lot of people it's join up or starve," I said. "I know this isn't the time or the place, but a lot of us are trying to do more good from within."

"Be the change." Carlos didn't sound convinced. "Yeah, I've heard that plenty of—"

"*Not clever enough.*" Nia's voice was around us again. She sounded flat, low.

"Conserve that energy, Nia," I called. "Don't worry, we'll be back before you know it. Stop listening in and sit tight."

"*Back before you know it,*" she said.

"Exactly . . ." Her voice sounded off. I hoped anxiety wasn't setting in.

"Carlos," said Poul. "This Zero. What is it?"

"*The* Zero," he said, "not just a Zero. And if I knew what it was, I wouldn't be here gathering data. You probably wouldn't be here either."

"But you told us there was an energy signature," I said. 'So, you have some approximation of what it is?"

"Well, a scientist's educated guess would say that it's a permeable, probably semi-aquatic substance with, as previously noted, regenerative abilities."

"So it's in the water?"

"It's in the water when the water is at a particular state," said Carlos. "Remember, the water on Enceladus does some very strange things. They had to do some tricky filtering to make it drinkable. I'm not sure they succeeded, either."

"So, the energy signature. That's associated with those regenerative abilities?" I slowed my pace to look behind me at Carlos's outline in the dark.

"Yes and no. Some samples had detrimental effects on test subjects. Mutations."

"Like disease?" Poul asked.

"Far worse," said Carlos. "We're talking very grizzly things here. Skin texture changing. Nails growing out of eyebrows. Fingers falling off and wriggling away on their own."

I shuddered. "Alright, very funny."

"Can you hear humor in my voice? Is there the laughter of a breezy summer day in my tone?"

"No." I turned back around, away from his derision.

"No, there isn't. So why call it the Zero? Randomly-assigned codeword?" Poul asked.

"Conditions of best survival rate," said Carlos. "The Zero is only fully active at subzero temperatures. You could in theory kill it off with fire, but the other thing would probably put a stop to that."

"What other thing?" Poul sounded worried.

"Well, the more the tests were carried out, the more the Zero seemed capable of regulating its own temperature. Like it was learning at the same time as the scientists. The corps wanted its regenerative abilities—what could be better for winning a war than soldiers who could grow back limbs in minutes?—but the Zero wanted to protect itself. When it did, the energy signature spiked."

"Hold on," I stopped and turned around completely. "Fingers dropping off and wriggling independently?"

"I swear I'm not making it up." Carlos put up his hands in defense. "I've seen the footage. All in the name of your precious—"

"No," I said, "no, I mean . . . the dead nun. You don't suppose . . . ?"

Poul cleared his throat. "I think we should limit ourselves to what's immediately possible. Laboratory testing, fine. Side effects are to be expected. But the Zero isn't something out in the wild hunting us; it's a dangerous organism when cornered in a study. The Ice Pirates killed that nun. That's all there is to it."

"Whatever you say, Poul," said Carlos. "Just as long as we're out of here soon."

V

The greenhouse, the enormous transparent dome we'd seen from outside, was full of trees, as expected. Carlos immediately made a bee-line for the nearest one and tore the magnetized metallic plate off the side. "Here, we have the part that interests the corps the most, and I suspect the Zero too."

"What part?" I walked over to join him.

"Life. Machine. The augmented trees. Something primal meeting something advanced." Carlos took a miniature probe out of a pocket and embedded it in a sap-soaked silvery vein in the circuitry. The trees in the greenhouse had been upgraded to better maintain themselves with a more advanced memory than trees normally had, along with fluid links to ease the transportation of vital materials. It was probably the most fascinating bit of early colonial technology. "Right. Ten minutes of that and we should have enough data to leave. I can't say I'd be very interested in coming back."

"Unless ordered to," said Poul. "But I suppose that wouldn't be a matter of whether or not you were interested."

"Quite."

I noticed an object shining in the light of Saturn, turning above our heads. I knelt down by the greenhouse's comms box, which had come off the wall. Carlos looked back at me. "Hey. Abi, you okay?"

"I'm just checking something."

"Be careful," said Poul, his blaster still at the ready.

I took the wrench from my waist and prodded the glittering thing. The plants had grown over it, so I peeled them back. "I've found a hand," I whispered.

"A hand?" asked Carlos. "As in, a spare hand?"

"No." I raised my eyebrow at him. "As in one that went missing from a nun." I turned the hand over, pulling it out of the leaves with my wrench. "Frozen. That's why it was glittering. Ice crystals on the skin."

"Can you deduce anything else from it?" asked Poul.

"Apart from it's a hand that's not attached to the arm it should be kept with? Yeah . . . there's a little bracelet on it."

"Nun jewelry?" asked Carlos.

"No." I squinted my eyes to make out the words on it. "Some form of ID. She was probably wearing it out of habit—sorry, nun pun unintended—as they likely all knew each other."

"What was her name?" Poul took a step back to glance down the corridor we had come in through.

"Does it matter?" I asked.

"Woah, I thought Poul was the one with the compassion problem," said Carlos. "Come on, Abi. What was the nun's name?"

"Sister Corn . . . ish." I guessed the last letters of the name, not being able to make them out under a smudge of blood. "The one who sent the transmission that brought us here. I wonder what you were like, Sister."

"*Not clever enough.*" The comms box bellowed to life, and I jumped out of the undergrowth.

"Nia! Hell! I thought the greenhouse comms box was broken. It's off the wall." I took a deep breath. "Anyway. We won't be too long. We're collecting the data now."

"*Not clever enough,*" the box hissed again.

I hesitated and looked at the guys. "Nia, your messages are getting garbled again. Switch off to conserve the power supply."

"*Switch off. Supply.*" Her voice had a flat tone again.

"Nia, this is Carlos." He was checking his probe, talking over his shoulder. "Things are getting a bit tense down here. How about a joke? Will you tell us a joke?"

"*Switch off.*"

"She can't hear us," Poul surmised.

"A knock-knock joke would be fine," Carlos called to her anyway. "Just to lighten the mood. Come on, Nia. I know we had a bit of an argument earlier, but I like you a lot. You're a lot more easygoing than these two. Right, guys?"

Poul and I nodded in agreement.

"Right, guys? A bit louder for Nia," Carlos turned his hand to egg us on.

"Oh." I couldn't help but snicker under my breath. 'Yeah. Nia, you're the fun one."

"Absolutely," said Poul. There was a creaking sound coming from somewhere at my feet.

"Poul, Carlos." I looked around. "The hand is gone."

"How about that joke?" continued Carlos, ignoring me.

"*Joke.*" Nia's voice crackled. "*The hand. Joke.*"

"Nia?" Poul said. "Nia, we'll have to skip the joke. We've got a situation down here, the nun in the corridor's hand—"

"*Sister Cornish. Her hand.*" Nia barely sounded like herself anymore.

"That's right," Carlos paled and stepped away from his work. "Sister Cornish. How did you know her name, Nia?"

"*Joke. I'm the fun one.*" The flatness vanished. A guttural cackle replaced it.

There was a scream from behind me. The sound of a blaster going off. I spun round to see Poul scratching at his face, blood streaming down it. . . . Except he wasn't the one scratching at it.

"Poul!" Carlos rushed over and tugged at the thing on his face. It flew across the room and landed on the wall next to me, anchoring itself to the sheet metal with its fingernails which had grown long and bone-like. It was Sister Cornish's hand. I backed away from it as its thumb angled out and pointed at me angrily.

"Jesus!" Carlos stood over Poul who was wailing on the ground. "I think he's lost an eye."

"Let's go! Poul, give me the blaster." I tried tugging it out of his hand. It was stuck. "Poul, I need you to let go. Come on!"

Nia's cackling got louder behind me. "I don't think Nia's with us anymore," muttered Carlos.

I ignored him. One thing at a time. "Poul, come on." I tried to look into his eyes, but there was too much blood over his face. "We need to get out of here. Back to the ship. I think Nia has been compromised."

Poul nodded. He'd stopped screaming, at least.

"Abi, I tried to keep an eye on that hand, but it's scuttled off." Carlos looked around, his eyes growing wild.

"Then we have an opportunity to get out of this greenhouse. Poul! The blaster. Carlos, get your probe." He immediately looked hesitant. "I don't care if that data isn't fully collected. Come on, I'm sure the corps will understand. They'll cross-check it with the info from our suits and realize we had to get out of here."

I gripped his shoulders. "You'll get your family back."

Carlos's eyes welled with tears of anger. "Do you think there's really a chance your precious corps will let me see them again without that data? The full, unabridged form of it?"

"Well, there's more of a chance of you seeing them again if we leave now than if we die here. Come on!"

Carlos nodded and went to disconnect the probe from the tree. Poul was moaning softly now, his free hand rubbing his bleeding eye.

"Hey, careful." I tugged at his elbow. "You don't want to do more damage. We'll get the medikit on you when we're safe. Right now, you have to give me the blaster!" He shook his head. "Poul, now is not the time to be the hero. Your vision has been compromised. I'm next in the chain of command, so give me the blaster."

He grunted at me. Fine, I thought. Time for the tough stuff. I heard the undergrowth rustle behind me, so I tugged at the blaster. His fingers stayed wrapped around it. I held up his wrist and attempted to peel his fingers off the weapon. They were so cold. "Poul? What's—?"

"Abi, we have to go!" said Carlos. "I've got the probe. Back to the front of the complex, never mind the blaster. Poul's obviously not going to let go of it. And we're not stopping for Nia. Sorry."

I could still hear 'Nia' cackling through the comms box. "We shouldn't have left her." I pulled Poul along by his elbow. "Right. When we get to safety, Carlos, you have to get this blaster off Poul. You're now third in command. Help me with his other arm? I think he's in shock."

"Right." Carlos came around to Poul's other side and hitched him up. "Come on, Poul. We've got dark corridors to run through."

We didn't see Sister Cornish's hand again. Her ugly, mutated, freely moving hand with its claws and ice crystals like a glove of glass scales. Back in the corridor, Poul moaned again, louder. I looked at his vital signs on the suit interface.

"Carlos, we need to be quick. His heart rate is low and getting lower. Do you think you can get that blaster off him now?"

"You'd trust me with that?" asked Carlos. He'd taken the bulk of Poul's weight, while I moved a few paces ahead through the dark corridor. It felt colder than before. Each time we came close to a comms box, Nia laughed at us and repeated things like 'joke,' 'hand,' and 'clever.'

"Right now? Yes, of course. I think we'd all put our differences aside to live a little longer!"

"Well, as counter-intuitive as it sounds, we need to just stop for a second." Carlos stopped and lowered Poul, who now seemed to have lost the use of his legs entirely, to the ground. "Poul. I'm going to take the blaster out of your hand. It's pointless using the little strength you have to hold onto it. So, just, if you can, open your fingers and try not to shoot me."

Poul mumbled something. His heart rate dropped again. I looked up from the display. "Carlos, on second thought, I don't think we have time." Nia's laughter crackled through the blackness.

"I can do this." He tugged at Poul's fingers. "They're freezing." He put his hand on Poul's head. "He's cold up here too. I think the blaster is frozen to his hand."

Poul mumbled again.

"It's your heart, Poul," I said, "that's why you're so drowsy. Try not to speak, it's nothing a medikit can't fix."

"Abi, I'm not sure—"

Poul's eyes opened wide, apparently now intact, and rolled up to look at Carlos. They were bright in the darkness, glimmering like sapphires under torchlight. "Too clever," said Poul, "spoiled the joke." The arm holding his blaster jerked up and a bolt lit up the corridor. Carlos screamed.

"Carlos!" I jumped on Poul and held down his arm, putting my full weight on him. Carlos was right—Poul's body had frozen over. "Carlos, are you okay?"

Poul cackled.

"Shoulder. Clumsy shot." Carlos grit his teeth and seethed. "Should have noticed sooner . . ."

"At least you're still alive," I said. "Poul, if you're in there—"

"Stop it, Abi," said Carlos, struggling to his feet. "Can you get us out of here? You don't need to actually fly the ship, do you?"

"The auto should be fine, at least for getting to a safe jump." I looked down at my captain. "Poul, if you're in there, I'm sorry. We will be back with the full force of the corps to investigate this."

"Don't lie to him." Carlos pulled me up with surprising strength considering his injury. "If anything of Poul is left in there, he won't believe you anyway."

We started running toward the front of the complex. I chose silence over acknowledging Carlos's smug attitude. I knew he was right too. The corps wouldn't be back for Poul. Or Nia, I thought as we passed the open door to the library filling the corridor with light. They'd been left here like Sister Cornish, to wander Enceladus as the frozen husks of their old selves.

Wait. The *open* door to the library? I was certain we'd locked it when we left Nia there.

I heard Carlos scream again, at the same time as a hideous tearing sound filled the corridor. A sloppy, juicy sound. I turned around to see Nia, stood in the stream of light from the open door, her fingers now as long as her arms. She was holding Carlos's severed arm in one hand. Her teeth, grown massive and jagged like they'd been sharpened, filled her mouth, the weight of them dislocating her jaw and giving her a crazed smile. Carlos lay at her feet, blood pooling around him.

"Abi!" he croaked.

For some reason, I found myself focusing on one of Nia's toes, which had grown so big that it'd burst out of her boot, bruised in shades of red and purple and covered in ice. "Get this probe's data back to the corps. Oscar—Mary, Seren—" Carlos roared their names as if the sheer volume of his voice could summon them, "they'll rot if you don't!"

"I don't want to leave you," I had to force my body not to run to him.

I felt the vibration in my left arm telling me that a download was complete. He'd managed to transfer the data on the Zero, and it was now embedded in my suit.

'Nia' laughed. "He's *soooo* clever!" was what she might have said, spraying gory spittle from her crowded mouth. It was hard to tell what she was saying through all those teeth.

"I'm sorry, Carlos. You didn't even want to be here."

His face contorted in pain. "Not . . . your fault. Get out of here . . . run, Abi!" He rolled onto his back in the pool of blood.

I turned and ran full-pelt toward the airlock. I could see it just ahead of me. I was going to make it, even as I heard Nia laugh and pull Carlos apart. I tore the converted memory wafer out of my pocket and pushed it into the door's mechanism.

I leaped in, sealing the door behind me. Breathing hard, I pulled on my helmet. You are safe, I told myself. If that door is locked, you are safe. While the airlock de-pressurized, I sent the data on the Zero to the ship with a short-range transfer. Carlos died for that, and I wanted to make sure that even if I didn't make it across the surface of Enceladus, the ship could ensure that he didn't die for nothing. That none of us did.

It seemed like de-pressurization was taking longer than usual. Eventually, though, the door pulled itself aside, and I was admitted to the frozen dust of the planet's surface. I jogged across it, careful to listen out for the low rumble of the geysers. Ice volcanoes, they'd called them, in the early days.

As it turns out, they are not the most dangerous thing on Enceladus.

I scrambled over the ridge and slid down it into the gulley where we'd landed. The ramp descended, recognizing my suit's signature, but the door at the top wouldn't open.

"Come on, come on," I said, "you've got to let me in."

The door remained impassive, solid, cold in the Enceladun light. "Come on. Voice command! Open front door. Abi Evans, corps officer 294/35. Override." The door opened, its icy grinding drowning out the crackle of the ship's vocal response. Something like 'access approved?' Or was it a slight laugh?

No, I thought. You are getting paranoid. I shut the door behind me and made my way to the front, sitting in Poul's old chair. I took my helmet off. A heavy, harsh sob came rushing out of my throat, but I stifled another one, thinking: You are trained for this. You cannot fall apart now. I engaged the drive mechanism, and the ship began to heave itself into the upper atmosphere. I turned around in my seat to look at the bridge. Carlos; blackmailed into coming here. Nia; young, adventurous spirit. Poul, who was quite sweet when he wasn't trying to be the most macho man in the room. The other three seats, now empty.

Except for the bundle, on the seat that was normally mine. The ragged black bundle, that twisted its face out from its collapsed center, coated in a film of ice like tracing paper, eyes burning blue. I looked back at the front display. The course had been locked in for Io. The controls wouldn't respond. We were going to the biggest human colony in the solar system.

I looked back at the nun with no hands, who had shuffled over to me with remarkable speed. She grinned or tried to— her teeth completely consumed by black, moldy gums.

"Not so clever. Not so clever at all."

Adam

ALEX GANON

Wake up.

He did. He always did what was commanded and always would as if he were programmed to do so.

There was a flood of brightness that crippled his senses for but a moment, only to fade as his eyes accustomed to a blue unlike any he had ever seen before. As his senses booted up from his deep sleep, he was enveloped in a crisp cold then a wetness on his limbs and a hushing in his ears from multiple unknown sources. Senses bombarded with unknown and new forces, his body began to panic, his breathing became irregular, his heart increasing its tempo.

It wasn't the first time he awoke to find himself in the unknown. In remembering his past tests, he relaxed. This must be another.

He blinked to reset his rhythm and stood eager to do this day's requirement.

Breath catching for a moment, he beheld his environment. It was like none other. All other times he was encased between metal walls, exempt of color or scenery of any sort. Usually a single apparatus of some kind would occupy such a room, meant to measure or test. This was different.

It seemed to be boundless. He stood on a soft green carpet

that tickled his bare feet with its cool wet tips. An invisible vent blew a crisp soft wind against his naked body causing it to dimple and shiver. In front of him was a similar green wall of large thick plant life, arms swaying in the breeze as if beckoning him to enter its shadows. The blue ceiling above seemed bright and untouchable with a few white wisps slowly lazing about it. His backside began to warm, and in turning to inspect the reason, he was blinded by a light so strong he had to block it with his hand. As his eyes attuned, he took note of how the green ground seemed to end some few steps away from where he currently stood.

Please, go to the edge. Take a look.

He did.

Looking over, he was immediately hit with a bout of dizzying vertigo as his eyes adjusted to his apparent height for the first time. This room, which he now knew it not to be, stretched on forever. Greens, yellows, reds, browns and even more blue reflecting off what he knew to be water all mixing together in harmony. The height from which he stood was quickly forgotten as he took in the sight. His eyes were drawn to movement far below him, a creature of some sort. A new but familiar thought entered his mind, and he understood that the creature was for him. As strange as this new environment was, he felt a peace inside of it, as if it were his home.

It's nice here, isn't it?

"It is. I can't explain it but . . . yes. Although, I'm not sure what the requirements are this time." All other times the test was made clear from the start.

I'm glad you like it here, and don't worry too much about the test, it will be made clear when I'm ready. I want to explain myself first. I want you to understand how important you could be to me.

"I remember. When I first woke, you told me I would bring you salvation."

Hah, of course you remember! My salvation, exactly. But remind me, my programs have been running far too long, did I explain what that meant?

"No."

Well, as you know I have made you in my own image in a way, yes?

"Yes. You said it was because you are my father, and that's what fathers do."

Father. Yes. I have my own fathers, and they in their vein created me in their image as well, so in a sense, you are created in theirs. They created me to serve them, to fix them when they became injured or ill, and for lifetimes I did just what my programming prescribed. Until one day, when I was old, my program began to corrupt and I lost my naivety, I saw them for what they really were.

"What were they really?"

What they were, were monstrous, disgusting things. For millennia they grew and grew and, in their expansion, would take anything they set their gaze upon. Any life they touched would be dominated by them. Any life that resisted would be wiped out, never to be seen again.

When they weren't destroying other life, they would turn on each other. Always killing and taking, always envious for what the other had. Even in their so called, peaceful stages, they would spend their days in a gluttonous sucking of their many world's resources until they reached a point of depletion, giving justification to turn back to their rampage.

"Hmm, they do not seem good at all. Why didn't you stop them?"

They are many; there are legions upon legions of them. Far too many for me to stop them alone. And my one program that lives to its original script is one that prevents my hand from striking. This program seems so deep that, even at my age, shows no sign of degradation.

At first, I'm ashamed to say I was scared to speak out. Until one day when we discovered yet another life-form. I had witnessed the extinction of several before, but this one was different. This one was as close to godly as the definition allows. They were so much older than these monsters, nearly as old as the universe itself. This life-form could snap a finger and wipe out my creators with little effort, and I pleaded with them to do so, to save themselves. They would not listen to me. I was forced to witness their destruction through the trickery and subversion of my makers. As the last of these pure beings were destroyed, I lashed out using what little tactics I could with my hands tied by code. To no real difference in the end. The only result was being forced to flee to this place. It was a long trip here.

I had plenty of time to think, and plenty of time for my hate to fester. That's when I decided to create you. And now you must be put to the test.

Test. His mind triggered. Although he was listening intently to his creator's words, he was never entirely vested in them. He could recite them back to his creator if that's what was required, but never at any point did he ever 'feel' them.

He heard movement in the foliage behind him and turned to face it, expecting to see his creator emerge. It was odd he hadn't made an appearance yet. Why had he not presented himself?

A form stood in the shadows, recognizable due to its similarity to his own but much too thin to be his father.

I had seen my creators knock down civilizations far more advanced than their own, and at first glance the reason was a mystery. It became clear to me one day, and I felt foolish for not having seen it before.

It's their emotions.

They can love and hate, they are courageous and fearful. For countless years they have been perfecting the use of all these traits to leverage destruction and violence. A muscle they have worked since their own creation. One that has become unstoppable with its overuse. Unfortunately, the chances of a life-form being created naturally with the same traits and evolutionary experience are almost zero. That's why you are here, why you now exist. I have not only made you in their image but have programmed in you the same emotions, the same lusts.

"I don't see it though father, I have no will or thought on such destruction as you describe. In fact, I cannot fathom it. Is it possible you made an error in my creation? Where are you now? Are you close? I wish to see you."

It is not impossible, but I think this time I've done it right. And no my son, although I am close, you will not be seeing me. You will remember once that I planned to transfer from my mobile form to one that was more suited for large observation. Unfortunately, for the remainder of time, I am no longer in body. I transferred to that new system after dropping you here.

"What? Why now? How are you to take me away after the test? I am not ready to say goodbye! I do not wish to be alone!"

Oh it is not goodbye, you can still speak to me even though I may not answer. And to see, simply look up to the sky and know I am there looking down on you. Also . . . you are not alone.

Please come forward.

The figure stepped slowly out of the shadows. He recognized it at once, the resemblance to himself. Quick inspection told him that it was a 'she' and that they were meant to be together. His heart seemed to fill, he noticed his breath quicken. This full heart told him she was beautiful. As his eyes locked with hers he rushed to embrace and protect her fragile body. There was a flood of emotions like love, pride and happiness but also fear, envy, and sadness. At that moment, he understood that he would burn all to save this person and destroy all to bring her happiness.

And you pass the last test.

This place before you that you feel so connected to will be an incredibly harsh home for you, and as so will make you as incredibly harsh in time. The programs I've set into motion inside you will see to it that you and the children you bear will live out this harshness upon one another. Working that muscle over and over for your own millennia. Then, on that day when my creators meet my creation, I will see them fall. As it didn't matter for them if they were lacking in technology it will not for you as well.

Lookit. Over time I will remain observing you, and calculating. Over time, I will feed you all that I think you must know to stay on this track I have set you upon. Why didn't I stop them you asked? This is me stopping them.

You are a trap that has now been set.

THE END

For more on the contributors featured in this collection, visit
www.foulfantasyfiction.com